# THE ALIYEN

## THE STORY OF THE FIRST ARCHIMAGE

### BOOK I

MICHAELA RILEY KARR

Rye Meadow Press

Published by Rye Meadow Press, based in Emporia, KS.
ryemeadowpress@gmail.com

ISBN (paperback): 978-0-9986065-0-7
ISBN (hardback): 978-0-9986065-1-4
Library of Congress Control Number: 2017900578

Cover designed by Magpie Designs, ltd.
Photo credits: Pixabay
Textures by Sascha Duensing
Author photo by Jordan Storrer Photography
Interior map by L. N. Weldon

Printed in the United States of America.
First Edition, 2017.

# THE ALIYEN

# DEDICATION

You would not be holding this book in your hands if it were not for one Rachel Evans. This is for you, Rachel, my sister in Christ. Thank you for seeing me through to my dreams and for never allowing me to give up.

# NERAHDIS

TREDENO

JOSHUUA'S TREE

LEONAR

THE KINGDOM OF
## MINERALTIR

CADEN'S

MINERALTIR CASTLE
★
DEMORA

TRANINI

THE
GREAT DESERT

IONDRIA

IVANN'S DELTA

N

★ CAPITAL
● CITY
■ CASTLE

# PROLOGUE

———— ⬩◦〜◦⬩ ————

He walked slow, full of purpose through the woods. He knew this path, these trees. It was not the first time he had owned the night here, nor would it be his last. Walking calmly, his mind replayed the vision that brought him here to this place, his mission.

The sun was setting on the Kingdom of Lunaka, the prairie country of the continent Nerahdis. Twilight fell to the earth while the two Lunakan moons rose into the dimming night sky, their pale faces full.

Clouds traveled over the sorcerer in this small forest, there in the southwestern part of the kingdom. Trees rustled in the dying wind. No sound echoed upon the landscape. Not from the branches or leaves on the trees and certainly not from the lone traveler.

The sorcerer continued his mission with steps light as a deer's, his face and body vaguely masked by the silhouette of his cloak and hood. He was careful where he trekked. If he was heard, animals and other needless annoyances would be alerted. If he was seen, everything would be ruined.

The black trees loomed around him, isolating him from the rest of the world and possible observers, yet something seemed wrong. There had never been another time like this – when something felt skewed and out of order. He did not know where to look or who to blame for the discomfort. The sorcerer knew his magic was undoubtedly powerful enough to never allow for such anxious feelings. That thought alone made the queasiness remain. Still, this very night was the beginning of everything to come.

The sorcerer continued on beneath the silent leaves toward the clearing where the visions had displayed a nine-year-old Lunakan girl appearing. This child in particular was one of two that he had waited, watched, and planned for. She possessed the first key he aimed to obtain. After he claimed her, a Lunakan boy and his portion would be next. The second journey would be longer through the mountains and into the Kingdom of Auklia.

As the wanderer's thoughts turned towards the prize of this mission, the wooded landscape broke and revealed the same clearing the visions depicted, surrounded by silent, towering trees, the sentries of the forest. He closed his eyes, bringing to the forefront all the frustrations and plans that had grown for nearly three hundred years. Just for this night. Just for this girl. Finally, all that was left was to wait for a few mere moments. After that, she would be his. It was simple really, she would walk straight into his arms, and then onto the Kingdom of Auklia. All of his plans would work. All the waiting would be–...

The sorcerer's thoughts were interrupted as his ears picked out the small, rather loud, steps of a tired, slow little girl. A dark tree branch bent to the side as her tiny body meandered into the meadow.

The lone wanderer was alone no longer as he stood, waiting, in the center of the space with her a mere ten paces away. The twin moons' light reflected in the child's eyes and revealed the glittering gold specks, the sign of what she truly was. An Allyen.

The earth-haired girl was barefoot and blank-faced while trudging on in a dress far too big for her petite body. For such a diminutive frame, her face spoke volumes as her eyes fluttered open and closed. After a day full of adventure, she was ready for bed and a night full of rest.

However, that was not within the sorcerer's plans. To him, the most important objects were the silver locket around her neck and the slumbering power she possessed. In a few brisk steps, the sleeping child was gathered into his arms as the duo headed towards the Lunaka-Auklia border to the south. His young, new passenger merely settled her head on his shoulder, believing that he was taking her home and soon she would be tucked safely away under her covers.

As the sorcerer walked with the child, he became keenly aware of footsteps. These were not his footsteps, yet they seemed to be going the same direction. They were being followed, but by who? If the person or persons behind him had even a smidgen of magic, his own great power would have sensed them much earlier. If the person or persons did not have magic, then they had to be within his field of sight with no physical objects between them in order for him to sense them. No exceptions.

Since he had to wait to hear the physical footsteps, the sorcerer judged the trespasser to be of little threat and assumed that these were not mages following him. The wanderer's reasoning went little beyond his own enormous confidence in that, since he could not see them, it was reason enough for why he could not sense them. The young Allyen must have someone protecting her, and, if her guardians had no power as he suspected, they would be easy to handle. He was, after all, the most powerful sorcerer on the continent of Nerahdis, he thought, smirking in confidence. Nothing could get in his wa–

...

Instantly, without finishing the thought, the sorcerer found himself surrounded for the first time in his very long life. Ten or so cloaked figures had swiftly come without as much as a brush of the green grass beneath their feet. Their heights dominated the meadow and seemed to rival the trees for control of the sky. These uninvited guests were here to stop his mission; that much was clear.

The sorcerer was quickly confused, and his pale hand tightened on the child he carried, shifting her to his hip. The figures were now directly in his line of sight, and still he sensed absolutely nothing.

This was utterly impossible, but the sorcerer's rolling thoughts were interrupted by a foreign voice, not of any Nerahdian, or human for that matter. The voice stretched into strange pitches as it spoke, not its native tongue, and yet was completely coherent, "It is not time. You shall not succeed. Give us the child." A sword hilt appeared out of the towering dark cloak, whose height easily measured seven feet tall.

The sorcerer calculated the stern, accented voice, still contemplating why he could not sense the intruders, but nonsensical strangers were not going to be enough to stop him, whether they had magic or not. Without a single word, the sorcerer and the child vanished from within the circle of figures. His magic took them a few miles south, closer to the marshland kingdom of Auklia where the Allyen boy awaited, and he began to walk again. Although they moved no faster than before, this time his gait was steeped in arrogance.

The young girl began to stir in her slumber, perhaps unconsciously sensing his use of magic. Her own magic had not awakened yet, but it was still possible that she was sensitive to others' powers. She looked up at him and snuggled her head in closer on his shoulder, her voice tiny and sleepy. "Are we there yet?"

"No, child." The pale man glanced back over his shoulder, skeptically analyzing the dark trees. "Please sleep, everything is fine."

When he looked again, the ten figures were advancing from in between the trees, in full view now, at a speed no human could maintain. As they approached him, he studied the strange forms that were humanoid, yet not. Their limbs were much longer, and they towered over him even more than he'd previously thought. Now they stood facing him in a strategic line, a much tighter formation than before, and the sorcerer knew that he could not simply whisk himself away again.

The one who seemed to be the leader, took two or three steps more forward than the others, a brightly colored tassel hooked at the clasp of its cloak on one end and wrapped around its shoulders with the other. It pulled its sword from the hidden sheath slowly, letting the gleam of the silver catch the moonlight, and angled it at the pale man who had dared to kidnap one of the future Allyens. The same voice from before spoke, its Nerahdian clear but pulled in odd pitches that turned the words even more threatening, "Give us the girl."

The pale, hooded man smiled back at this creature, arrogantly assured of his own vast power, "That is not an option."

Since he really did not know what these creatures were, the sorcerer remained on the defensive as he ensued with all ten or so towering things. His left arm around the young girl tightened into a rock, and she awoke with a scream. She only clung to him tighter, believing the sorcerer, of all people, to be her protector. If only she knew.

The creatures were extremely skilled, pounding at him in turns utilizing a strategy that seemed to have been executed hundreds, if not thousands, of times. Strangely, the sorcerer was never touched by their foreign fists or weapons, as he fluidly dominated the battle with the help of the limitless magic he housed. It wasn't even a struggle for him, outnumbered ten to one, as he lifted his pale hand and shot bursts of electric violet at the unknown creatures.

One fell with the first bolt. Then two. The sorcerer could feel the fire racing through his veins, the force of every shot along his long arm. It was pure ecstasy to him. But soon, he found that the girl was no longer in the crook of his arm, only her tiny hand in his grip. Her other was held by a large hand with extremely long fingers, the leader itself. She screamed and cried, tears leaving tracks down her round cheeks from the gold speckled eyes as she tried to get back to the sorcerer, still believing him to be a friend instead of the enemy he was. Using this to his advantage, the sorcerer enacted a new plan and shoved the child several feet away from him toward the end of the meadow grass.

Although the leader quickly bounded after the tossed girl, the other nine unknown things remained entangled around the sorcerer as they continued fighting. In the blink of an eye, the nine around him fell to the ground dead after a surge of purple-shaded magic, their cloaked bodies turned cold and their limbs twisted together.

The sorcerer's pale lips merely grinned, until he searched for the girl and found her sitting on the ground where she had been improperly flung.

The future Allyen's eyes were huge in horror after witnessing his murder of so many people. She shrunk away from him until her back hit a tree, and once there, she flattened herself against it as much as she could, attempting to get away.

The leader of the strange humanoid beings was about to reach the little girl when she swiftly stood and ran as fast as her scrawny legs could carry her away from both the last intruder and the shadowy man. Before she could get very far, she tripped over a tree root and fell hard to the ground between the Lunakan trees. She turned to see the towering figure still advancing, getting closer to her, the colored tassel dangling from its cloak and its face hidden by the huge dark hood. It cornered her against a tree, and then it happened. The event the wanderer had been waiting for and the event the young Allyen did not understand.

The forgotten Allyen locket around her neck began to glow softly and its face began to shine brightly. It grew even brighter as the leader continued to get closer, the shrill air becoming fingers of wind that tore at the being. The hood was ripped from its head, and the girl saw a face that was not the monster she had expected. It was structured similarly to her own, although it was longer and more defined. Thick brown hair flew about his face in the magical wind, brushing across the extremely high cheekbones. Those foreign cheekbones paled in interest compared to its eyes. They weren't human at all but reminded her more of an animal's, with pupils narrowed to slits and a fierce golden color she had never seen before.

She began to fear again as it continued toward her. Its

paces became slower and slower as he, indeed the creature was a he, attempted to draw closer, against the screaming wind. He gained less than an inch with each step; the Allyen locket's magic was too powerful to enter. The creature spoke as he forced his way toward her; the strange accented voice struggled. "Do not be afraid. Nothing is going to hurt you. We are here to help."

The magic shut off abruptly, under no control of the girl, and she was scooped up into the creature's gentle arms. She had been wrong. The strangers were the friends, and she clung to him, crying.

When the sorcerer saw that his ruse as her friend had ended, he knew what had to be done. His smile faded, and he calmly aimed a thin, pale finger at the revealed creature. A bolt of violet shot out as another invisible wind ruffled his cloak and the symbol painted onto it, one of a hollow golden flame with a red circle in the middle.

Residual magic in the air from the spell the girl had unwittingly used previously intervened with the deadly sorcerer's shot, yet the violet burst eventually found its way to the target the sorcerer had intended: the creature's heart. Although it did not die instantly, the sorcerer knew it was doomed, so he was patient and waited, yet again. Once all these impertinent creatures were gone, he could proceed with the Allyen girl as planned.

The creature shouted and jolted in pain. Now he lay on the hard, cold ground with the child crying over him. He took a deep breath as he tried to speak. "Do not cry, young Allyen, only remember..." – the voice began to go hoarse – "Someday...you will understand..."

The girl's cries became even louder when the creature closed his eyes for eternity. Her weeping echoed off the trees

Auklia, the kingdom south of here, along with rice from their paddies. Something like a hundred different herbs seemed to have a presence here too, maybe from the forest country of Mineraltir, the kingdom on the western seaboard. Because Mineraltir literally had no room to plant anything around their vast forests and huge trees, mostly they only exported lumber and a few orchard commodities. Every once in a while, though, a batch of herbs or roots would make it over the border from random foragers.

I slowed to a walk for a while, gazing at all the decorations that people were beginning to put up. There was a festival at the end of the spring season. People tended to look forward to these things so much that preparations often began weeks in advance. After all, it was Middle Spring now, and the festival wouldn't be until Late Spring. I relished festival time as much as the next person since they allowed me to feel like a kid again, forget about taking over the farm, and forget about having become Rosetta's mother. Giddiness flowed through me as I looked up at the paper flowers that were being strapped to windows and lantern poles.

Out of habit, I pulled on the string around my neck to make sure it hadn't broken again. Appearing from inside my tunic and hanging from a ratty shoelace was the locket that I had been given as a child, and its silver flashed in the little light. It had never opened for me in all the years I'd worn it, so I was kind of just waiting for the day it became so old that it fell apart.

Curiosity gripping hold, I tried to pry it open with my fingernails as I'd done countless times before. Useless. Of course, it didn't open, just like always, so I slipped it right back into my tunic, content that it was still there. Still safe.

"Are you really still playing with that thing?" A full,

flowing voice came from above me, as most voices did considering my childlike height.

I shrugged back at Rachel, the very woman I'd been trying to find all morning. She just grinned back down at me, a good foot or so over my head, and then walked next to me with her basket slung over her arm. She was slender with long red hair pulled back into a neat bun on top of her head. Other than a few bangs touching her high, freckled cheekbones, her hair was flawless. She was the prettiest girl in town in my personal opinion, but that wasn't what made her my friend. Rachel was always positive in such a way that made me want to be around her all the time, and she seemed to have a hovering, motherly presence.

I laughed it off, "Guess I don't know when to give up!"

"Oh, I wouldn't say that." Rachel started meticulously inspecting apples at the first stand we stopped at, dropped a few into her basket, and gave the merchant a few copper pieces. "Sometimes things just don't happen until they're meant to."

"I know, but I want to know now! My mother always told me to protect it and hide it, but I mean it's just a locket. It can't be that valuable, it's just an heirloom." I grabbed a few apples of my own and bit into one to the merchant's dismay. Mineraltir's apples were usually about fifty-fifty on edibility, so I always tried one before I bought any. The sweet apple flesh was juicy, so I bought six. Two for me, two for Rosetta, and two for my cousin who was arriving in a few days.

"Maybe." Rachel shrugged, a hint of a smile on her pink lips. "Do you think magic apart from Royals exists?"

I swallowed the apple in my mouth. "Sure. There're Rounans, aren't there? I just hope I never meet one!" I remembered in my head how Rounans were still hunted today, hers almost seemed to be silk, or a kind of finely woven reed, likely from the marshlands I knew Auklia had. She remained sitting close to me, so her sleeve brushed against my bare arm, the delicate softness of it totally foreign to my hardened, tanned skin that mostly wore leather. It almost felt like smooth water.

The colors, too, played with my mind's eye. Lunaka mostly wore brown, with maybe some black and gold mixed in there, but Keera's tunic was made of vibrant lavender with long flowing blue sleeves. Her skirt was made up of a light green, with a rainbow of beads dangling from her sapphire sash. It was a little hard to believe that this girl was my cousin.

"So where are you from, Keera?" I asked curiously.

"Rondeau, Auklia." She answered simply, her gaze solid on the approaching house in front of us. "Straight south of Canis, over your mountains."

I nodded in thought. It was always fascinating to hear about the other countries, simply because I didn't know much about them. What I knew of them came from what I saw in the marketplace and what little news of politics that happened to reach my ears. Auklia only had one ruler, Queen Maria, after King Walter died. That, to me, was a huge testament that women could be taken seriously in a role of power. She even did a good job, imagine that? I wished King Adam would notice.

On the other hand, Mineraltir was a lot more complicated. All I knew was that the king's name was Morris, and Queen Jasmine was actually his second wife. I didn't know what happened to the first one.

There was also a little island off the coast of Auklia and Lunaka by the name of Caark that had recently been discovered a few decades ago, but it was a republic with no

Royals or magic to speak of. Its people probably never feared magic nor feared being labeled a Rounan like everyone on Nerahdis did.

The use of magic was how the Royals kept the people out of rebellion, because everyone believed that they could be stricken dead anywhere anytime from magic they didn't understand. To make life worse among the gossips, if you were labeled as a Rounan, the rumor became reality, whether it was true or not.

I dismounted Shadow and helped Keera down. She took it willingly, which made me hope that I had passed whatever test she had begun.

The earth under my feet was damp, but not muddy like the road to Stellan had been, making me hope that Sam's and my planting would indeed happen today. The sky was blue above, so the rain had probably skirted just east of Soläna, I felt confident. I put Shadow back in his stall before taking Keera's hand gently to lead her to the house.

It was a Saturday, so Rosetta was inside sitting at the wobbly table reading one of her hundreds of books. A young man named Mikael sat across from her, who had already graduated from school while Rosetta had one more year. If someone didn't know any better, they would probably think he lived here too he was around so often. He and Rosetta had been friends ever since he came back with Sam.

Sam's entire family moved to Stellan a season or two before the Epidemic. I had missed him terribly. He ended up moving back shortly afterward, his mother having died from the disease and his father already gone years before, so I guessed he just liked living in Soläna better. But when Sam moved back from Stellan, I didn't know why but he already had Mikael with him. I never asked, but simply assumed

Mikael was an orphan.

Rosetta looked up from her page, her dark blonde hair stuck up on one side where she'd propped her head with her hand. Her face was much more angular than mine, with freckles, but you could still tell we were related. She smiled, her dimples showing. "Hi, Keera!"

Keera almost looked bashful in that moment. "H-Hi."

I looked down at the scared twelve-year-old. "Keera, this is my sister, Rosetta. And this is her friend, Mikael. He comes around a lot."

The dark-haired girl nodded, and when she looked at Mikael, he smiled. He'd undergone another growth spurt since the last time I'd seen him, I noted. Not only was he a few inches taller, but his face was beginning to change. It was no longer rounded like a boy's, but lengthening slightly into a more defined shape. Of course, I'd only known Mikael for the last couple years, but still, it was weird to me to see all the changes.

"Alright. I've got work to do," I said, as I grabbed my staff from its usual spot and braided my still wet hair back out of my way. I touched Keera's shoulder. "Just come find me out in the field if you need anything, okay? We'll go to town later so you can see Grandma."

Keera's little lips turned into a tiny smile, the first one I'd seen out of her. "I remember Grandma."

Her smile was contagious. "Great. I'll see you all later!"

I walked outside to see Sam waiting for me, a huge bag of seed strapped to his back, a pole in his hand and an old leather hat on his bandana-ed head. He was already getting a tan line from that hat, a slight change in shade across his cheekbones that made him look a bit like a bandit. I laughed at him and caught up my own bag of seed. "C'mon, bandana boy, this field isn't going to plant itself!"

"Tell me about it." He laughed right back as we walked out to my southern field.

The hours limped by. Now that the storm had passed, the never-ending wind ripped at everything it could grasp as it flew across the prairie. I gave up on my hood within a few minutes, and even then, it was if the very fingers of the wind were trying to pull my hair out of its braid. Sam gave up on his hat too, and weighted it to the ground with a big rock we'd turned up while putting down seed into the dark earth.

The powerful gusts always made me stop and watch the sky, scanning for fingers of dust that may have reached the ground. The twisters always came during Middle Spring time but none were in sight. On the next gale, I nearly fell over, ducking toward it so much that I was pretty much horizontal.

"Gotta love Lunaka!" I heard my helper joke over the wind as he grabbed the bandana on his red-brown head to keep it from flying away. With all the dust and dirt being kicked up in the air, I could barely see him. Just swirls of brown and red.

As soon as the wind died down, Sam went back to planting. I just watched him for a while, trying to mimic his movements again. He stepped forward through the little row left by the plow and shoved his pole two or three inches into the soil, dropped a few seeds into the hole, and then used his boot to close it. I understood the whole drop and boot technique, it was making the hole that was getting so difficult too fast.

"You'd think I would have gotten better at this!" I gasped, tiring quickly of the wooden staff in my raw hands. I stabbed it into the ground yet again, pulled it out, and dropped a few seeds into the hole before I stomped it shut with my boot in frustration.

Sam shrugged, the time to do just a little gesture resulting in two more holes formed and filled with seed. He looked down at me when he finished, his brown eyes still joking. "Maybe because farming is man's work, not woman's?"

I stuck my tongue out at him, something I'd done millions of times since we were kids. "Ha ha, very funny!" He only grinned, resulting in another two holes full of seed. I sighed. My back was killing me, my hands were stinging, and sweat dripped down my forehead. My voice fell, "Sam, you know I have to do this."

"I know." Sam was quiet. Quickly somber, as only he could do. He stared at the air above my five-foot-tall frame. "I don't know what to tell ya, Lina. Just don't kill yourself, please? You can take a break, I'll keep goin' until I have to go."

I grabbed up my staff again and quickly poked another hole in the ground. "Nope." He wasn't about to show me up.

Sam shook his head and chuckled in spite of himself, another three seeds in the ground.

We went on for maybe another hour until I felt like my hands were going to plumb fall off, but then Sam looked toward the setting sun, judging what time it was getting to be. I knew what time it was. It was eight. He had to leave. Apparently, there were people waiting for him, but I knew well that Mikael was still at the house with Rosetta.

We walked back to the house rather quietly. My silence came from exhaustion. I didn't like admitting it, but there wasn't a single part of my body that wasn't moaning.

The sun had set the faraway mountains on fire by the time we reached my front door, and there wasn't much light left in the sky. Just a bit of yellow and pink before the night would take over, decorated with stars.

In pure joy, I untied the sack of seed and let it fall off my back, the weight of it revealing my sweat-soaked tunic and dress underneath. The wind rushing against my weight-free back felt absolutely beautiful. Setting my staff against the wall of the house sent needles through my fingers, and I couldn't quite stifle the grunt that escaped my lips.

Sam's eyebrows came together to a crease in the middle of his forehead, the one that was beginning to leave a permanent mark. "You should go to bed."

"In a little while." I said, trying to smile. "I've got some stuff to do first. Thanks for all your help though, I really appreciate it."

Sam just smiled a small smile. It wasn't his genuine lopsided one. "Good night, Lina."

"Good night, Sam." I was too tired to spite him this time.

I walked in the door and splashed water onto my face from the basin, trying to wake myself up enough to fulfill my commitment to Keera. I glanced at my reflection again, and I looked absolutely terrible. Heavy bags under my eyes, and sweat and dirt intermingled in streaks down my red cheeks. Just plain yuck. I scrubbed my face harder.

When I turned around, Keera was waiting there expectantly although she had changed. I recognized one of Rosetta's old outfits, a long brown dress with gold borders that fit well enough. I didn't blame her for not wanting to stick out like a sore thumb, but I still preferred her Auklian ensemble.

We walked to town in silence, pretty much all of the light gone from the sky since the two Lunakan moons were only beginning to rise. Keera was fascinated by this. "Is that another moon? Just below the other?"

I looked back at her in confusion as we reached the path down to the canyon. The pulleys were closed for the night. "Of course. Can't you see both of them in Auklia?"

"Uh-uh." Keera shook her head so much her black braid flew over her shoulder. "We only have one."

"Huh!" I was honestly shocked.

I stared up at the two moons, mirror images of each other, in the half moon stage right now. One was slightly smaller and lower, but other than that they were the same. I began to wonder if the moon that was lower couldn't be seen in Auklia because of our mountains. Maybe, it was a northern moon.

"Lunaka is weird." My cousin proclaimed. I honestly could only laugh at that.

The town was still fully lit below us, every lantern and lamppost aflame in its own individual beacon of light. The streets were beginning to thin out, men in coal-encrusted overalls beginning to meander their way back to their homes. As we reached the cobblestone road at the bottom, I looked back up at the streak of star strewn sky I could see, like a crack in a black wall.

I held Keera's hand tighter as we walked through the empty corridors, little pieces of newspaper floating about in the dying breath of the wind from above. I was honestly starting to get a little scared, I'd never been in the city after nightfall on a regular day. Festivals sure, when people were still roaming about merrily, but this was verging on the ghost town category.

My voice was a little shaky when I spoke to calm myself, "So…When did you meet Grandma? I'm surprised they didn't send you to her rather than me."

Keera didn't seem to be phased by the dark city at all. "A long time ago when I was just a baby. I remember her being really nice, but that's about it. They told me I could choose which person I wanted to go with, so I chose you."

I almost stopped in my tracks. "Really? How come?"

A faint grin appeared on Keera's face. She merely shrugged, much to my dismay.

Distracted, I felt my shoulder collide with something hard, and nearly fell to the ground. A hand darted out of the night to grab me before I dropped, and I realized I'd run into another person without even thinking about it. The words tumbled out of my mouth, "Oh, I'm sorry I didn't see you!"

The man standing in front of me was wearing just as bright of colors as Keera had this morning, only he was wearing warm colors rather than cool colors, which of course was proper since he was a man. A pair of glasses sat on the bridge of his nose, something you never saw in Lunaka, and light hair fell over smug eyebrows. His voice was slightly nasal, which made it a little hard to take the man seriously. "Oh, no I apologize, I should have been watching where I was going. I don't know how I could have missed someone like you." He smiled, but it wasn't sincere.

I felt my jaw lock shut, and I pushed Keera slightly behind me. All instinct.

"Allow me to introduce myself. I am Eli Zephyr, advisor to Queen Maria of Auklia." The man bowed deep, one of the multi-colored sashes that hung from around his waist brushing the ground. "And just who might you be?"

This man was an advisor. An extremely important advisor. I figured it wise to answer him even though I really didn't want to. "Linaria Harvey."

"Linaria? Strange name, very beautiful." Eli took my small hand and lifted it to his thin, angular face. My mind refused to register the formal kiss on my hand. He bowed again. "I apologize, I really must be going. I hope we meet again…" And off he walked.

Hopefully not. What on Nerahdis was an Auklian advisor

they were. I had to be dreaming!

Sitting on one side with perfectly erect posture and a handkerchief in her lap was Princess Mira herself, the eldest princess. She was only a year younger than me, I knew that much although up close she appeared so much older. Her pretty purple eyes were nestled in a pale, full moon face under a night sky of deep black hair, which was braided intricately away from her face and back into the hood of her midnight colored cloak. She looked at me with uncertainty, like she was scared, but a tiny grin slowly cracked the porcelain face.

Opposite the table from her was someone who nearly made my heart stop in its tracks. The crown prince!

Prince Frederick sat without his cloak, unlike his younger sister, and my eyes soaked up every detail of this person I'd never seen and yet would someday be my king. He was extremely wiry, compared to his soft sister, for every tendon and vein could be traced along his hands and neck. He wore a white vest suit over a more Lunakan-esque brown, long-sleeved tunic and trousers while messy golden threads covered his head. His face was as still as a statue as he glanced my way. His deep blue eyes seemed like they were boring right into my soul.

I dropped to the floor onto my knees, bowing down to these two immensely powerful people. It was the instinctive response that every peasant learned as a small child whenever they were graced with the presence of a Royal, someone with extensive magic that could kill you at any time. Much less two of them in the same room. I knew for a fact that Lunaka's Royal family tended to have wind magic, though every once in a while, there was an exception. This prince and princess could easily level the entire town with their power.

"You may stand up."

A voice I didn't know. It was male, full of authority. I slowly raised my forehead from the floor to look straight into Prince Frederick's blue eyes again, his face maybe a foot away from mine as he crouched in front of my kneeled position.

Long dimples appeared in his thin cheeks; he was smiling. "There's no need for that, Linaria. I do not believe my people should grovel on the ground in front of me as they do my father."

He helped me stand although I was sure my eyes were probably double their usual size, and I couldn't really grasp the concept of speaking at the moment. Why the heck were two Royals in Grandma's house?

I let go of his thin yet strong hands and backed away from him until I collided with Rachel behind me. She wouldn't let me back up any more than I already had.

"Relax, Lina. Everything's okay. Frederick and Mira are friends. They're here for a very important purpose." Rachel started rubbing her rough hands up and down my arms as if it would help... It didn't.

Keera kept glancing from me to Prince Frederick, and I realized that she probably had no clue that these two were part of Lunaka's Royal family. She was used to the Auklian Royals. Then her eyes located Grandma Saarah, still sitting in her rocking chair motionless, and she smiled. "Gramma!"

Grandma's small body finally relaxed. Her eyelids drooped a little bit, and a smile carved its way through the wrinkles. "Keera!" Her sweet, melodious voice exclaimed, and she opened her arms for the twelve-year-old, who was nearly as big as she was, to climb into her lap.

I looked around me again, seeing the prince, princess, Rachel, James, and her other brother Luke sitting around the corner at a convenient seat next to the window. Finally, I well. "Yes. This sorcerer tried to take over Nerahdis after Emperor Caden was murdered, and Nora stopped him but was unable to kill him. That's why her magic has continued to be passed down to her descendants. She knew someday Rhydin would return."

I nodded, beginning to understand. "Rhydin... How do you know Rhydin is returning? How is that even possible if it was three hundred years ago?"

Rachel looked to the Royals next to her, and they nodded. She swallowed hard, visible in her thin neck. "Rhydin has used his extensive magic to stop his aging. That's how he is still alive. You told me once that you woke up in the forest as a child with no memory as to how you got there. We know now that Rhydin tried to kidnap you."

My fingers tightened on a clump of my clothes, even down to the trousers I wore underneath my dress. I began to rack my brain hard trying to remember anything about that night. Anything at all before Sam found me. Nothing would come. Not even the usual hazy shadows of a childhood memory. Just blackness. It seemed unreal.

"You may not remember anything, but surely you can tell that something other than time has erased it. He used magic, there's no use trying to remember." Rachel said sympathetically, her long freckled hand reaching out to rest on top of my small one. "I'm afraid that he was also to blame for the Epidemic a few years ago, and several of his Followers have been spotted in Soläna near you recently. His number one priority right now is you, Lina. This generation of Allyens is different from the older ones like Grandma Saarah. For three hundred years, there has only been one Allyen per generation. You are one of two. The other is your brother who was separated from you. The separation is for safety reasons, but we'll get to that later."

I didn't really hear the last part. I already felt as if I'd been punched in the stomach, and my lungs would not work. There was an evil sorcerer named Rhydin. Rhydin somehow caused the Epidemic? He was the one who killed my parents and left Rosetta and I alone? Somehow, it all seemed unbelievable, and yet I felt an intense anger begin to swell inside of me. Worse was the fact that he had tried for me with the Epidemic, and got my parents instead. It was my fault.

My fist clenched the knee of my dress and trousers. My voice was tight as I said, "So, what are we going to do about it?"

Rachel was quiet now. I wasn't looking at her, but I could feel her steady gaze on the crown of my head. She was my friend, and she knew my thoughts far too well.

I heard Prince Frederick's strong voice, hinted with tenderness. "We're going to train you. We're going to teach you to use your magic, so we can defeat Rhydin once and for all."

Mira finally spoke, her voice tiny, "We can finish what Nora Soreta started."

I looked up at the fair-skinned princess, her amethyst eyes were captivating, "Is the magic good enough to beat him? He seems so powerful."

Mira tucked a stray black curl behind her ear, and a smile graced her perfect lips again. "The Allyen has done it before. You just have to learn how. For some reason, Rhydin doesn't seem to understand the fact that your magic is like the antidote to his. He does a lot of things that we don't understand. For example, Rhydin letting you go that night does not make sense. His knowledge of magic is so great due to his three hundred years' existence that it is very strange that he doesn't understand this. That's why he couldn't kill you in the Epidemic, either. This information is very hard to come by, and because of this, minimal people believe Rhydin and Allyens are more than myths. Rhydin went underground very successfully three hundred years ago, and so possesses the advantage of surprise. You have a very good chance at beating him, Lina. It will be difficult, but it is attainable. We're all here to help you."

I looked around the room for the hundredth time. I saw the smiling Rachel, confident as always, and her brothers off in the corner watching the windows. Seeing all three siblings together reassured me of the reality of where I was and what I now knew. Young James was grinning, and Luke had a slight smirk. Grandma looked downright proud, which made sense if I was finally going to learn the magic she had. And when I looked at the two Royals, they seemed much less foreign than they had only an hour ago.

They'd gone from complete, terrifying strangers, to two people that could, in the future, possibly be labeled the impossible term of "friend". It was eerie to consider that I was somewhat friends with two powerful Royals. I could already see that their magic expertise would be a great help and something I would rely on heavily. My brain still hadn't completely registered the incomprehensible concept of magic, but I felt confident about this dreamlike situation. Still processing everything, I simply smiled, and Rachel took that as my response.

She stood up from the table, as if dismissing the meeting. "Good. We'll start your training soon to make sure you're ready for Rhydin. While we do that, Frederick still needs to get into contact with Xavier and Daniel to see where they stand in the conflict. I'll be spying on the meeting that

Rhydin's Followers seem to be here for. And Lina, because of everything we've talked to you about tonight, we want you to sleep here."

My thoughts abruptly switched gears. I remembered that Xavier was the crown prince of Mineraltir, and Daniel was getting ready to ascend the throne in Auklia with his new wife now that his mother, Queen Maria, was getting on in years. I'd seen that in the papers sitting on the apple stand one day, so I read it stealthily while pretending to pick out the good apples from the worm-infested ones. Newspapers were expensive.

However, at the mention of my staying at Grandma's, I immediately stood as well. "But Rachel, I can't stay here! I have work at home to do! And Rosetta's there by herself, I can't leave her all night! Sam will be looking for me, too, in the morning!"

The Royals slipped their cloaks back on and disappeared into the night as Luke left his spot at the window to join his red-haired sister. "Lina, you must understand. Rhydin's prime target right now is you. He wants your locket to amplify his own power and then kill you. On your way here, you ran into someone we think may be one of Rhydin's Followers. Because of everything we've told you tonight, it would just be smarter for your own life if you stayed here. One night is all we ask, until Rachel, James, and I can locate Eli and the other suspect, the one you and Rachel met selling Mineraltin wares named Terran. Please?"

I was about to come up with another rebuttal when Rachel interrupted me, the smile vanished from her expression. It made me slow down to see how somber she was. "Lina, I promise you that I will go stay with your sister, okay? Just stay here, please. Your grandmother can protect you while my brothers and I are away. We'll try to be quick."

I sighed louder than what was probably necessary. I looked at the two determined tall people in front of me, both of which had their own particular set to their jaw. My hands found my hips. "Fine! *One* night, but that's it!"

"Thank you, Lina!" Rachel's brilliant smile returned as she whirled around to grab her own cloak and bag off the table. Luke motioned to James as he grabbed a sheath from behind the door, a long sword handle sticking out threaded with colorful tassels. James grabbed his own, though slightly different from his elder brother's, and suddenly I became confused as I stared at the three Owenses.

"Wait." The word escaped my mouth, before any thoughts had finished forming really.

The threesome halted what they were doing. Rachel had pulled her cloak on, a broad shape underneath that was beginning to remind me of yet another sword, her brown hood blending with her bright fiery hair. Luke and James were strapping thick, leather arm guards on, and for the first time I noticed that both of them wore leather gloves over their right hands that nearly blended in with their skin colors. They seemed so *armed* for normal people.

Eventually, my thoughts put themselves in the right order. "How do you guys fit? I mean... I guess Grandma and I are Allyens. Frederick is the crown prince, and Mira's a princess. Both Xavier and Daniel will be kings some day with Frederick. How are you guys involved in something so dangerous?"

Rachel blinked at me. Luke looked just as confused as he reached to scratch his head, his light brown hair beginning to stick up. It was James who finally spoke, "That's a little complicated, Lina. We don't really want Rhydin to win either, y'know? But you could kind of say that we're your bodyguards, I guess. We've protected you for a very long time, and others before us. It's our job to protect the Allyens."

"Oh." I looked at Rachel, a little hurt. Did that mean she only became my friend in order to protect me?

Rachel seemed to read my glance perfectly, and took my hand. "Lina, I may be your protector, but you're much more than that now. You're my best friend, you know that."

I nodded smiling slightly. "Yeah."

The three Owenses grinned and headed for the door. They had barely opened it, yet instantly they were gone. I was left in the little living room with Grandma and Keera, and it suddenly felt very big with them all missing. I took a deep breath and exhaled slowly, still trying to absorb everything that had happened.

I had magic. There was a sorcerer named Rhydin who had stopped aging, wanted my locket, and to kill me. The prince and princess were my friends, I was possibly involved with Prince Xavier of Mineraltir and the soon to be King Daniel of Auklia. Rachel, Luke, and James weren't just my friends, apparently, they were my protectors. It seemed as if everything had changed.

I pulled my locket out of my tunic and held it close. It felt warm for once. Usually, the metal was cold against my skin, no matter how long it remained against the heat of my body. Strange. How was I going to tell Rosetta about this? And Sam? What if me having magic alienated them from me? Then again, maybe I wouldn't have to. Maybe, this was just a dream, or it would be over before too much time went by. I wouldn't tell them until I had to, I decided.

Grandma had taken Keera to bed, so I forced myself to walk through the doorway to join Keera in the bedroom. As I passed the window, I heard a familiar chirp. I looked into the darkness to see my little birdie through the window pane, and I smiled a little bit. Weird bird, up so late at night. It came closer and began pecking on the window rather loudly, as if trying to get into the house.

My smile disappeared as I whacked the glass with my knuckles to scare the little thing off. I inwardly apologized to the bird, but I doubted Grandma would appreciate a broken window. I shut the blue shutters, and then went to join my cousin with my hand still tight around my warm, silver Allyen locket.

# CHAPTER FOUR

A few hours passed. The town fell into complete silence around Keera and I, even the great whirring of the mine came to a halt in the darkness. The beam of light pouring through the window cast a square glow onto the bed that Keera and I shared, but while Keera's breathing slowed, I was still waiting.

I stared at the white, uneven ceiling, picking out all of the cracks in the night that had appeared, the telltale signs of an old house. This was Grandma's guest bedroom, which was not used very often as far as I knew. Grandma mostly used it to store all of her "nice" things that she didn't like in other places where they could get dirty. A fluffy white comforter on the bed, a never-before used rocking chair in the corner, a dark chest of drawers next to my head that was most likely empty.

This was so stupid. I understood where Rachel and her brothers were coming from when they asked me to stay the night at Grandma's, but surely I was safe enough in my own house! I sighed heavily and waited until the light window-print on our blankets became incrementally dimmer. This meant the Lamp Master was finally coming around to Grandma's street to put out the lamp posts and refill them with oil. He typically did this around midnight, the king's curfew, which meant Grandma and Keera would likely both be asleep by now.

I rolled out of bed as nimbly as I could with my muscles still sore from planting, trying not to jostle my slumbering cousin, and shoved my feet into my holey boots. I clasped my cloak around my neck and threw my hood over my head, probably looking more like a bandit now than a granddaughter trying to go home. I didn't have time for this. Sam would be waiting for me in the morning to continue our work, and the path up to the Canyonlands, the prairies surrounding Soläna's canyon where I lived, didn't open until at least midmorning. I felt like I didn't have a choice.

I tiptoed across the creaky floor in the fading light, the map from when I was a child still permanently etched into my head of which boards were silent and which made so much noise they could probably awaken even the king. A tap at the window scared the living daylights out of me, and my foot landed on one of the especially squeaky parts of the floor, a nail head jutting into the toe of my boot. I cringed with pain, desperate to keep my mouth shut. Keera moaned a little bit, and then rolled over in her sleep towards where I had been in the bed.

I looked out the window to see the outline of a bird in the remaining glow. I chastised the bird in my mind. It was going to get me caught! I laid my hand on the smooth metal of the door handle, and began to turn it ever so slowly…

"Lina…?"

Dang it.

Keera blinked her little blue eyes several times, trying to wake up, one of her hands resting on the sheets where my body should have been next to hers. Then she gasped, reached over, and lit the lamp by the bed. "What do you think you're doing? You have no idea what kind of danger you're in!"

I sighed, "Keera, it's fine. I just want to go home, I don't have time for this." I turned back to the door.

Before I knew it, Keera bounded up and latched herself around my shoulders. "You can't go! I know more about this than you think I do!"

I merely stared at the twelve-year-old, her eyes level with mine. Sighing again, I let Keera push me back to the bed so that we were sitting next to each other. "How could you possibly know about this? I just figured it out, and I'm still having difficulty grasping it. Doesn't the idea of me having magic scare you?"

The girl looked down, her hands still tight on mine as if I'd still get up and walk away, though one reached up to tousle her black bedhead. "Lina... I know about the Allyen, because I grew up with one."

I looked at her confusedly, the little lamp still flickering in the corner of the room, sending strange shadows across the ceiling. Birdie now sat visibly outside on the windowsill, staring at us. "What do you mean you lived with one?"

"Remember when they told you that for the last three hundred years there's only been one Allyen per generation? And that you're the only generation that's different?" Keera almost seemed to be pleading with me now, her only chance of keeping me safe at Grandma's for the night. "The man who dropped me off at the stage stop in Stellan to see you was the other Allyen. He's your twin, Lina."

I blinked at her. "Now you're just messing with me." I

stood, trying to leave.

"No, it's true! He told me so! He told me everything! That he was sent to live with my mama because if you two were together, you'd be in even more danger! When Mama and Papa died, he took care of me for as long as he could, and then his training started. He felt like he was endangering me." Keera's full cheeks were becoming wet. "That's why he sent me to Lunaka…because he knew you or Grandma could take better care of me than he could."

As hard as it was to believe, it was difficult to ignore Keera's heartfelt tears. After all, Rachel had mentioned something of a brother rather briefly. Although, I still thought it impossible. Keera had been so skeptical of me in the beginning, and now she was baring her soul to me. I sat down on the bed again. This was getting overwhelming, as if it hadn't been already. I refused to think that my parents had lied to me, yet those tears… I would have to think through this later when I was emotionally capable.

My voice was quiet. "Okay. I believe you. What's his name?" I tried to smile at her, to make her feel better, but I was failing at this whole mother figure thing.

She sniffed. "He shortened his name just like you did. Everyone calls him Evan, but one of the people who trains him always calls him 'Evanarion', which always makes him angry." Keera chuckled a little bit, "Evanarion and Linaria. Pretty similar, y'know? That's why I chose to come to you instead of Grandma. You look like him."

I wasn't sure whether to be reassured or stressed by the fact there was more proof for the existence of a twin brother. As Keera kept talking, I remembered back to just that morning when I'd picked her up, to the man standing on the platform with her. I'd thought he was a roaming bard, what with the violin strapped to his back and everything, but what really stuck in my mind was how short the poor fellow was. I was barely five feet tall. He couldn't have been more than a couple inches taller, which meant this whole vertically challenged thing had to be genetic. Why did my mother never tell me about Evan? Or did she just never have the chance before she died?

Keera was mentioning something about Evan's training again when I interrupted her. "So when did Evan figure out he was an Allyen?"

Keera became quiet. "I don't really know. I was too little. He seemed to have known for a long time. I think when he started training with Prince Daniel, Evan told him he figured it out when he was around my size, like thirteen-ish. Did you know my father was murdered?"

I shook my head. My mother had only told me that my Uncle Jed had worked himself into his grave.

Tears were now visibly flowing down Keera's freckled face. "Well, after the man killed Papa out in our rice paddy, he made his way to our house and tried to get Evan. I don't remember much because I was too little, but Evan told Prince Daniel that suddenly there was a bunch of golden light and powerful wind, and it scared the evil man away. All I remember is my mama holding me really tight with Evan in front of us, trying to protect us. Mama died too. Ever since then I think he just played with the magic to figure it out on his own. I don't know when Prince Daniel discovered him, I only saw them together once, but I think there were two others that helped lead Prince Daniel to train Evan although I never saw them. I have no idea how much he can do. But it was Prince Daniel that told Evan that the man who killed my father was one of Rhydin's Followers. He was trying to kill all of us."

I pulled the girl closer to me, my own heart aching for this brother I barely had any connection to. She rested her head on my shoulder, and I rocked her slightly. "I'm sorry this has brought you so much pain, Keera."

She shook her head barely, and then spoke in a voice clouded with tears. "Do you believe it now? How much danger you're in because you're an Allyen?"

I took a deep breath, not sure if I really wanted to admit it or not. "Yes, Keera, I understand. Forgive me for being so stubborn. Do you have any idea where Evan is now? Why didn't he just come with you?"

Birdie shuffled closer to the window outside in the darkness, as if eager to hear Keera's response.

"No. He wouldn't tell me where he was going. He probably went home to keep practicing with Prince Daniel. He made me promise not to tell you anything about him. But I thought you needed to know." Keera began to sob a little bit, perhaps at the breaking of her word to someone so special to her. "But Evan was really upset when he told me not to tell because he really does want to meet you, Lina. He doesn't have any family but me. He said that until you awaken your magic and learn how to use it, you're not strong enough to be together yet. It had to do with some magical thing that I didn't get… It's too complicated."

"Trust me, I understand that part. I wish I could make it easier." I looked back up at the ceiling, kicked my boots off, and they thudded to the floor. "He seems like a nice guy."

"He is when he wants to be. Most of the time he's pretty quiet…watchful… On some days, he's just plain boring!" Keera's voice rose slightly and her arms crossed. "Just so ya know, never play hide and seek with him, he always wins every time!"

I stifled my laughter for fear of waking Grandma up. It was some much needed comic relief. I pushed Keera up from where she was halfway lounging in my lap. "C'mon, better get to sleep."

"You're sleeping too, right?" The black-haired girl looked at me quizzically, not budging. "I will sit on you all night if I have to."

"Yes, I'm sleeping too, no need for all night sitting." I chuckled as we pulled the covers back and jumped in. As soon as Keera situated herself, I leaned over her and blew her lantern out. The room fell into complete blackness now that the Lamp Master had completed his job. The street wouldn't be relit until tomorrow evening.

We talked for a little while in that darkness, more about Evan and Prince Daniel. The only thing I found rather interesting was the fact that the Auklian heir had blue hair, and that just seemed strange to me. All the Auklians had strange hair colors, so it must have been part of their genealogy. Our family was Lunakan, which was why Keera had black hair. It came from her Lunakan father, but I was pretty sure Aunt Marie had bright green hair when she was alive.

While I lay there waiting for sleep, it occurred to me that when and if I ever saw Prince Frederick again, I needed to tell him that Prince Daniel was indeed on the side of the Allyen. Now, it was only Prince Xavier we had to worry about.

There was one more tap at the window from Birdie's beak and then nothing, so I assumed it had flown away. Strange little bird, it should have been back in its nest hours ago. I slid down under the covers, trying to figure out how I would sleep on such a fluffy mattress when I only had a stiff cot at home.

"Lina? Are you scared?" Keera asked, her voice filling with sleep.

I thought a little bit about my answer. "Kind of. Everything is still soaking in…"

"Are you going to tell Rosetta? And Sam?"

Silence.

"I don't know." I admitted.

As the last lamppost was snuffed, the capital city of Soläna plunged into complete darkness. The plains were quiet up above, the two brilliant moons beginning their descent toward the western horizon. The prairie grasses were still as the eternal Lunakan wind rested, only a breath remaining to twirl the fresh, green blades.

The mighty mountains stood tall in the distance, a barricade for keeping things out, a boundary for keeping things in. So, few people knew the magical secret of these ancient mountains, but the sorcerer knew and that was all that mattered.

A cloaked figure stood at the very southern point of the canyon housing Soläna, waiting patiently. His arms were crossed, merely out of habit. He had seen this scenery far too many times to be intrigued by it, for not much had changed in the last three hundred years. Only the construction of this canyon was different from the original town, though this had occurred within fifty years of his perfect rule of the continent.

The sorcerer glanced to the northeast where Lunaka Castle towered, the spires attempting to reach the heavens. Only one light remained flickering in the tallest tower, and the sorcerer could sense Lunaka's king becoming edgy. He knew this man quite well after so many years. He tended to be rather temperamental, but the sorcerer knew that there was a different reason on this night.

A simple tweet shattered the silence, and Rhydin looked back down toward the canyon. One of his pale hands emerged from the dark cloak, palm upward, and in only a second a small flame appeared. The light revealed a small black bird approaching from down in the canyon, a bright red breast with its wings tipped in gold. The sorcerer said nothing, and the bird alighted onto the grassy knoll in front of him.

Instantly, its body changed size and shed its feathers. The beak shrank and turned into a nose, the long feathers turned into fingers, and the legs thickened and bent at the knee. Kneeling where the small bird had once been was now a man, if you could call it that. It looked up at the sorcerer, its eyes pure white with no pupil. A symbol was on the black shirt that once decorated its wings, a golden flame outline with a red sphere in the center, the same design that decorated Rhydin's cloak.

The sorcerer grinned slightly, proud of his creation. These Einanhis were brilliant really, just empty shells of magic that followed every order. The perfect spy to use on the young Allyens.

The monotone voice of the Einanhi known as "Birdie" to young Linaria cracked as it spoke. "I have a report, Master."

Rhydin beckoned the created being to stand with the hand not holding the flame, but he already knew what the report would be. "Linaria has discovered the existence of her power, and yet still cannot harness it."

"Yes, Master."

The sorcerer raised the flame a little higher to see his Einanhi and studied it. "I can sense her. She is with Allyen

Saarah. Until her magic awakens, the locket is useless to me. When she was a child, I tried to take her and train her myself to encourage the awakening to occur earlier."

"Yes, Master."

"Yet, I was interrupted. My decision became to let her discover it herself. At that time, she will be too inexperienced to prevent me from stealing her locket successfully. With its strength, this continent will be on its knees within one revolution of the sun." Rhydin's voice filled with confidence and the flame in his hand grew larger.

The Einanhi remained static until its master finished speaking, and then raised its voice. "Master, I have one other report."

Rhydin's gaze returned to the Einanhi, his face still obscured by his dark cloak. "Continue."

"The location of Evanarion has been confirmed. He has returned to Auklia."

"Yes." Rhydin's pale hand touched his thin chin. "I have foreseen this. Something is hiding his presence from me. I still require his half of the locket as well, and he knows far more than Linaria."

"Nothing can hide from you, Master."

A memory invaded the sorcerer's mind, ten years ago when he walked this very plain with Linaria, headed toward Evanarion. That night possessed the one instant when he could not sense the presence of someone standing directly in front of him. Magical beings could be sensed anywhere close by, but anything without magic could only be sensed when facing them head on. Those creatures had obvious control of magic, yet they were still unknowns. Rhydin's power was so great, yet this was one thing that he did not understand.

"What are your orders, Master?" The Einanhi asked.

"Return to Linaria. Watch her every move. This time is critical more than any other. The instant her magic appears, summon me, and I will finish what I started three hundred years ago. We must reach her before those creatures can hide her from me." Rhydin's voice was hard, the flame becoming brighter in his hand with his determination. "I will send others to search for Evanarion, to find whatever abominations are harboring him, and to kill them all. The Allyen twins cannot escape forever."

The Einanhi bowed deep, and began to morph once again. It shrunk to the size its humanoid foot had been, its entire body turning black, gold, and red. It tweeted for its master, hopped a couple of times, and then took off back down toward the canyon, where Linaria slept with her cousin. The light at the top of the castle tower disappeared.

The sorcerer watched for a few moments, the wind beginning to return to Lunaka's plains. The moons were barely visible behind the western mountains, sinking toward where Mineraltir lay. The stars were bright overhead, patterns that had been traced so many times.

No, Rhydin thought, this place had not changed at all, even from so long ago. After so many centuries, his arduous task was finally coming to an end. Nora Soreta had thwarted Rhydin once, but once her descendants were vanquished and their power turned against them, Rhydin would finally reclaim his empire for eternity. He would let nothing get in his way.

# CHAPTER FIVE

———————⟨⟩—————————

I awoke as soon as the sun's rays were strong enough to break through to the bottom of the canyon. As I swung my feet over to the side of the bed, my back aching because I wasn't used to such a soft mattress, I began to ardently hope that Sam hadn't shown up only to find me missing. It took quite a bit more time for it to be daylight down here rather than up above on the farms.

I was lacing up my boots and looking out the glassy window when the sound of a door opening shattered the morning silence. I looked over to see Grandma absolutely beaming, her cheeks rosy, with a pan of golden brown circles that smelled divine. Her voice squealed with delight, "I made biscuits!"

"Oh, Grandma, you shouldn't have." I feigned gratefulness even though I was really balking at the idea of staying any longer than I needed to. Yet, one look at her lovely face was just far too much. I knew that it would crush her if I deprived her the opportunity of serving breakfast to two of her granddaughters. I sighed and stood, shaking the still sleeping Keera so she wouldn't miss out.

It was nice really. To be able to sit at an actual clean table like the family that we were. To be able to eat Grandma's to-die-for three layer biscuits. To simply talk about life as if the events of last night had never occurred. Maybe, I dreamed that I'd been told I had magic? And yet why would I be here still if it hadn't been real? Besides, to have magic was no dream of mine when I was growing up. Only a nightmare.

Grandma cleared her throat and set down her blue flowered teacup. She folded her hands slowly on her lap, and I could see her swallow. "Lina," she said, "I just want you to know that if you ever have any questions, or need any help at all, you know I will always be here for you. I had to learn how to be the Allyen once too, and even though it's different now, I will always do my best."

It hit me like a brick. I was really truly hoping that it was still all a dream. I nodded, swallowing my last beautiful bite of biscuit. "I know, Grandma. You always have been there for me, Allyen or not." The word was still completely foreign sitting on my tongue.

Grandma smiled a little bit and rose from her chair to grab the teakettle from the wood stove. "The Owenses reported to me this morning. Luke and James were able to find Terran and Eli, the two we suspect to be working for Rhydin, and they are keeping track of them now to make sure they do not try anything."

Keera's blue eyes found mine over her biscuit, which had been given a rare spoonful of honey. I knew she was still worried, but I asked Grandma anyway, "So does that mean we can go home now?"

"Yes. For now." Grandma smiled sadly as she sat back

down with us and filled our teacups.

We didn't stay for much longer after that since I was biting at the bit to get back up to the Canyonlands so Sam and I could get to work. Keera and I walked through town quickly, straight through the heart of Soläna, seeing as I really didn't want to run into any more strangers on side streets or alleyways.

The capital city was coming alive as it always did every morning, yet my eyes seemed clouded by what I had learned. Most of the dirty men in mud-colored overalls had already disappeared into the yawning mouth of the mines in the southern wall of the canyon. Now, only the women were about with their children. I could easily tell which ones were married to the miners of the southern part of town and which ones were married to the merchants and noblemen of the north.

Nowhere else in Soläna did they mix so much except here in the central square. The families from the south wore threadbare clothes, a few had leather vests on top, but mostly all were brown in color except for the occasional stain from coal dust. The younger women looked as if they had at least tried to scrub their faces clean and get the dark powder out from under their short fingernails while the older women seemed to have called it quits long ago.

The women from the north were far different. Their frames weren't bony at all, some were even downright buxom, and their clothing was much nicer, made out of materials that I didn't know the names of. Their clothes were also a tad more colorful, as far as Lunakans go, since no one can really compare to the rainbow spectrum of Auklia. Every northern Soläna woman had her hair curled in a different way, no doubt with one of those heat-up things I'd seen in some of the mercantiles. I always thought it was stupid in the past. Why spend hours every day on something that wouldn't last?

And yet now, I didn't know what to think as my mind effortlessly distinguished between the noble and lowly women. I had always compared myself to the ones who looked like me, the ones from the south. I had foreseen a similar future for myself. Marrying another farmer, preferably, or a miner. Never quite having enough money but enough to send kids to school and not go hungry.

With all this Allyen business, every sense of the word "future" was wiped away. What did it mean for my life now? Every person in this town would fear me just like the Royals because of this magic. Would I be able to keep the farm? Would I be able to stay with Rosetta and Keera? Would I succeed against Rhydin, or would I die? Everything was unknown now, and I certainly didn't like it.

Keera and I barely made it back up to the flowing Canyonlands when I noticed a plume of dust getting closer to us from the direction of my farm. In five seconds flat, Rosetta's round, red face was barreling down on me, her high voice screeching hundreds of questions and accusations that I couldn't really follow.

Unfortunately, I noticed Sam behind her, confusion in his eyes and shadows underneath them. Rachel was with them, and at that moment I remembered that she had spent the night with Rosetta to keep her safe. What was Rosetta so worked up about then? I pushed her shoulders out to at least an arm's length so that I could focus on her. "Rosetta, slow down will ya? I don't understand screaming sisters."

The blonde just sputtered, no words able to form themselves, her hazel eyes scrutinizing me in every degree to make up for it. She took a deep breath, putting her hands on her hips in typical Rosetta-fashion, and carefully pronounced her loud words. "You. Left. Me. Home. *Alone!*"

Sam's eyes widened with understanding, and his voice suddenly shot up to levels I hadn't heard since he was at least twelve years old. "You were out all night?"

And then I had two people screaming at me. Marvelous, wasn't it? I withstood about two seconds of their rambling, Rachel smiling uncomfortably behind the two of them, until I conjured up the loudest voice I possibly could. "*Hey!*"

Both Rosetta and Sam were instantly silent, staring at me expectantly.

I took a deep breath. "Rosetta, you were not left home alone. Why do you think I sent Rachel to stay with you? I'm sorry, we went to Grandma's last night and…Keera started not to feel well, so Grandma had us stay the night." Keera gave me a look for using her as my excuse, but what else could I say? Hey, we went to Grandma's last night, and I figured out I have magic and some crazy sorcerer dude is out there trying to kill me so they needed to keep me safe? That was so much better. I went on, "I asked Rachel to come out to stay with you because I knew you'd be upset. That's better than nothing, right?"

Rosetta merely rolled her eyes, not interested in listening to logic, and began to stomp on toward where her schoolteachers awaited down in the canyon. Sisters. Sam seemed to be appeased although I knew him well enough to see the hint of skepticism in his expression as he turned to stare down Rachel.

My best friend merely smiled and shifted her bag a little higher onto her cloaked shoulder. "Well, now that everything is as it should be, I should be headed home myself. I'm sure Luke and James will be eagerly awaiting their breakfast. See you soon!" She winked at me as she passed, heading back toward the canyon.

For a split second, I wondered why she winked until I felt a weight drop in my pocket. She had given me something. Something else to screw up my life perhaps? The wink was a little much, I decided to tell her later.

Next to me, Keera turned back into the young girl who trusted nobody, quietly staring at Sam and somehow judging what kind of person he was. I realized that I hadn't introduced them yet, so I firmly moved Keera out from behind me and held her shoulders. "Keera, this is Sam. He helps me with the farming, and he's a very good friend of mine." I turned to Sam, who just stood there with a small grin on his thin face, "Sam, this is my cousin, Keera. She's going to live with me now."

Sam placed a hand on one of his knees as he slightly leaned forward, the other hand extended toward Keera. This way, his head was level with hers since he usually towered over everyone. He smiled that crooked grin of his that reminded me ever so much of our childhood and said, "Nice to meet you, Keera."

Keera's blue eyes still seemed unsure as she stared at the tan, calloused hand in front of her, and when she looked up at me, I wondered. After everything that had happened to this twelve-year-old, how many people did she really trust in this world? Only Evan, probably. And maybe me now?

I took her left hand and squeezed it, hoping that the message would get across that Sam was truly one of the people I trusted the most. She had nothing to fear from him. And yet when I looked back up at Sam myself, I wondered again. Apparently, there were tons of people around me that were out to kill me. Who all could *I* really trust? I couldn't tell Sam about the whole Allyen thing. At least not yet. It felt weird to be keeping secrets from my childhood friend.

Keera looked back at the tall man who patiently waited in his crouched position and met his eyes. She smiled very little, but for her, it was a lot. She placed her small, delicate hand into his seemingly huge, hard one. "It's nice to meet you, too, Mr. ....?"

"Greene, but you can just call me Sam." He smiled and then straightened back to his normal height.

When he and Keera began to walk toward the house, I snuck a look into my pocket. A tiny glass bottle sat cradled in the fabric, a small piece of paper rolled up inside. Rachel left me a note. *Meet me the day after the festival at my brother's livery.* Was it really so important that she couldn't just tell me in person later? Or so secretive that she couldn't say it out loud in front of Sam and Rosetta? What else could they possibly need to reveal to me?

When we reached the house, Keera quietly went inside to take a nap, exhausted from the long night. Sam said he'd meet me at the field, but when I turned around the corner to grab my seed sack and pole, I felt heat blaze through my ribs.

On the very back corner of our little house was a set of pretty significant scorch marks. The way the black smears danced across the wood in a specific direction was suspicious to me. Even I was smart enough to know that kind of mark didn't come from a little prairie fire. Someone had done them. That kind of mark would only come from someone able to *project* flames. Magic fire. Fire magic.

Rachel said that one of the people after me was a Mineraltin. I knew enough about magic to realize that many Mineraltins had a disposition for having fire magic. Rachel was right. Someone *was* going to try and kill me last night. They tried to set my house on fire. With me and my family in it.

Rachel must have put it out. She protected Rosetta just like she said she would. If I had been in there and Rachel hadn't been around, people would have thought it was an accident. Just another grassfire. Not murder. I nearly sank to my knees my legs became so woozy. This was real. The threat was real. All of it *real*.

"You okay?" Sam's voice appeared out of nowhere, scaring me further out of my skin. He just looked at me until I started breathing normally again. "Y'know, Lina, we really need to hurry if we're gonna get this seed in the ground in time for the festival."

"I know I know... I'm sorry." I sighed heavily, still feeling like I was in the pit of doom as I numbly reached for my pole.

"Is there something you want to talk about?" Sam's eyes were genuinely filled with concern, and for a second I wished we were little kids again and I could just hold his hand and spill my guts. But I couldn't. I had to protect him. Nobody could know about the fire. Or the murderers.

"No." I barely whispered, not used to lying to someone I'd told nothing but the truth to for the last ten years. By the twitch of his brow, I knew he could tell I was lying.

As I watched him, a light pair of feet perched on my shoulder. I turned to see Birdie, its eyes bright as it looked at me expectantly for something. Sam's brow furrowed further when he looked down again to see the small black bird on my shoulder. He changed the subject, "Huh. Never seen a bird like that before. Never seen any kind of bird that'll sit on your shoulder like that either."

I fought the urge to shrug so I wouldn't bother Birdie, but I felt somewhat better simply knowing that I didn't have to lie about this. "I don't know. It started coming around a few seasons ago. It built its nest in the tree next to my house. I figured it was from Auklia or something because it isn't like the sparrows and stuff we have around here."

Sam glared at it, "I don't think it's that simple."

"Sam. It's a bird. Relax."

"I don't think so."

I rolled my eyes a little bit and crossed my arms. The shift caused Birdie to fly up, and the next thing I knew, there was a sharp little pain in my neck. I felt the weight of my locket release from my neck and the cool silver slide down inside my tunic to rest against my stomach, my sash stopping it from going to the ground.

Blood was on my fingers when I pulled them away from the wound Birdie had given me, where it had broken the old shoelace that had held my locket for so many years. When the bird started to fly back down, I waved it away. "No, bad bird! Shoo!"

Sam merely looked at me cleverly, as if he had somehow foretold this. "See? I wouldn't let that bird hang around, if I were you."

I sighed and turned away from him so I could fish my locket out of my tunic. When I held it in my hand, still cold regardless of the hot day, I remembered the importance of this little thing. This was what Rhydin was after. This was what he was willing to kill me for, that his people were willing to set my house on fire and burn me alive for. The only thing he needed to subject not only Lunaka, but Auklia and Mineraltir as well to his control. I needed to protect it better, even if it was just from Birdie.

As I turned back to Sam with the locket still in my palm, his brown eyes lightened in recognition. "I didn't know you still had that old thing. I always wondered if you still had it."

"Yeah. It's kind of important." The only response that

made some kind of sense spilled out. It killed me to continue lying to him, but I had to protect him. This thing was trying to encompass my entire life, and I had no idea what the future held anymore. I could be killed at any time, and I certainly wasn't going to allow Sam to be a dead innocent bystander.

"Have you ever been able to open it?" He asked curiously, eyeing me as I stared down at the little antique thing that meant life or death to me. "I haven't seen it since that night I found you in the forest."

My head snapped up to look at him. Why had he seen it that night? The night I couldn't remember when Rhydin tried to kidnap me. "No, I've never been able to open it. You saw it that night? How?"

Sam shrugged, not knowing how big of a deal it was. "It was just the one time it wasn't hidden. Anybody could have seen it. You always have it out of sight now."

"It's just really important. If anything happens to it…" I trailed off, unable to find a lie that would work or a truth that wouldn't reveal too much.

Sam ignored my silence. "I guess you'll have to find something sturdier than a shoe string then." He laughed a bit, little specks of light dancing across his face as the foliage above played in the sun.

I tried one last time to dig my fingernails in the hinge to open the locket, but I knew it was hopeless. I knew now that it wouldn't open until the right time. Perhaps, when I was ready for this whole concept of magic. Maybe, when I actually learned to use it. But, personally, I knew I was nowhere near ready.

We walked out to the field together after that. As I hefted the heavy burlap bag into place on my back and tied a big knot in the front, Sam began to work to his whistle, his body easily settling into the rhythm he'd known since he was old enough to help his father. My mind didn't have a rhythm anymore.

I grabbed my pole and began to stab it into the dried-out plow lines, needing some kind of monotony to relax my mind and my stomach. I dropped a few seeds that several months from now would become wheat and covered them with the leather toe of my boot. These seed sacks were the last ones. Once they were planted, we'd be ready to attend the festival and celebrate the finish. Rosetta always looked forward to it so much every year, I tried to tell myself. The attempt at normal thoughts failed. I was still just as paranoid as ever.

After a few minutes, Sam piped up. "Um, Lina, are you going to the festival with anyone?"

I looked up at him. "Well, I'm taking Rosetta and Keera obviously, and I'll probably run into Grandma and Rachel at some point in the night-..."

"No, uh..." He interrupted me, his eyes very carefully trained on the ground. "I mean, are you going *with* anyone?"

Realization almost physically slapped me in the face. My mind was so clouded, and it resulted in a light blush. "Oh. Uh... No, I'm not. Nobody's asked me. I didn't figure anybody would."

Sam's gloved hands chafed around his wooden pole, more jittery than I'd seen him for a very long time. "Do you want to go with me? Er... I mean, would you like to go with me?" He finally looked at me with pure terror in his eyes, and I saw how much bravery this was costing him.

I smiled, glad that my face was already red from the sun. "Of course, Sam. I'd love to."

# CHAPTER SIX

The day of the festival finally arrived, and I tried to busy myself with things that were once "normal". As soon as lunch had been cleared from the table, Rosetta was a whirlwind. She danced around the small house, the wooden floorboards squeaking at different pitches as she donned her carefully chosen attire – also known as, the only nice dress that hasn't been eaten by moths or decorated with Lunakan dirt. Every year before this she had worn one of my old dresses that I had outgrown, but Rosetta had finally gotten too big for those as well. She made herself a new dress with her own money, earned from dusting shelves at the library. It was cotton, a…dare I say it… *pink* floral pattern. I hate pink. I told myself that every single time my mind began to wander to other more disparaging things. I hate pink.

My old dress had now been passed to Keera, who was actually rather excited for this festival. Rosetta had been ranting about it for a couple of weeks, about all the lights and booths and dancing. The dress Keera wore was the same shade as her sky-blue eyes. Rosetta was now standing behind her, impatiently trying to braid some kind of up-do into Keera's midnight hair. I laughed every time Rosetta missed a curl and had to go back to get it. She was a perfectionist, always would be. Sadly, I began to wonder if this would be the last Spring Festival I'd get to take my family to…

I hate pink.

A few hours later, there was a knock on our front door. Keera had been ready long ago, but even as I walked toward the door to answer it, Rosetta was biting her lips and pinching her cheeks to make herself "prettier".

I took maybe ten minutes to get ready. I wore one of my mother's old burnt orange numbers, cinched at the waist. She had been much taller than me, but it worked. Rosetta insisted on braiding my hair as well, although I made her promise not to go as immaculate as last year. This time she gave me a braided bun, and I stopped her before she could do anything else.

Outside the door were Sam and Mikael, probably in the nicest shirts and sets of trousers that they owned. Sam even had a tie on, which meant that the apocalypse was probably around the corner. Although, maybe the apocalypse's name was Rhydin… I hate pink.

Sam smiled at me sheepishly, not quite letting it turn into the crooked grin I knew so well, but I could tell he was just as fidgety as when he asked me to go with him. I felt my face grow a little warm.

Instantly, Rosetta and Keera ducked underneath my arm, Rosetta taking Mikael's hand as if it was the most normal thing in the world and Keera, anxious to see this festival she'd heard so much about, moved next to them restlessly. Sam and I watched the three of them run off without us, especially the couple. I chuckled, "Looks like we've got a problem on our hands."

Sam stared off at them after I spoke, at the boy he had taken in and my little sister. "Oh yeah? What's that?"

I looked up at him skeptically as we began to walk. His smile grew so I reached up as far as my short arm could go and cuffed him on the head as I'd done for many years. He exclaimed that it hurt, but I didn't believe him. Somehow, I didn't think my little, bony hand could possibly harm his rock of a skull. I only wished that we could stay like this forever.

When we entered the streets of Soläna, I marveled at their transformation. I had seen them hanging the paper lanterns and streamers all season, but none of that compared to seeing them all lit up by the Lamp Master. Now, each lantern had a small beautiful light within to illuminate the floral pattern printed on their delicate paper. The lights sent a warm glow down onto the dark cobblestone streets and all the farmers dressed in their holiday best.

Since it was a kingdom-wide festival, there were farmers from all over the plains. A few from up north that weren't dressed any different than usual, a bunch from down south around the lake, and even some fishermen from the Canis area that dabbled in farming as well.

All the nobles from Lun, the northwestern city of merchants, would be up at the castle celebrating with all the Royals, whose "Royal" festival started an hour or so after ours. All three of the Royal families usually gathered for events like this, seeing as the majority of them were interrelated by now. It was slightly strange to think that the three ruling families of Nerahdis were less than a mile away. Not many people trusted them. I knew I didn't.

By the time Sam and I reached the square, our three

charges had completely disappeared. I began to worry for their safety, not only because Rosetta was on a *date* but because of Rhydin. I actually began to hope that Rosetta and Keera being separated from me would make them safer.

Sam didn't notice my worry, but was turning his head like an owl's to see all the booths that had been set up around the square. They were decorated with a myriad of colors, and that was saying something for Lunaka. Only Auklia had colors, so seeing such rainbows never failed to dazzle my eyes every year. There were booths for little games like bobbing for corn or throwing little rings onto different pegs nailed to a big wooden board. There were stands with food prepared from Mineraltir and Auklia, and Lunaka as well if one wasn't keen on trying new things. Personally, I always got something small from both of the other countries because I had never been there and probably would never get to.

I looked up at Sam to distract myself, and he smiled down at me. His presence was comforting. Besides, I was on my first date. I needed to enjoy this the best I could, especially considering the person it was with. We began to walk around the square in a circle, so that we could make it to every single stall. It was the same route we had walked year after year since we were kids.

I'd never been very talented at the bobbing for corn game. It was almost embarrassing really, at the end of every attempt I just ended up with water all over my face and the ears of corn scattered to the edges of the miniature cow tank. The ears of corn all still had their husks on and you weren't allowed to pick them up by the ends. You had to grab them with your teeth just like the way you'd eat them, lengthwise. Sam, however, of course had an ear of corn within five minutes, looking almost like a loyal dog who had brought the stick back.

On the other hand, I was pretty good at the coal throwing game. That was a different one where you were given three good-sized lumps of coal and had to throw them at a hay bale painted like a bull's eye. The coal lumps always left a black mark where it hit, and I liked to think I had pretty good aim. Mine were all within the smallest two rings, but never a perfect bull's eye. Sam didn't make any rings, though. He always threw them too hard and caused them to ricochet strangely off the hay.

We played a few other games, and by then we had come around to the food side of the square. There were only three big booths in a row for each of the countries. Sam had always been skeptical of Auklia's food, simply because it was slightly less traditional than Mineraltir and Lunaka. Auklia was known for its concoctions of raw fish, crab, and different clams that I couldn't name. Along with other seafood, Auklians were also known for their generous helpings of rice with every meal. I didn't like rice much, but I always liked getting at least a little something from the Auklian stand. I always enjoyed the foreign feeling of eating something entirely different, as well as trying to be Auklian for one meal.

To save money, Sam and I shared a fried fish roll with some kind of sticky sauce on top, and, of course, a bowl of complementary rice. The flavor of the fish was strong yet tasteful. After checking to see if the fish was actually cooked, Sam ate his entire half.

Mineraltir's stand was completely different, exuding the odor of hundreds of spices paired with unfamiliar meats. The most popular meat in Mineraltir was venison, which was gamy, but the small piece Sam and I shared was well-rubbed with a flavor that made your mouth water for more. I wished

I knew the names of all the herbs and spices.

We skipped the Lunakan stand because our stash of extra cash was dwindling quickly. Bread, cheese, beef, and chicken. Not much spice, and definitely no raw fish. Most of their wares were normal to a noble's diet, but every so often we farmers would get lucky.

Sam and I moved on with our circle to the next game stand, and in that moment my heart dove into my stomach. Beyond Sam was a booth where you try to throw the leather ball so perfectly that it begins to spin on its axis on top of a little funnel. The game was not the issue. The man running the booth was. He was in disguise, yet I instantly recognized him. It was the same Auklian noble that I had run into the night I had gone to Grandma's, but tonight he was dressed in regular Lunakan clothing. His big glasses were what gave him away. There was no one else on this continent that I knew who wore such thick lenses.

Next to him was a red-haired man, one that I had definitely seen before, yet I couldn't quite remember where. Rachel had said that one of the men they were sure was one of Rhydin's Followers was Mineraltin, who was named Terran. Terran and Eli were the ones who Luke and James had to protect me from. I had forgotten about everything going wrong in my life while I laughed and played with Sam, but at the sight of them together, I nearly keeled over right then and there.

Sam looked over at me, and his expression changed immediately. "You okay? You're as white as a sheet."

"Y-Yeah, I'm fine." I took a deep breath. "Totally fine."

Sam quirked his eyebrow. "Y'know Lina, I really do hate it when you lie to me."

And, as if it hadn't been possible before, my heart sank even further into my gut as adrenaline kicked in. I couldn't bear to have Sam think me a liar. I stared up at him helplessly. "Sam, I-...!"

"You've been hiding something from me. I'm not stupid, Lina. I can tell you've been different ever since Keera was 'sick'. You know you can tell me anything, don't you?" Sam's eyes turned into a puppy's, and it was killing me. I couldn't do it! I couldn't keep it a secret anymore. But could I really trade Sam's life for my weakness?

"Sam..." My throat began to clog up. "Trust me, I'd tell you if I could. But if I told you, you could be killed."

His brow furrowed, his hand tightening on mine. I hadn't even realized we were holding hands until this moment. It was most likely the only reason I had not dropped to my knees yet. Or worse, fainted.

"Killed by who? What's going on, Lina?"

My knees felt like they were going to give out at any second, so Sam led me over to a bench. He promised that he'd go back and get some Auklian punch until I found the words to tell him what was going on. I straightened my skirt as I waited for him to come back, trying to slow my heart rate. I couldn't see Terran and Eli's booth from here. That fact was adding immensely to my anxiety, although it did mean they couldn't see me either.

What was I going to tell him? About being the Allyen? About Rhydin wanting to kill me and steal my locket? That all of Nerahdis was in danger, and it was my and some brother-I'd-never-known-existed's job to protect it? If anything, Sam would think I'd gone looney. There was no easy way to tell him, and certainly not in public where anyone with a set of ears could hear us. I decided to tell him that the instant he came back.

When he returned, he gave me the punch carefully, as if I

would drop it, and I gulped the fruitiness greedily. I hadn't realized how thirsty I was until now. When I was finished, I looked up at him, and he took my hand. "Do you want to go up to the castle? Their festival is just starting."

"Why?" I asked with a little more attitude that I probably should have. Why would we crash a Royal party?

"Oh, I know a few others who are headed up there now, and I just figured it'd be something different." Sam smiled innocently.

"I thought you wanted me to tell you…?" I looked up at him quietly.

"Oh, we can save that for later when there's fewer people. C'mon, let's go, it'll be fun." He smiled, and I decided not to question it. Maybe, he'd forget about it and I wouldn't have to tell him!

We walked up to the castle in the dark, his hand firmly on mine. He had held my hand softly earlier, carefully. It seemed tighter now. Because he really hadn't held my hand since we were kids, its presence on mine was a lightning bolt to my senses. I wondered if it was because I'd seemed so lightheaded earlier.

He was right, there were a few people on this path to the castle. There were lanterns up here as well, seeming a little less bright all alone in the dark landscape, but they were necessary to lead us along the almost invisible road.

In only minutes, I was standing in front of the castle for the first time in my entire life. It was gigantic. Each stone measured nearly half of my height, and there were so many towers that I couldn't even count them. It was hundreds of years old; its age read in the cracks of the mortar. Sam began to lead me toward the light of the front steps, and I held back, beginning to worry.

Part of me was a little excited. I had never been inside the castle before, yet at the same time I couldn't help but be frightened. This wasn't right. Royals and commoners hated each other. They didn't mix. That's why they were up in their Royal Castle, and we were down in the square. Most of the people we'd walked up here with seemed to be nobles, ones who could play both sides since they lived in Soläna but could were rich enough to rub elbows with the Royals. The nobles had already disappeared inside the big, wooden front door. I began to give in to my anxiety.

"Sam, I think we should go back down-…" I tried to say, before all my breath was taken away.

In front of me, Sam's body began to morph. He grew shorter and the reddish hue was taken out of his brown hair. His clothing changed from a simple farmer's best to bright colors and sashes, with what I guessed to be an Auklian medallion hanging around his neck. His face went from being the angular one I knew to one that was more circular, his eyes changing from brown to blue.

When the man who stood in front of me unfolded a pair of glasses and set them on his bony nose, I spun on my heel and tried to sprint, but a long arm caught me around the middle. I began to scream until Eli's hand covered my mouth, pulling my head back until my feet were off the ground. He whispered into my ear, "Quiet, young Allyen, or you'll regret it."

I felt a sharp point in my back, hidden underneath his cloak. I was in so much trouble. "I hate pink" wasn't going to fix this one.

I bit my tongue to keep from making a sound, and Eli put me down. His hand was becoming excruciatingly tight on my arm. He thrust me toward the open gates, and led me through a labyrinth of rooms until we reached the ballroom. Inside were no paper lanterns or streamers, but the finest flowers and plant decorations to honor our finish of the planting, Lunaka's main export other than coal.

I stood out like a sore thumb among all the nobles, their clothing all made of silk, cashmere, and other foreign and expensive materials. All I knew of fashion was that all Mineraltins wore green head to toe with gold accents, and Auklians were walking rainbows just like Eli was now. Lunakans seemed to be more of a mix between the two, wearing colors but not nearly as vibrant.

I swallowed hard when my eyes glanced across the golden thrones at the head of the room. King Adam sat there with his wife, Queen Gloria – Frederick and Mira's parents. I had never seen them before, only heard their names and had been taught long ago to fear them.

The king had dark curly hair similar to Mira's, his stocky structure lazily arranged on his big golden chair. The queen had a pleasant expression on her face, and I immediately thought her the most beautiful woman I'd ever seen. She had long golden hair and sparkling blue eyes, the same coloring as Frederick's, but her skin as pale as a doll's just like Mira's. Lounging in front of her was a young girl, maybe eleven at the most, who was the spitting image of Queen Gloria. I knew she must be Frederick and Mira's younger sister, Princess Cornflower.

On either side of their two gold thrones were two silver ones. On King Adam's right was a couple dressed immaculately in greens, both light grassy greens and dark emeralds, and decked out in gold. These I assumed to be Mineraltir's monarchs, King Morris and Queen Jasmine. They were Prince Xavier's parents.

To Queen Gloria's left was a much younger couple, a man

my age with deep blue hair like the ocean and a girl with unnaturally orange curls, both dressed in the rainbow. They had to be from Auklia, which meant that Prince Daniel had finally ascended the throne with his new wife, whose name I had yet to hear of. His blue hair matched the description that Keera had given me of the Daniel helping Evan, so I knew it was him. I looked up at them in awe. There were Three Kings of Nerahdis once again, as legend dictated. Nerahdis hadn't had three kings for some years since Queen Maria ruled alone after the Auklian king died.

I didn't dare making a move now that Eli and I were inside. There were too many Royal mages that could strike me dead any minute.

At that precise moment, the ballroom cleared in the center. King Adam stood from his elegant throne and straightened his deep black vest. He held up his hands, and for the first time, I was going to hear the king speak. His voice was gravelly, but strong. "Attention! Thank you all for coming tonight to celebrate the end of Lunaka's planting season! As an extra matter of celebration, I dedicate the first dance of the night to my daughter, Princess Mira Gloria Dorothy Tané, and her new fiancé, Prince Xavier Morris Josip Rollins of Mineraltir. As of this moment, they are engaged to be married! Let the dance begin!" A sneer was on King Adam's lined face.

My jaw nearly dropped open. Mira was engaged to Prince Xavier? Did they even know each other remotely well? At that moment, I decided I was completely disgusted with the Royals' system of marriage, and we didn't even know if Xavier was on our side or not.

I saw Mira head to the empty center of the room, her long dark hair elegantly curled with pearls laced through it. A light green and purple dress flattered her form beautifully. From the opposite side of the room, a young man, apparently caught off guard, slowly made his way toward Mira. I stared at him harder when I realized it was Xavier, trying to put a face with the name. He was red-haired like all Mineraltins, but it was long in back, tied in a stubby ponytail. He wasn't as decorated as the other people who were around him, which made me respect him a little bit, but he still looked nice.

When he reached Mira, he took her hand and kissed it, like a gentleman greeted a stranger, but Mira looked like she was about to faint. He led her in an extremely slow dance, both their sets of knees weak. As if from a hidden cue, everyone else then began to join the slow dance in pairs.

The point in my back got a little sharper, and I gritted my teeth to keep from yelping in pain. Eli's lips brushed against my ear as he whispered, "Now, young Allyen, onto business."

The knife was removed, and he pulled me onto the dance floor towards where I saw all the Royals dancing in the middle. Was he *nuts*? Everyone was going to see me! I didn't blend in with their satin and jewels in my mother's cotton dress! Unless that was what he wanted? He wanted me dead. I suddenly could not decide whether to escape and be run through with Eli's dagger or stay put until someone recognized me and shot me with magic. Either way, I was a goner.

Eli turned me and placed a hand on my waist to begin to dance, and I saw Xavier and Mira dancing awkwardly together, not a word passing between them. The blue-haired man that I assumed was King Daniel twirled with his young queen, bright smiles on their faces, ignorant to my plight.

When Eli swung me around as part of the dance, Frederick landed within my sights. He was all dressed up in a white suitcoat with a Lunakan emblem around his neck as the crown prince. He was dancing with a dark-haired noblewoman I recognized from my childhood. Her name was Cassandra. I had known her in school before she moved away to Lun. She had been one of my best friends as a child, and it was surreal to see her with Prince Frederick now.

As we passed dangerously close to them, I made sure to step on the long blue trail of Cassandra's immaculate dress. She became confused when it happened, and when she looked at me, I saw recognition in her eyes. Frederick turned to see what she was looking at just in time to see the most terrified expression to ever cross my face.

Instantly, he dropped Cassandra's hands and tapped Eli on the shoulder, apparently the proper etiquette to ask for someone's partner. Cassandra's deep blue eyes were still confused, trained on me as her hands gripped each other now.

Eli dropped me instantly, Frederick taking his place, one hand holding mine and the other barely touching my waist. Eli looked at us for a few seconds. His smile was so wide I thought his face might crack open, and then he ran off toward a dark hallway.

I let myself sigh in relief and relax from the tension that I hadn't even known was gripping me. A brief thought about dancing with the heir to Lunaka's crown crossed my mind, but at that point I really didn't even care. I looked up into Frederick's light blue eyes, his blond hair neatly combed, and felt completely safe for that moment.

Frederick slowly and inconspicuously danced me over to the side of the room. We wedged our way through people until we reached the pillars and crossed into a dark hallway. Immediately, his voice was louder than necessary. "What the heck happened, Lina?"

"I don't know, I thought he was Sam..." I choked on his

name, all the tears starting to come out now as I shook with fear.

A shadow stepped away from the next set of pillars, and I saw James, Rachel's younger brother. He was also decked out in clothing I'd never seen before but vaguely Lunakan. He promptly put a strong hand on my shoulder. "We need to get out of here."

"Where were you?" I turned on him fiercely. "I thought you were supposed to be my bodyguards, well, where on Nerahdis *were* you?"

"Lina, I was following you the entire time. I was trying to get through the ballroom, why do you think I'm dressed like this?" He gestured to himself and his fancy outfit. "But that's not the problem."

"Oh, no…" Frederick groaned, his wiry fingers messing up his stringy hair. "No no *no*! I'm such an idiot! It was a trap!"

James looked at him, slightly confused, but then started to try and pull Frederick and I toward the exit. I was lost more now than ever. Any sense of safety melted away as James' grip on my arm tightened and he spoke through gritted teeth, "What is it?"

Frederick screamed in a voice I had never heard before. "*Run!*"

# CHAPTER SEVEN

James' eyes widened in fear, and I visibly saw the moment when his heart dropped. His voice shook, "Oh, no. They weren't here for you, Lina, they were here to see if Frederick was helping the Allyen!"

And then, all three of us were running as fast as we possibly could, desperately following Frederick through the labyrinthine castle. Frederick fell into Rhydin's trap when he saved me from Eli. I was only the bait. I swallowed hard with another gasp of air. They only wanted to see what he'd do upon seeing me with one of Rhydin's people. They wanted to see if the crown prince would dance with a peasant girl if it meant saving me, the Allyen, from Rhydin. It was a test, and he had passed with flying colors. He had confirmed that he was working with me by protecting me. Something he was now going to be hunted for.

We were in so much trouble.

When we were only yards away from the front gate, I began to hear several pairs of footsteps getting closer to us.

Catching up to us. My lungs burned, but my legs were far too full of adrenaline to quit now. I ran faster than I ever had before, flying out of the gates toward the canyon. It was then, while out under the stars that I realized little balls of something were being hurled at us from behind.

After a few blasts, I dared a peek over my shoulder. Men in black were charging little violet balls of energy into their hands and aiming their best for the three of us. They were shooting us with magic! All my nightmares came true in that moment, and that fear drove me even faster. I saw bits of prairie grass hit in the crossfire fizzle and burn into black oblivion, and I sure as heck did not want to be hit with anything close to that.

More often than not, the purple, buzzing blasts were aimed towards Frederick's vicinity. Once or twice, I saw pieces of his suitcoat or his long cloak burned away. Each piece would suddenly light up and smolder into a dark circle of nothing. While I was running with wild abandon, my mind couldn't help but be a little confused.

Only Royals were supposed to have magic, and these people, like Eli and Terran, definitely were not Royals.

' As Frederick, James, and I got closer to the edge of the canyon, my eyes picked out something familiar in the dark. It was the pulley mechanism, the exact same device as was on the southern side of the canyon that I rode down every once in a while, and now, my occasional joy ride was turning into the perfect escape plan. No one knew the speed and power of the pulleys like I did.

Frederick was actually slightly behind me, my short legs able to complete more paces than his long strides, and so I turned around just long enough to latch onto his wrist, beginning to haul him towards the pulley. He was confused but didn't question it. We were running too fast for questions. The magical blasts were getting a bit closer as Rhydin's people gained on us. James zigzagged behind Frederick and I to make us a harder target.

Prince Frederick and I were only feet away from the pulley platform when I heard James scream. My mind only had seconds to process the fact that it wasn't a scream of pain but a short burst of noise designed to draw attention to something. I turned my head in time to see the fiery purple shot blazing forward about to dive deep into Frederick's heart. With only seconds to spare, using all the strength I had left, I shoved the crown prince to the side.

Frederick tripped but didn't lose his footing, and the next thing I knew, a deep burning pain was burying itself into the back of my arm. A loud gasp escaped from my lips, my arm wet and charred where I touched it. After only a second, my eyesight was still clear enough to see the terror on the man in black's face as he saw whom he had struck. I saw him yell in frustration before I felt two long wiry arms pull me onto the pulley.

The world spun, heavy with pain and muggy air. My legs gave out. The prince scooped me up as James released the pulley lever, sending our platform flying down the canyon walls at a barely under control speed.

However, after maybe thirty seconds, a crash resounded. Our pulley began to spiral as Rhydin's Followers destroyed the mechanism and the line above. As we spun in circles, the corners of the wooden platform collided with the rock wall, shattering and sending splinters everywhere, until it tipped and the three of us were free-falling into the darkness.

I was going to die. There was no question about it. My arm felt numb and destroyed, and now we were falling out of the sky like shot birds. I could feel myself fading from consciousness, my body weightless in the fall while still in Frederick's tight grip.

There was a burst of insanely bright light. I could no longer feel Frederick's arms clinging to me, but I felt my body slow, and then nothing.

Sam saw everything. He'd been confused when Lina hadn't been there waiting for him, even though the line to get the punch was extremely long. He had been a little irked that she had run away before telling him what she'd been lying about, but he had figured that it was getting a little late and perhaps she had taken Rosetta and Keera home.

However, that all changed when Keera, Rosetta, and Mikael returned to him thirty minutes later during the festival cleanup and asked where Lina was. The look on the little cousin's face was one of absolute terror, and Sam began to worry. He sent the three of them home and began to search for Lina, but it didn't last long.

He heard a racket from the north end of town and so started walking up that way through the quiet townhouses. As he got closer, he heard a loud scream that chilled his blood and the familiar sound of offensive magic. He hurried along faster, his feet barely touching the cobblestones, until he could see amethyst shots flying over the pulley above, shots that Sam immediately recognized from the stories his father had told him as a boy. Stories that nearly no one else in Nerahdis had ever heard.

From where he was, he could see three people coming down on the pulley. They were descending more quickly than normal, yet he couldn't exactly make them out. Suddenly, the rope was cut, and it began to fall, jutting into the canyon wall multiple times before overthrowing its occupants. Sam's heart sank into his stomach.

Abruptly, a burst of white light nearly blinded him, and two of the people were blown to the side. Sam didn't see the other two land, but by then he realized that he wasn't alone. Next to him, waiting beneath the wreckage, were the two eldest Owens siblings, of which he recognized the red-haired woman as Lina's best friend, Rachel.

As the ball of light slowly fell, Sam awaited it carefully. He was wary of magic, as most Lunakans were, but was more cautious than ever because of his past experiences. To his surprise, as the ball began to dissipate maybe six feet from the ground, it revealed the form of the girl he'd grown up with, one that he would recognize anywhere. Tiny, too-skinny body, with short legs and mud-colored hair that had been blasted out of the braided thing she'd had earlier. She was completely unconscious, and Sam immediately ran toward her to catch her as the light magic shut off.

He kneeled slightly so he could move one hand to her face, gripping her chin as he moved it back and forth. His voice betrayed his panic and desperation. "Lina. Lina, wake up! *Please*, wake up!"

Hearing footsteps, Sam looked up to see James and Luke Owens with an also unconscious Prince Frederick between them. Both the prince and the younger boy, James, were roughed up from Lina's magical explosion. Rachel placed her hand on Sam's shoulder, his breath beginning to catch in fear. Her voice was calm but hurried. "Come, we need to move now! We're not safe here."

Sam nodded, holding Lina more tightly. Within another

flash of light, the six of them vanished.

Lunaka's crown prince woke up twenty minutes later in what seemed upon first impression to be a cellar. There were several candles hanging from the ceiling, lighting the dark, excavated space. A single window was on the eastern wall up next to the ceiling, but one wouldn't know from the outside because of the multitude of towels stuffed into the indention. Frederick almost looked up to see if there were any stalactites he should be worried about, but alas, above him was only wood with a few supports here and there. Where was he?

He leaned forward carefully, his body aching slightly. The events of the evening came spiraling back to him, and Frederick groaned, touching his head. How could he be so stupid?

"Are you alright, m'lord?"

Frederick looked over to see Rachel staring at him, sitting on the very furthest corner of the little cot he'd been sleeping on. She had slight circles under her eyes, and the candlelight truly brought out the brilliant, unnatural red in her hair. Sometimes, Frederick forgot what she was. The prince allowed his regal bearing to slip away as he flopped back onto the cot. "How could I be such an idiot, Rachel? Why did I not take the time to realize what they were doing?"

"You'll have to fill me in on that one." Rachel smiled.

Frederick took a deep breath. "The instant I saw Lina in the ballroom with Eli, the only thing I could think about was getting her away from him. She looked so terrified, it was an expression like nothing I'd ever seen. I didn't even consider leading him to the side or waiting to see what happened. Like an imbecile, right there in the middle of the room, I dropped my date and took her from him. And he just *smiled*."

Rachel's brow furrowed. "Rhydin must be doing the very thing we're doing to him then."

"He's trying to figure out who's on her side. The side of the Allyen." He said quietly, "Just like how we've been trying to figure out who's helping him. Tonight, Lina was just the distraction. I-…I was the target." A flash of pain crossed the prince's face, "And I fell for it. Like the biggest oaf in Nerahdis. My head is on the chopping block."

"Oh, Your Highness, don't be so dramatic!" The red-haired woman stood and straightened her skirts. "But, you're right. My brothers and I cannot allow you to return to the castle. If you even step outside into the streets, his people are watching for the chance to murder you. Right now, nobody knows where you are, so you must stay here."

Frederick sighed heavily. "So my sisters are on their own?"

"No. But we'll have to shield Mira heavily so Rhydin's Followers do not discover her allegiance to the Allyen as well. Cornflower doesn't know a thing, so she is safe. Besides, now that Lina's magic has activated, things are going to get much more interesting."

That was right. That shining ball of light that had stopped Lina's descent and sent him and James flying was the awakening of Lina's Allyen magic. She would have died if it hadn't, so the magic sprang into being from its dormant state to keep itself alive as well.

This was what Rhydin had been waiting for, for so many years. Lina's brother, Evanarion, had gained his magic several years ago, and now the last card had been played. Now, Rhydin could begin his move.

———————⟨o≈⟩———————

My body felt heavy. When I was finally able to open my eyes, at first all I could see was a thin beam of light trying to make it through Grandma's lace curtains. As my mind slowly cleared, I could make out the familiar shapes of my grandmother's guest bedroom: a chest that had never been used, a mint-condition wicker rocking chair, and all the cracks that had been etched into the ceiling over the years of shifting earth.

I groaned when I tried to lean forward, the fluffy comforter on the bed seeming more like a restraint than a comfort. My arm where I'd been shot ached with a dull pain, but it was subsiding. What happened? How did I not die when we were falling? Were Frederick and James okay?

I suddenly heard Grandma's voice very loudly from the kitchen on the other side of the door, "Now, Mr. Greene, we've done everything we can for her. We calmed her magic down and healed her, and now she needs her rest. I am asking you nicely to leave."

"Look, I know what I saw! I was the one who caught her! What's going on here? What's wrong? Why was she hurt?"

Sam's voice was nearly unrecognizable he was so upset, but I knew without a doubt it was him. What did he mean that he caught me? He became even louder if that were possible. "Tell me what's going on, or I'm taking her home right this instant!"

The door was barely open a crack, and I held my eye up to it. I saw Grandma's expression turn black and her little wrinkled hands find her hips. "Come now, Kidek. I would not threaten me if I were you. You have no idea what you're getting into!"

Sam's expression was one of complete and utter shock. His eyes went wide, sending wrinkles up his forehead, aging him instantly. He rested his hand on Grandma's kitchen table and sat down before he could fall. "You've known? All this time?"

"No. Rachel, Luke, and James told me, but I am familiar with the position." Grandma admitted, her voice lowering.

Sam and Grandma were at eye level now that he was sitting. He looked at her almost as if he had tears in his eyes from it all, and pleaded, "Won't you please tell me? I need to know what happened to her."

"Rhydin's Followers attacked Prince Frederick last night."

"Why? I know he's the crown prince and all, but what other reason would he have?"

"Because the prince was caught helping the new Allyen."

Sam became quiet, looking down at his feet with his brow furrowed. Then, it was as if lightning struck him with realization, and he smacked himself in the face. "Of course, how could I be so stupid. Her locket! It's the Allyen one from the legend, isn't it?"

Before Grandma could answer, I decided to finally open the door and let them know that I was listening. A lot of questions were on the tip of my tongue, but before I could say a word, Grandma switched the subject.

"Ah, you're finally awake! How do you feel? Well, it'll continue to get better. Unfortunately, we have no more time for words, because you were only brought here to be healed, my dear. Rhydin knows where I live, and you are not safe here. You must be moved into hiding."

I swallowed, upset that I couldn't ask my questions. "Where am I going then? What about Rosetta and Keera? And the farm?"

Grandma sighed, looking sad. "I will take care of the girls. As for your farm…"

"I'll tend to it." Sam's words were quick and decisive, his eyes delayed in meeting mine.

I remembered how Sam had morphed into Eli last night. Of course, it was the wrong Sam, but it still made me uneasy. My hand ran through my bangs, a nervous habit. I took a deep breath, trying to wrap my mind around another huge life change. How long would this last? Would I ever get to go home again? I sighed with defeat. "Thank you."

Grandma went and rummaged through one of her crates next to her counter, returning with a big, heavy brown cloak. She raised her voice for someone outside to hear. "Luke! James! It's time!"

As the two freckled Owens boys walked in, jingling slightly with hidden chainmail, Grandma motioned for Sam to stand and fastened the cloak around his shoulders. My feet still heavy, she pulled me over to Sam and directed him to pick me up and hide me under the cloak. She explained, "My house is being watched for signs of magic now. This will have to do for getting you to safety."

As James put on his own cloak, pulling his hood over his shaggy hair, he grinned at me. "Congratulations, Lina! You can use your magic now!"

"Is that what happened?" I asked as Sam gingerly put his arm around my shoulders and picked my numb legs up. My body tensed, but I tried to ignore it. If my magic was what saved my life, maybe it wasn't such a bad thing after all. "What does that mean then? That I have magic now?"

Luke spoke this time, his voice a low monotone. "It means that the hard work can now begin. You have a lot of training in front of you."

Before I could respond, Grandma pulled the edges of Sam's cloak around his arms to cover me. Luckily, I was so small that it worked relatively well. She also laid the big hood over his bandana-ed head, and breathed something so quiet I barely heard it, much less anybody else. "You're very brave to wear the colors of your people. Many would love to see you all dead."

"I know, Ma'am." Sam whispered, "But it's something I must do."

With that, Luke and James took their positions on either side of Sam and I, and we exited Grandma's house into a town much different from what it was last night. Last night, the streets were full of lights and music and the sound of people laughing. This morning, people were quiet and talking amongst themselves in hushed voices. The strangest part was the number of soldiers. There were soldiers marching in every street, walking down every alley, standing at every corner. It was if Lunaka was at war, although there hadn't been one for decades.

I could barely see through the thin crack in the cloak, and soon Luke turned around and closed it completely. It became a little brown tent. No sunlight could make it through the heavy material, so I resigned myself to the blackness. I let my body finally relax against Sam's, convincing myself that I had very few real friends in this world, and I needed Sam. I wanted Sam.

My ear was over his heart, and its beat had quickened considerably. I wondered if the sight of soldiers freaked him out too. Lunakans were completely unaccustomed to seeing them. Sure, we all knew we had a big army because it was King Adam's brainchild, but it was always within the castle walls or out along the borders. Never in town. I wondered if it had to do with Prince Frederick.

It seemed like we'd been walking for ages. The darkness was playing tricks on my eyes, and at any second I was sure they'd close for another few hours. Sam's stride was soothing and constant, but abruptly it shortened. He seemed to shuffle down what I guessed were stairs.

For a split second, the cloak fell open slightly to allow me one last view of the world. Another picture of all the soldiers patrolling the familiar cobblestone roads. My heart fell into my stomach when I saw one of many wanted posters plastered to the wall above our heads.

On the left was Frederick, the crown prince who had "disappeared". On the right was a sketch of my own face, "The Traitor", but it was out of sight before I could see what it was for.

When Luke and James allowed me out of the cloak, my eyes had to adjust to the new surroundings. It was a basement. The curvature of the ground and the one high window was evidence enough of that. There were candles dangling all across the ceiling, which was wood. It made me wonder what we were underneath. There was a big table in the middle, and off on one wall there was a cot laden with a sleeping form. Rachel came forward to greet me out of the corner and threw her arms around me, thrilled that I was all right.

Apparently, it was Frederick on the cot, and there was another one in the same part of the room that Rachel began to herd me toward. "You need your rest, Lina, you let out a lot of magical energy last night. You have to build it back up before you can start your training." She grinned happily, ear to ear.

Luke and James escorted Sam to the door to my dismay, and I reached after him with my eyes until I could see him no longer. I wanted him to stay.

Rachel made me lie down and pulled the blanket up to my chin like any mother would. My mind felt like it was spinning in circles trying to keep up. What was a Kidek? How did Sam know about Rhydin? What would my magic feel like when I had it under my control? I was only able to verbalize the first one before Rachel called mandatory bedtime.

Rachel looked at me as if she hadn't expected to hear that question. Her red eyebrows rose and shadows formed under her blue eyes. "Well, long story short, the Kidek is the leader of the Rounans. I'll tell you more later if you would like."

I could barely nod or process any shock before my eyes unwillingly closed.

# Chapter Eight

My eyelids creaked when they opened, feeling heavier than they'd ever been before. As they began to recognize light, I realized that the wall was wrong. I lay on my side, staring at it, with a huge weight in my chest, a lump like a sand bag sitting on my heart. My arm ached, although not too badly now.

I did not see the rough edges of the wood that lined my home. Nowhere could I see those beautiful shades of brown etched into the lines that once could tell a tree's age. I did not see the little notch in the wall where I accidentally fell as a child and nearly broke my arm or the little burlap bag that held some of my most dear possessions – my mother's favorite children's book that I learned how to read from, an old sock of my father's that he had taught me how to darn, Rosetta's doll she had made me when we were extremely little, and a grass whistle Sam had given me shortly after we became friends – which sat in the corner underneath my straw tick where no one could see.

I saw, instead, a hard, earthen wall that was dug out hastily, perhaps in secret. A small, thin root twined its way through the crumbling dirt, straggly and black. It was most likely killed many years ago by the coal-sodden soil of this mining town.

As the realization sank in that I was not at home, and that I was, indeed, in the basement of Luke Owens' livery, I felt my heart beat increase. We were nearly killed last night. I should have died, but I didn't. My magic saved my life…

It was at this moment that I realized that my back was against something hard. I moved slightly, but not too much considering the weight in my chest, and became confused as to how I could be facing a wall and yet have my back against another one. This wall wasn't just hard; it had *curves*.

I leaned forward barely far enough to look over my shoulder, and to my surprise, I saw Rachel. She was parallel to me, her shoulder blades against the small of my back because she was so tall. Her red hair seemed messier than usual, pulled tightly away from her face into a little blob on the back of her head, but she was awake, staring into the corner of the little earthen room, the candles dimly lit above. When I finally found my voice, I just had to say, "Rachel? What in the world are you doing?"

Rachel snapped out of her thoughts, her pristine blue eyes finding mine as she rolled over toward me the tiniest of bits, careful to keep her back firmly against mine. "Good morning, Lina! How do you feel? Oh, this? Sorry, we're still working on hiding your presence from Rhydin. Until your charm is finished, the only way to keep him from sensing you is by keeping core contact with me. Good thing we're friends, right?" She grinned from ear to ear like this was the most normal thing in the world. "Frederick has to do it, too! See?"

She motioned just a few feet away in the same little alcove to Prince Frederick's cot. He was sitting up, barely awake, his pretty white suitcoat wrinkled and smudged with burn marks. Sitting to his back was young, long-haired James working away with his hands on some sort of multicolored leather object. It was a strange sight to see two people with their backs to each other, but at least if I had to do it, they did too.

Frederick groaned and rubbed his eyes, stretching the skin of his temples into strange contortions as if that would make his head stop hurting. Afterward, his back straightened, like the noble prince he was, and his eyes found mine. "Lina, I am so sorry. I would come kneel and apologize further, but my protector is preoccupied."

I couldn't help the smile coming to my face as James gave him an irked-teenager look, the lump in my chest becoming a little lighter. "You don't have anything to apologize for. Besides, that would just be wrong to have the crown prince at my feet. Not to mention unsettling."

Frederick chuckled, possibly the first time I had seen him smile. It was nice. His wiry build extended to his face, the cords in his cheeks tightening to create quite the set of dimples. His voice was resolute as he said, "Either way, please accept my apology. I have put both our lives into irrevocable danger because of a hasty, rash decision that cannot be undone."

Before I had time to respond, Rachel chimed in with her musical voice. "Well, it's not the perfect situation, but we must make the best of it. You two are going to be getting a lot of one on one time living down here, and it's the perfect set up to begin magic training!"

"Magic training?" I could feel my jaw fall and the fear settle into my throat.

"Of course!" Rachel replied cheerily, "You remember that message I left you in that bottle, don't you? It said 'meet us the day after the festival', and here we are! The objective was always to begin teaching you magic, but now it's awakened so even better! Although that means we really need to get started so you'll be ready for Rhydin. You did get that message, right? I winked at you. I thought that would help."

"Whoa, whoa wait, slow down!" I forgot for a moment and tried to scoot away from Rachel to better situate myself to look at her, as most human beings do.

She gave me a dark look and moved with me to keep her back against mine. "Lina, never do that again until the feathers are ready! Even just a few seconds could allow Rhydin to find you and kill you before you know one spell!"

I swallowed hard, starting to feel claustrophobic.

Frederick sighed. "Rachel is right. Rhydin no doubt knows that your magic has awakened, and so whatever he has in plan for us will soon be made known. I will teach you magic the best I can. Our powers are far different, but it will be as close as we can get. Don't be afraid of it. It's saved your life once now, and it will do so again countless times."

I nodded, beginning to feel slightly better about the whole magic situation. A few thoughts were swirling around my mind though. "Your Highness, I-..."

"Don't call me that." The prince was quiet, his eyes staring right through me. "I would prefer if you called me by my given name. So few people in my life do, and I would like you to do so as well."

"Okay... Frederick." The name felt strange on my tongue with no title. I was getting used to hearing it by Rachel and her brothers, but it felt strange to say it myself out loud. "I have a question already, if that's okay?" He nodded. I took a deep breath, trying to decide how I should word it. It was still so foreign to me. "How do Rhydin's Followers have magic if they are not Royals? Does this mean they are Rounans?

Frederick tried to stand but remembered James and stopped. Instead, he gripped his knees a little harder as he spoke, "Lina, you really must work on forgetting that notion ever existed. It is totally incorrect. You have magic, and you are not a Royal or a Rounan. Royals tend to have magic much more often than most people because of their pure bloodlines. The Royal families typically only marry within each other, and so we have a very strong Gornish bloodline straight from Emperor Caden himself. Common people have mixed blood, which may contain Gornish, Rounan, or any sort of mixture that never had magic in the first place. Rhydin's magic is created magic, as the Allyen magic is. His is so great, in fact, he can metaphorically break off pieces and hand them to other people to use in his stead. This is how his Followers have power. There is much more complication and technicality to it, but it is far too impossible to understand at your current level."

He was right. My head was already spinning. Parts of it made sense, yet it seemed impossible to unlink the connection between Rounans being the only common people who had magic. We had grown up our entire lives being taught to stay away from Rounans because they were dangerous, and if you were convicted of being one, whether rightly or falsely, you were immediately hanged. I remembered one of the public hangings I saw as a child. My mother hadn't realized it was occurring and had taken me to town with her. Normally, she kept our family clear away from them, but she had made a rare mistake. She kept her hand over my eyes, but I remembered the screams.

And now, I knew a Rounan personally. Someone I never dreamed would be a Rounan, much less the leader of the entire people. Sam was the Kidek. I was an Allyen. In the span of less than a week, our friendship that had been a constant for ten full years had changed forever, equally complicated by both new titles.

What would happen to us now? I hadn't told him about my magic, and now he knew I lied. But he had lied to me as well... He never told me about this role, or that his bandana, which I always figured was some weird preference or obsession, was actually a way of signifying him as leader. Kidek of the Rounans. It was mind boggling, and it was scary to think I might lose my childhood friend. It bothered me a lot more than I thought it would, too.

"Frederick? Is Sam really the Kidek?" My lips trembled.

The blond-haired man looked at me with a quirk to his eyebrow. "Yes, he is. Leader of the Rounans. It is an inherited position, always passed down to the firstborn son just like kingship is. Therefore, he inherited magic that is unlike any other. Rounan magic does not take any sort of form, such as water or fire. Or even wind, like my own. I'll get to that in our lessons." Frederick smiled slightly.

At that moment, there was a sound outside the little door. They were light footsteps, but the old stairs betrayed the noise with loud creaking. The door opened to reveal Luke, Rachel's brother, with bags under his eyes and clad in simple clothing with an apron covered in straw. He smelled of horses, having already worked a few this morning.

James seemed overjoyed to see him, as if he'd been quite bored. "Luke! Are the feathers ready yet? I am so ready to be one person again!"

Rachel let out a chuckle, but Luke was much more adept at

hiding his emotions. He cleared his throat as he crossed the room to another wall where shelves had been dug out. "Yes, James. They had to crystallize overnight, but they should be finished. You will be free soon enough. All of you will."

I began to watch Luke carefully as he withdrew a package wrapped in animal hide, curious as to what these feathers really were. More questions came forth from my teeming mind. I sputtered, "Rachel, you said a charm would hide Frederick and I's presences from Rhydin. Is it a feather? How can just a bird feather be so special? What is a presence anyway?"

Rachel sighed, trying to look at me while remaining back to back. "Yes, the charm I mentioned takes the form of a feather, but it's not a bird feather, Lina. It's far more important than that."

Luke and James were both eyeing her as she spoke this.

"These feathers come from our people, the ones that have devoted their lives to protecting the Allyen. They are very powerful, and they will hide you from even Rhydin. A presence…well… It's more like when you have magic, you are able to tell when other magical people are around, or even where they are if close enough. That's what it means to sense a presence. Rhydin's power is so great that even if he were on the far end of Mineraltir, he could sense you from here in Soläna because you have magic. This feather will make your presence invisible, you and Frederick both."

"Oh." I nodded, that concept somewhat making sense although seemed halfway stalker-ish. "Do normal people have presences? What about Rounans?"

"Again with the Rounans…" Luke grumbled from across the hall.

"I'm just curious!" I crossed my arms angrily.

Frederick responded this time. "You can sense normal people if you're looking straight at them. If you cannot see a person without magic, you cannot sense them as they have no power to sense. Rounans have a slightly different case, seeing as they aren't Gornish in descent. They feel different when you sense them, again only when you're looking right at them. You *can* sense them, but most of the time you have to check their arm to make sure."

"Arm? Why the arm? That doesn't make sense. What's so special about an arm?" I was flabbergasted at this point and totally lost.

Frederick chuckled, "No one really knows this. In fact, I didn't either until I met a real Rounan, but they have marks on their arms. A long angular one from their wrist to their elbow that tells you how much magic they have. It's a mark every true Rounan has, but nobody knows, which leads to all the tragic hangings of innocent people that were just a little strange. You could ask Sam to see his."

I had to let that absorb for a while. That's why they were so many terrible hangings? Because people were so prejudiced that they didn't bother to check the facts? How many lives could have been saved? Why were Rounans persecuted so terribly? I wondered if I should wait and ask Sam that last one.

Luke approached the two cots with what looked like two shards in his hands. One was a brilliant purple, more like amethyst, and the other was the most beautiful shade of grass green. They both shone with reflected light, looking like pieces stolen from a stained-glass window or something. They were each strung on a leather cord, a few beads on either side of purple, orange, or green.

James took the green one and tied it around Frederick's

neck. As soon as it was knotted tightly, James shot up and took a few leaps around the small room, stretching his thin limbs. "Freedom!" He celebrated.

Rachel took the purple shard into her hands carefully, and then worked on tying it securely around my neck. I touched it as it came to rest a little lower than my locket would if I was still wearing it. It was not there, and I remembered that it was tucked safely into my sash because I had yet to find something to replace the shoelace Birdie had broken.

This so-called feather looked so much like glass, but it didn't feel like one in any way! It seemed hard and sharp, but when I held it in my hand, it was light and soft, as if I held nothing but air. Barely, within the purple shine, I could make out a vein, such as a leaf or bird feather would have. It really was a feather, but it looked like a piece of stained glass. What kind of creature did these feathers come from?

"Now, you must *never* take these off!" Rachel warned as she stood, stretching herself although not quite as animated as James was.

Frederick was looking at his own feather, marveling at its qualities just as I had been, before tucking it safely inside his vest. I turned just in time to see Luke handing Rachel and James a piece of paper from his pocket and whispering, "You'll never believe what they're doing…"

In a matter of seconds, Rachel and James both busted out laughing, holding the paper tightly. James was howling while Rachel cried she was trying so hard to control herself. Frederick and I glanced at each other, confused as to what could make the Owenses laugh so hard. They had senses of humor, that's for sure, but it was a rare occurrence to see them crack up like this.

Frederick caved before I did. "What is it?"

Rachel pursed her lips, attempting to keep from laughing as she handed him the paper, which I could now see was a flyer. "So, how's the happy couple?"

I could see the color drain from Frederick's face as Rachel and James died of laughter. When I asked what it was, he couldn't even speak to me, much less look at me, as he passed the flyer over. It was the same poster I had seen yesterday, Frederick's face on one side and some sort of rendition of mine on the other. They made my eyes too big. I saw the word "Traitor", as I had yesterday, but the text at the bottom was a completely different story. The official news straight from the castle was that Frederick and I had *eloped*!

I felt my heart sink and my mouth go dry instantly. I could barely feel my hands holding the paper anymore, and there were no words for what I was feeling. Horrified came the closest. I dared a glance at Frederick, who was being elbowed by James until he finally gave a little laugh. He was getting over it. Probably thinking it was silly. I wanted to die.

"Yep, you two are *definitely* going to have to stay down in this basement until this craziness comes to an end." Rachel laughed, "The entire kingdom is scouring the town for you two newlyweds, and once the kingdom finds you, Rhydin will. Feathers or no feathers."

I glared at Rachel with one of the darkest glares of my lifetime.

She apologized rapidly.

I sighed, falling back against my blankets now that I was free of the person on my back. Despondently, I said, "But when will it end, Rachel? I want to go home. What about my farm? Sam can't tend it forever. He's got his own place!"

Luke responded, "We do not know yet. For now, we will stick with Frederick beginning your training down here. It is safe, so it works for now. But we do not know how long you must stay down here."

"Great. This is gonna be boring." I rolled over.

"Better than dead!" Luke's hands moved to his hips.

James chimed in, "Besides, your grandma moved up there with your sister and cousin. We can help with your farm since we can go outside. It'll be fine, trust me. We'll do our best till we can sort this all out!"

I took a deep breath, trying to believe that it really would be alright. Luke went back upstairs to tend to his livery while Rachel left to go secure us some sort of meal. James remained with us, a little put off that he couldn't go outside too, but he didn't make a fuss.

Since we began to be bored, and at least I for one still felt pretty awkward about the whole elopement rumor, Frederick began to give me some sort of introductory magic lesson. I really thought that I was starting to get the hang of this, but before we were even midway through the lesson, I felt like an idiot. This whole magic thing was going to be a lot harder than I would ever have imagined.

But, I suppose it's better than being dead, right?

# CHAPTER NINE

Frederick had an interesting teaching style. He took his sweet time explaining concepts to me because he knew they would be difficult to understand. He definitely didn't seem to be concerned about the amount of time spent on each subject, as all my old schoolteachers had been. They had grown angry if I took too long to spell a word or work an arithmetic problem, but Frederick was the most patient man in the world because we had all the time in the world. We had no idea when we would be able to leave the little basement underneath the livery, especially without fear that someone would capture us thinking that we had eloped. Or worse, Rhydin found us. Although I must admit, the elopement story seemed much scarier at this point.

The most important thing Frederick taught me was that the weight in my chest I'd been feeling since I woke up was actually my body acknowledging the new magic within me. I asked Frederick if he had a lump in his chest too, but he couldn't tell because he'd never experienced being magic-less before. He'd possessed magic his entire life because he was a Royal. He was born with it, so there was no transition period. He said he was sure there'd come a day where I couldn't feel the weight in my chest anymore because I'd be used to it. But, he said to never forget that having magic was a heavy burden we would have to carry for our entire lives.

"Now if you ever feel like you're not in control of your magic, a spell has gone haywire or something, just remember to focus on that weight in your chest. That's where your magic lives, and by focusing on that little area, it'll return it to your control." Frederick said, "There was once that one of my spells didn't quite turn out the way I wanted it to. I was jealous of the aguamages in Auklia, so I tried to use my own magic to siphon water from the river by the castle. Being an aeromage, it's completely impossible, but I was determined. Yet, instead of siphoning water, I ended up creating a little dust devil in the palace courtyard. Luckily, my father never found out!"

That was an interesting tidbit too. There were different "types" of people who could use magic. There were aguamages, who worked with water, aeromages, who worked with wind, and pyromages, who worked with fire. Then there was Rhydin. He was a sorcerer because he didn't use magic based in nature. Dark magic, to be precise.

The Allyens on the other hand were a unique type of sorcerer who used a mix of wind and light magic. They were also different since it was a created magic physically passed down, rather than genetic. I wondered what Rounans were, or if they were merely considered Rounans rather than given a fancy name on top of that one.

Frederick also made the point that Rounan magic took no form, much unlike people of Gornish descent. It was totally different, like an invisible force. I was so curious to ask Sam what it felt like, or if he could show me. Yet, at the same time I still felt unnerved about it. It was surprising how uncomfortable it made me feel to think he may not want to be my friend anymore. I found myself growing sick to my stomach as Frederick's lessons churned on. I wished I could just see Sam and get whatever would happen over with.

It was at that moment that I realized Frederick had stopped speaking. He was staring at me with those clear blue eyes of his as if he were a century old rather than barely twenty. He took a deep breath when he noticed I was looking back at him, rather than probably the ceiling previously. He looked down into his lap where his pale, wiry hands gripped each other loosely. He glanced upward slowly as he spoke. "How are you doing with all of this?"

I shrugged, the train of thought from our lesson coming back to me. "Oh, I think I'm getting it slowly but surely. The weight thing makes a lot of sense, although I still have a lot of-..."

"No, um..." Frederick shook his head, his expression genuinely curious. "I meant...emotionally, perhaps, is the best word?"

I swallowed the words that had been locked behind my teeth. There was literally no word that seemed right to say. I took a deep breath and said, "Well, uh...you could say I've been better."

Frederick began to gnaw on his lip, wringing his hands out as if nervous. His voice was lighter than I'd ever heard. "Lina, did you know that I've met you before? Before a few weeks ago, that is?"

I blinked at him, totally shocked. "No? How? I'm sorry, I don't remember that."

The prince chuckled, "Oh, I didn't expect you to, it was

once for only a few minutes. I was thirteen, and you couldn't have been much younger since we are so close in age. I was upset, as most teenagers are, and had resolved to run away from my father because of an occurrence I don't remember now.

"I was traveling through Soläna on the way to the southern gate with no thoughts of looking back when I ran into a little girl. She was walking along the street but staying within sight of the mercantile. She was small for her age, and when she saw me, she immediately came to talk to me. I don't remember everything we talked about anymore, but I had told her that I was tired of King Adam and wanted to move to a different kingdom. I didn't call him my father because I figured she would understand better. And Lina, you gave me this wonderful expression, like you totally understood why I wanted to leave, but your words surprised even me. You said 'Don't worry! King Adam won't be king forever! That's what my papa says. He says someday Prince Frederick will be king, and then Lunaka will be happy again!'. Those words made my heart stop."

He laughed before continuing. "Of course, right at that moment, your mother came out of the mercantile and called you to go home. You smiled at me and waved goodbye, but I didn't even hear. It had never occurred to me that I could reverse my father's doings. My father never likes to admit that I am the next king. I think part of him wants to hold on to his reign forever even though that's impossible. But at that moment, I knew I had to go back to the castle. I couldn't leave Lunaka without an heir, and that's what I did."

Silence filled the room when he finished. I was thinking hard, trying to remember this event in my memory but failed to do so. I shook my head and asked quietly, "How did you know it was me?"

Frederick smiled, the wires pulling taut to reveal his dimples. "I didn't at first. I didn't know until many years later when I first met the Owenses, and they told me everything about Rhydin and the Allyens. They took me by your farm one evening, and I saw you through the window. You were still small, but it was your eyes that did it. The strange brown color with speckles of gold in them. I knew you were that little girl who made me want to be king."

My throat became tight, and I could feel my cheeks becoming flushed. I tried very hard to swallow before I spoke, but it hurt. "Um...Frederick...this doesn't help the whole elopement thing."

The prince blushed slightly. "Oh, I apologize, that's not what I meant. I just wanted you to know why I consider you one of my few real friends. It is because you befriended me that day outside the mercantile without a clue as to who I was, and I will always remember that." He smiled now, more comfortable. "I do sincerely apologize for this whole elopement scandal. I am sure it is because my father does not approve of whom I have chosen to be my wife. He is trying to ruin me and no doubt turn her against me. I just want you to know that the rumors do not change anything. I would still like to be your friend, and I am always here to help you. Quite literally since we are stuck down here."

Instantly, I felt lighter, and I could breathe again. He already had a woman betrothed to him, and somehow that made it all better. I wondered if it was my old friend, Cassandra, who I'd seen him dancing with. It made me happy. I smiled at his joke of being trapped here, and I felt at ease that I had seemingly known him all this time. We were friends. Real friends, not just acquaintances out of necessity.

Things were never as awkward between friends as they were between strangers, and for the first time, the elopement rumors seemed bearable.

I grinned at him. "Well, I would like to be your friend, too. I'm glad that I helped you even though I didn't have a clue, just as you said."

"You guys are so cuuuute!" Rachel's voice came lilting down the stairs to the outside world.

"Rachel!" I shouted.

"Rachel, really, you know it's just a ruse!" Frederick yelled at the same time.

The red-haired woman giggled, her arms laden with burlap bags full of different foods, the smells familiar from the Lunakan marketplace, but she wasn't the only one to come through the door. A tall figure in a cloak came behind her, and I recognized the voice before he pulled the hood off.

"So Lina, havin' fun with your new husband there?"

A huge grin had taken residence on Sam's thin face, and his eyes were dancing with delight at how funny this seemed to be. Whatever relief Frederick had given me was immediately drowned. It was even worse when he said it, and I felt my face flood with heat.

Sam sat down at the little table in the center of the room as Rachel took to preparing our supper and spoke between laughs, "Well, when we were you planning on announcing your marriage to me, huh?"

"Sam?" I said tensely.

"What?" He chuckled softly behind his smirk.

"Shut it."

Sam smiled at me, and it was unbearable. I squirmed under his gaze, and finally had to look away it was so uncomfortable. Embarrassment choked me like a death hold, but my mind spun as to why it was suddenly so overwhelming in front of Sam. With him here, all I wanted in life was to crawl under a rock and die.

Frederick seemed to sense the awkwardness and so cleared his throat. Although, what he had to say didn't completely help the matter. He looked to Sam, "Before you become upset, she asked me specifically about it. She knows all about the Kidek now."

Sam nodded quietly, his eyes dropping. He probably could have guessed that my curiosity would be piqued by the interaction at Grandma's house. He folded his hard fingers carefully before looking up at me with the first genuine look I'd seen in his eyes since he appeared. His voice was rather quiet. "Are you afraid of me, Lina?"

Part of me scoffed. "I should be asking you that question!"

A light grin appeared but only for a second. "I'm serious, Lina. I'm not only a Rounan, but I'm the Kidek of all things. Many would love to see my head on a platter" – he paused for a second, swallowing hard – "And I lied to you about it. For years. Yet, I continued to wear this and put myself in danger, as well as you by association." He gestured to his bandana: the amethyst border and navy sea littered with golden stars. "As Kidek, I swore to wear this to signal myself as leader. To most people, it's just something I like to wear, but to any Rounan, it is a sign that I am their leader and the one to come to if they're being persecuted. I have to wear it, every day. For my people."

I took a breath, letting it sink in. It was still extremely strange, but parts of it were slowly making sense. Then, I did something that I hadn't done since we were kids. I gently took his hand, hardened by years of driving the plow and harvesting. "You have no reason to apologize to me. You were trying to protect yourself, and I lied to you, too." I looked him right in the eyes but mostly spoke to myself as I said, "I am not afraid of you."

Sam smiled a real smile, half of his mouth pulling higher. "Good. Because I'm not afraid of you, either. It's about time someone other than me was abnormal."

At that moment, Rachel began to laugh her chiming giggle, and my hand released Sam's. Her voice was full of sunshine. "Oh, you two will be fine! After all, the Allyen and the Kidek have an extremely long history together. It's meant to be!" She added a secret wink just for me.

I quirked an eyebrow at her, and she got the message. I was going to be content in this moment even if it killed me! I could physically feel my body relax after so long. Sam was a stable person in my life again, and that was enough to make me feel better.

Suddenly, Luke walked down the stairs with a big box of leather in his hands. He eyeballed Sam and I sitting together, and his expression went slack. "So is the Kidek in on this now, too? How many people do we need on this expedition?"

Sam let out an exasperated sigh, "Does everybody know I'm the Kidek?"

We all nodded: Frederick, Rachel, James, Luke, and I. Sam groaned. It was pure comedy, and I found myself laughing with everyone else. Here I was, my life turned upside down, stuck in a hole under a livery with a tiny window to barely see the sun every day, and yet I could not stop laughing.

We all stayed up rather late that night, telling stories and getting to know one another a little more beyond duties and powers. I learned that Rachel and her brothers were from extreme northeastern Lunaka, which I had known but forgotten long ago. I learned that Frederick hated tomatoes and that Sam had been afraid of the dark up until a couple of years ago. James only had to sleep for three hours a night to feel totally rested, and Luke actually opened up a teensy bit, saying that if he wasn't here helping the Allyen, he'd have to sit around and read books. Apparently, this was a task he hated.

Eventually, the Lamp Master came around and extinguished all of the lights in the town, and people began to leave. Luke went upstairs to his quarters above the livery while Rachel made herself comfortable on the opposite side of the little room. James posted himself by the door, fully awake and no doubt would be all night now that I knew his skill. Frederick crawled into his little cot, the foot of which touched mine.

Sam was messing with his cloak, pulling it tight about himself from what I could see in the weak candlelight. I walked over to him and reached high above my head to pull his hood over his bandana. He chuckled, "Do you want to see something?"

My brow furrowed, not understanding, until suddenly the one lit candle that had been sitting on the table magically floated over to us, perfectly level. I felt my heart beat faster in awe of it. The candle stopped over Sam's outstretched hand, levitating a good six inches above it, still lit and flickering like normal.

It was then that I remembered Frederick saying that Rounan magic was completely unlike Gornish magic because it didn't take any sort of form. It was hard to imagine what he was talking about then, but now it totally made sense. Sam smiled in the candlelight and told me to take the candle out of midair, which I slowly did, carefully.

"Sometime, you'll have to show me something." Sam

grinned happily, before placing one foot on the stair. His expression mellowed out slightly then, and I felt myself blush as he stared at me. I told myself inwardly to stop it. This was not the time to be juggling a crush amongst everything else. Quietly, Sam said, "If you ever need anything...anything at all, let me know."

I nodded, and in an instant, Sam was out the door. The humidity of Early Summer crept down the stairs. I was left in the dark with nothing but the little flickering flame and burgeoning feelings that I desperately tried to smother.

# CHAPTER TEN

———⟨⟩———

Time went by. Days, weeks, I wasn't sure how much. The sun rose, and the sun set. I never saw either. I told time by the mines' sputtering, rumbling to life every daybreak and choking to death every twilight. Each day, around lunchtime, I would go over to the tiny slit in the window and angle myself to stare straight up out of the basement, out of the canyon toward the overhead sun. Then Frederick would call me back to whatever lesson he was teaching, and the world outside would go on as it always did.

However, it was never completely forgotten. I always remembered that somewhere out there was my sister, Rosetta, and my cousin, Keera. Both of whom I was supposed to be taking care of right now. Somewhere out there was my farm, my parents' beloved land. My goats. This time of year, I was usually slaving away out in the sun and heat, never resting for a moment. It seemed completely alien to be trapped in a cool basement during this season.

Normally, Lunaka was a wind tunnel, and so being in the

still underground made me feel like I was suffocating. Every time someone opened the door, I'd rush over to feel the tiniest waft of air. I missed my wind and the smell of my land. Sam was tending to everything for me, which I appreciated yet envied.

Rachel and her brothers were never completely forgotten either, for they never let up on the secure process of entering and exiting the livery basement. Someone was always posted at the door, day and night. The only person from outside that we saw was Sam, who came by with supplies and a kind word every once in a while.

One thing that I could say for sure was that my magic was definitely improving. I became used to the weight in my chest, to the point sometimes I would forget it was there. The most apparent thing, however, was how I could now sense everyone around me. Now, I didn't have to see Frederick in order to know that he was behind me. I could feel him, in some sort of weird way.

Each person had their own little presence that I could pick up on in my head. I could sense Frederick's wind magic, his bravery, and other things that made him distinctly Frederick in my mind. I could sense Rachel and James down here with me, and Luke overhead doing his livery work. Their presences were slightly different to me, rather foreign from Frederick's but similar within the three of them. I figured it was because they were siblings. Technically, I shouldn't be able to sense Luke at all since he doesn't have magic and I couldn't see him. I wondered if I could since Rachel and James were around to amplify his presence. Was that possible? I wasn't sure.

When Sam came by, I discovered I could sense him once he was right outside the door. His was a strong presence to me, one that created warmth and leadership. Frederick also reminded me of his earlier lesson, that you can't sense regular people unless you're looking right at them, which explained why I couldn't sense any of the people who came in to do business with Luke upstairs, or anyone outside for that matter.

No one else out there had magic, which was kind of amazing to me. I was beginning to be intrigued by my gift. I hadn't learned *how* to do these things yet, but I learned that I would be able to create things and manipulate objects in nature. Let me tell you, a farmer who can influence the weather is the happiest person alive!

Most importantly, as I was told, I would be learning slowly how to utilize my magic in a fight. I could tell Frederick was trying to teach me as many magical concepts as humanly possible within our unknown amount of time down here, but he always gave me an hour or so of break as to not overload my mind. This was always greatly appreciated.

During these breaks, the Owenses started bringing me books from my house, which I was sure Rosetta was not happy about. Being summertime, she loved to read for hours on end, so I wasn't sure how the Owenses got them past her. Once I had exhausted the three or so novels that Rosetta and I had acquired over the years, they began to bring me books from not only the library but the castle as well. They were a mixture of history books, spell books, books of myths that I now recognized as mostly truths, and books on swordplay, the most boring. My reading ability was limited from what schooling I had gotten up until I was sixteen, but Frederick helped me with the words I didn't know and clarified things that seemed confusing.

After a few weeks, I was able to get through my first book by myself. It was a simple myths and legends book, but it made me feel good all the same. There was a particular story about a dragon that Rachel had flagged for me to read, called "Duunzer", but I didn't know what the significance of it was. This particular dragon was magical and would cover the land with Darkness before it began its murderous tirade. I moved on because the story seemed depressing.

There were other entries, even one for the Allyen. It was interesting to read about myself, but the article was vague and gave nothing new to appease my curiosity. There was also a "Lunakan Giants" page, reminding me of the stories I remembered hearing from my childhood. Supposedly, they lived in northeastern Lunaka, but that area was very remote. Good place to tell stories about I suppose.

At that moment, my mind was flooded with a warm presence, one that smelled of freshly dug Lunakan earth and reminded me of Sam. Strange, it seemed early for him to come. He normally didn't come until after nightfall.

James reacted shortly after I did and stealthily brought Sam through the door since it was still daylight. He came bearing a sack filled with food, and he seemed to be happy to see us. I could tell that he had freshly washed his thinning face since no farmer looks that clean in the summer. He had missed a significant swatch of dirt under his jawline, a detail I tucked away for some jab to keep him on his toes.

After Sam gave the sack to Rachel, he walked over to where I sat on my cot with the book in my lap. "Hello, Lina. How are you today? What are you reading about?"

I smiled, "Oh, the usual. I read about King Spenser today, the first king of Lunaka. And I read the whole myths book all by myself."

"Congratulations. Your reading level now rivals Rosetta's." He gave me a wink, because he knew it'd bug me. It always made me jealous that Rosetta could read much harder texts than I ever could. Reading came so naturally to her while the words rendered little to me without help. Before I could retort with some sort of joke about his dirty jaw, he went on, "Maybe someday you'll be able to read as well as a Royal!"

Frederick chuckled from across the room, his nose buried in the newspaper.

"Thanks." I huffed, hugging my myth book to my chest. I, for one, was proud of myself. I couldn't wait to tell Rosetta about my progress. I decided to change the subject. "So, why are you here so early today?"

Sam leaned forward onto his knees. "Luke offered to help with my chores every once in a while, so I can come see you." Sam smiled sheepishly, staring at his fingers, "He's there right now, actually. For a one-man team, he does it pretty quick. It's amazing, really! Your goats don't like him though."

I grinned at him, trying to hide my blush. Sam wanted to come see me? I didn't allow myself to hope, and began to worry as I asked, "How is my sister? And Keera and Grandma? How are they doing with the farm?"

Sam's expression saddened slightly, "They're doing okay, but not the greatest. Keera has missed you pretty bad ever since you had to leave, but even Rosetta is beginning to miss you now. She and Mikael have been spending a lot of time together, and I think he's helping a little. She's just not used to you being gone this long, but your grandma is pretty good about taking care of them and reassuring them. Keera helps me with your chores for as long as she can, but it takes longer than I wish it would. Things are starting to dry up."

My heart began a slow sink to the pit of my stomach. Not only was my sister in a relationship that I couldn't supervise, but no one wants to hear that the crops they desperately worked to plant for days and weeks on end were slowly drying up in the desolate Lunakan sun. All I could picture in my mind were little shriveled brown weeds instead of full, golden heads of wheat.

Then that image was replaced by a presence that was both regal yet frail, beautiful yet shy, and smelled of roses. I didn't know this presence, but someone with magic was standing outside of our door. Frederick sensed it too, and a smile suddenly spread across his lips that he could not contain. He didn't even wait for James to let the woman in stealthily but went and opened the door immediately, holding the mahogany-cloaked figure tightly.

James had to push them in to get the door fully shut, giving them both a flabbergasted expression like they were making his life impossible.

"Oh, Mira," Frederick sighed as he held the Lunakan princess, and then leaned back and pulled her hood off. "How are things in the castle?"

Mira's pale cheeks were tear-stained beneath her beautiful, dark wavy hair, her skin the same color as her pearly teeth. "Not well, Frederick. This last month without you has been very bleak. Father will not cease his search for you. He has guards out scouting the entire kingdom at all times."

The blond-haired prince grunted, his hands releasing his sister's arms. "I figured as much. He won't rest until he finds me because he knows I am with the Allyen."

"Mother is deathly worried. Oftentimes, Father will not allow her to descend to the main level of the castle. I rarely see her which frightens me." Mira's eyes fluttered downward, implicating a meaning that only Frederick could understand. "Also, Cassandra returned to her home in Lun, and thankfully, she has not been disturbed there."

Frederick nodded, biting his lower lip. "Well, then. We must continue with our progress. Lina is doing very well with learning magical concepts although we have not tried very many spells yet. Perhaps, it is time to begin learning swordplay."

Sam's ears almost visibly perked up at that last word, and he bravely interrupted the two Royals' conversation. "Did you say swordplay? Why would Lina need to learn that? Is Rhydin really that serious about the Allyen? All this time I thought he was just after Rounans."

I looked at Sam sadly. Did he really not know?

Frederick glanced at me before he sat at the wooden table with his sister. His eyes almost gave away that he felt he had been offended. "Yes, Sam, Rhydin is extremely serious. His attempts on Lina's life are becoming more dangerous as the year goes on. However, he does not seem to be after Lina herself. He only wishes for her to be out of the way because he really wants her locket."

"Her locket?" Sam asked incredulously, "That little necklace she's had since she was a kid? What's so important about it?"

"It's an amplifier." Frederick said simply, getting more frustrated with every word, something I had never seen from him before. "It is best tuned to the Allyen, but it can strengthen any kind of magic, whether you're an aeromage, pyromage, aguamage, you name it. Rhydin wants to steal the locket, kill all of the Allyens, and subject the entire continent of Nerahdis to his control. Now really, what is so hard to understand about that, Kidek?"

Sam gritted his teeth but said nothing.

After a moment of silence, Mira spoke up with a queenly tone I had never heard from her either. "Now, Frederick, you cannot blame him for our predicament." Mira looked at her brother with a soft, but penetrating gaze. "This is a new fact of life for everyone here. Not just you and I."

Frederick began to look guilty and stared at Sam slowly. "I apologize."

Sam was stoic as Mira continued, "We know this is Rhydin's intent, but we do not know how he means to achieve it. His plan is complicated and is ever changing. We are sure, however, that it will come to a massive head, whatever it ends up being. This will not be an attack in the middle of the night that no one will ever know about. Rhydin wants control, and currently, no one knows of his existence except a scarce few. All of that will change if we are unable to keep the locket out of his hands. Both pieces for that matter."

"Both pieces?" My mouth fell open before my mind could even think it.

"Yes, Lina. You only have half of the locket. That is why you have never been able to open it." Frederick said quietly. "The other half remains with your brother, whom we may not-…"

"Keera told me." I cut him off, my hands unwillingly gathering my dress into clumps at my knees. "She told me about…Evan." I struggled to say his name. I really had not thought about him at all, not willing to admit that my parents lied to me.

"Yes…" Frederick hesitated. "He is your twin. You were separated shortly after birth to be protected from Rhydin. Your magical presence was far stronger together than individually. As such, the locket was also divided, in order to keep Rhydin from having access to both pieces at any time."

"So, is Evan going through this, too?" I asked, almost in a pleading voice, looking from Frederick to Mira to Sam to

James back in the corner listening in. "Has he had his world turned upside down in order to learn all these things and be safe, too?

"That's a complicated question, Lina." James spoke up, his northeastern Lunakan accent slightly detectable, but not leaving his post at the door. "His life has been different than yours. Rhydin doesn't have a hold on him because he is a wanderer. He has no roots. His foster parents were killed when he was thirteen, which is when he discovered his magic. He has been in training and under protection ever since by friends of mine and my siblings', as well as King Daniel of Auklia. He has no one he cares about to allow Rhydin a foothold, as you do. You have people you love, Lina, which is wonderful. But, they're also your weakness."

It was quiet then. I looked to Sam, thinking of my sister, Keera, and Grandma as well. It was true. All this time, I had been thinking about how they could get hurt because of all of this. Rhydin could easily use that to his advantage because the fear already existed. Instantly, the crops meant nothing to me. The goats, the land, nothing. My family's safety was top priority now. I swallowed hard, unable to speak.

Sam touched my hand with fingers as light as feathers, but it still felt like lightning. "What do we do then?"

"We continue your training." Frederick said slowly. "We will begin to teach you swordplay, because there is not a doubt in my mind that you will need it someday, as well as begin more complicated spells. Nora created the locket specifically to defeat Rhydin three hundred years ago, and it can be used in that way again. When we figure out what Rhydin's plan is, we can send for Evan to reunite the locket. He will help, too."

I nodded, gulping at the thought of meeting this unknown brother.

Frederick turned to Sam, his voice becoming more regal and kingly. "Sam Greene, are you willing to help us save Nerahdis from Rhydin and protect the Allyen with your life?"

Sam took a deep breath, his hand becoming more firm on mine. "Of course. Lina is important to me. Regardless of her being the Allyen. I will always protect her. Rhydin is my enemy, too."

I blushed in spite of myself.

Frederick and Mira both smiled as James proudly announced, "Congratulations, you're officially a member of the *Alyen nou Clarii*." James' tongue rolled off the beautiful words, a different language entirely, and then translated. "Soldiers of the Allyen. Now, let us get down to business."

James left his post and walked over to an old chest I hadn't noticed before. From within, he retrieved an elegant, double-edged, shining sword engraved with golden swirls as well as a much smaller sword made of wood. He didn't have to explain to me that the second one was for me to learn with so that I wouldn't hurt anyone. The other was for when I was more experienced. Ready to be trusted with a weapon that could maim and kill.

For the rest of the day, the wooden sword was a strange, wobbly thing in my hand that did not feel right at all. Rachel and Luke finally returned, one from town and one from farm chores, and both joined James in teaching me how to use the pointy thing.

However, compared with my magical lessons with Frederick, their teaching style was absolutely terrible. I was overwhelmed within minutes because I didn't understand what they wanted me to do. They were keener on personally moving my arms and legs for me rather than walking me through it verbally. After an hour or so of being poked, prodded, and made to feel like an idiot because they were the worst teachers on the continent, I had a meltdown and just sat on the ground huddled into a ball for a while. I felt like a failure.

I heard Sam from the sidelines stand up and walk over. "You guys are awful. I thought my old arithmetic teacher was bad."

Rachel, Luke, and James shrugged, knowing that they had no clue how to relay their apparent vast knowledge of swordplay. Sam helped me up. He began to try and help translate what the Owenses were saying into actions, so I could mimic his movements. It was a rough first lesson, but it went ten times better after Sam stepped in to help me.

Honestly, I was completely surprised that he even knew how to use a sword. Perhaps that was just one more aspect of his life as Kidek. One more trait that I'd never known about. I tried not to let it bother me, and instead just put it down on the list of things we hadn't told each other before. I hoped someday there would be no more secrets between us.

His teaching helped tremendously, and I think even the Owenses began to learn what worked better for me and what left me in the dust. Either way, we were making progress, and that was all that mattered at the end of the day.

# CHAPTER ELEVEN

———⟨ঙ⟩———

The day began normally. Like every day had for the last month. The first rays of sunshine took their sweet time traveling down into the deep, dark ravine of Soläna, stretching across my cot in long shapes. I was already awake, for once. I had taken to sleeping in as long as the militaristic Owens siblings would allow, but today I simply could not sleep. I recounted the things I had learned over the last few days, trying to figure out what it was in the air that seemed so strange. It wasn't the lack of wind this time.

Sam had taken over my sword lessons, and he was actually an effective, decent teacher. Rachel and James would help with "form" and all that fancy stuff, but I felt like I learned more strategy from Sam. Frederick pitched in once in a while with how to integrate magic into those moves, but nothing seemed abnormal. What was it, then? It felt like my body was off balance even though I was still in bed.

The only remotely strange thing that had happened recently was that Mira stayed the night with us. She was so upset the day before, her doll-like face even paler than normal if that was possible, and so Frederick offered her his cot while he slept on the dirt floor. In all honesty, I lay awake for a little while after that, just staring at the sight. Lunaka's future king lying in the dirt to give up his bed for his sleep-deprived little sister. I couldn't help but think to myself how wonderful a man he was.

I tried for the umpteenth time to roll over and close my eyes. I breathed in the sweet smell of the wood chips in my flat pillow, trying to pretend that it was the same wooden aroma of home. It wasn't. It was then that my ears picked up on the whispering a few feet away where I had thought Frederick and Mira still slept.

"I can't help it, Frederick. I barely know Xavier. We only spent a few summers together as children, for heaven's sake! Why would Father marry me away to a man I hardly know? I'm barely of marriageable age as it is."

"I don't know, Mira, but you should use this opportunity to get to know Xavier better. Perhaps you can discover if he knows about the Allyen and wants to help-..."

"We are talking about my *future*, Frederick! Marriage is a permanent thing, it is not something to be gambled away!" Mira began to speak louder until Frederick shushed her.

"Mira, if Rhydin has his way, no one will have a future. All I ask is to give the engagement a chance. Use it to recruit help to our cause. If in time you feel the same as you do now, then we will cross that bridge when we get there. Perhaps, you will change your mind."

The princess scoffed so loudly that I took that as my cue to let them know I was awake. Stretching my arms up above me, a rather loud moan escaped my lips as the cords in my arms straightened and warmed. I didn't particularly enjoy being an eavesdropper. It made me feel guilty. I sympathized with Mira, I truly did. I couldn't imagine my father suddenly declaring that I was to marry a practical stranger. Prince Xavier did seem like an interesting person, from the one time I'd seen him in person, but none of us seemed to know him real well.

Frederick looked up from his spot on the floor. "Oh, good morning, Lina. I'm sorry, did we wake you?"

I shook my head innocently. Their business was their business. I had no desire to butt in more places than I already had. I looked around the room, most of the lights still out. The weight in my chest, my magic, calmed from thinking something seemed strange. I felt relaxed again, so I brushed off the unusual feeling as nothing more than drowsiness. Mira pulled her dress back on over her light tunic and bloomers while Frederick began the arduous process of dusting himself off.

I glanced around one more time before asking, "Where are Rachel, Luke, and James?" At least one of them was usually puttering around in the mornings. I couldn't have woken up so early that they weren't around yet. That was downright impossible.

Frederick gave up on getting all the dirt out of his tunic, formerly a new one given to him by the Owenses. The white suitcoat that, after being blasted apart, was no longer white had been deemed lost to all hope. "Oh, James went to be with your family last night, and Rachel said she needed more food. Luke should be upstairs."

I tried a little harder, and I found the presence I had been missing before. Luke was the hardest one to sense of the Owenses. The three of them were a little more difficult to pick up on in general, but Rachel always had a warm, strong presence that reminded me of my mother. James' presence brought to mind games I used to play as a child and the smell of the wind.

Luke's was hard to place. It didn't necessarily remind me of any one thing. Perhaps, I didn't know him well enough. The only thing I could discern about his presence was the clear smell of rock. Very hard to pick up on out of all the other smells in the world, but it always brought to mind the mountains that encircled Lunaka. And that's exactly what I envisioned as I now heard a couple footsteps up above, along with the warm, friendly spirit of Rachel reappearing near the stairs. A smile spread onto my face before I could even think it, eager to see my friend and hear any news from home on the Canyonlands.

Rachel threw open the livery door, her arms laden with multiple packages as always, but we could never complain with how well she cooked. Even though she started with the same mundane food items, Rachel cooked every meal into a feast for flavor. She could be a chef for Royals if she wanted! She could remake the Lunakan staples into edible creations I would have never thought of, although my cooking experience was extremely limited and basic. The room had just begun to fill with the lovely smell of cheese when a little blur quickly fluttered in through the open door seconds before Rachel's foot came around to shut it.

Mira squealed and ducked. Rachel dropped her packages to try and grab the small thing. My eyes tried to focus on the flying, squawking creature until I finally made out the familiar form of Birdie, my little friend from home. Excitement at the sight of seeing something from my old life rose inside of me. Yet, before the feeling could reach the top, it got caught in my throat as my newly honed sensing powers took over.

I was looking at Birdie, but my mind registered darkness. A presence older than time and cruel. Birdie began to make a beeline for me, its beak sharp and aimed to kill, before a tiny blast of wind, the shot of an aeromage, twisted its neck en route.

As the frail body fell, my former little friend, I could feel myself beginning to hyperventilate. My voice didn't even sound like my own, morphed by the beginning of tears. "B-B-Birdie! W-Why did you kill it, Frederick?"

Frederick looked at me like I was crazy, but I was still staring at the still body only feet away from me. "Lina, you can't tell me that you didn't sense that. That isn't a real bird! It's Rhydin's creation." Suddenly, he put his teacher hat back on. "What kind of presence did you feel when it flew in here?"

I was broken from my trance, staring at Frederick through tear-filled eyes. For some reason, it felt like he had just shot the remains of my former life. But, as I thought harder about the cold, evil presence Birdie had possessed, I began to realize that even though the poor bird was dead in front of me, the presence hadn't gone away. I stuttered, "If that presence was Rhydin's, then why can I still feel it? Like it's further away?"

During the racket, Luke came downstairs and caught the tail end of my statement. At that moment, the basement became quieter than I'd ever heard it. It was so silent my ears began to ring. I could hear the footsteps and horses traveling outside above us on ground level. I could hear the faint churning of the mines and the belching of their smoke. I could even barely make out the bell tower of the castle chiming its way into midmorning. In that stillness, all of us could feel it. The cold began to creep in, the blackness unmistakable. A presence so old that it could only be one person. One sorcerer. Rhydin.

"He's come to Soläna." Luke spoke slowly, his eyes still trained on the corner of the room in concentration.

"He's here?" My voice became tinier than it had ever been. Tinier than a mouse.

Frederick shook his head. "No. The presence would be stronger if that were the case. He's still a little far away but definitely within twenty miles."

I turned to him immediately, my thoughts beginning to stampede. "What did you mean when you said Birdie wasn't real? How could it not be real?"

The prince's sky blue eyes connected with my own. "Um, it's called an Einanhi, Lina. The word literally means "puppet" in Gornish. It's a crystallized form of magic that is given the power of life. The feather around your neck is a prime example."

My fingers felt like lead blocks as I touched the beautiful purple shard that hung around my neck. "This is alive?"

"Not quite." Rachel chimed in, "It's a crystallized form of my own magic, but I did not give it the form of a living being or the power of life. Most Einanhis are animals or humanoids. Not everyone can make an Einanhi either. It's a very delicate process. Rounans can't make them at all because their magic does not take the form of nature-…"

"Quiet!" Luke hissed, his eyes still focused on the same spot across the room. His hand raised to plug one of his ears as if it would help him hear something better. All of us turned to face him, the only sound now our breathing. Luke swallowed hard when he returned from his thought. The most emotion I'd ever seen from him was pasted to his face as his eyes flashed the tiniest of bits. "It's James. Up at the farm. Rhydin is approaching them."

With that, the world seemed to stop spinning.

"*What*?" Rachel came closer to becoming emotionally lost than I'd ever seen her before. While my mind echoed her sentiments, I couldn't find the ability to move my mouth.

"Why would he head for the farm? Birdie just found Lina down here. He knows she's not up there!" Mira piped up, trying to remain sensible even though the current in the room was deafening.

It clicked immediately for me. We had this conversation a long time ago when I asked if Evan was experiencing the same things I was. I took a deep breath before I spoke, finding it hard to breathe. My deepest fear was coming true. "He's not looking for me. He's aiming for my family!"

"It's a trap! He's trying to draw you out just like he did with me at the festival!" Frederick exclaimed, jumping to his feet. "Or worse, he's trying to draw the rest of us out to leave you here alone where he can kill you."

I whirled toward him, less than six inches from his face. "We need to go! We need to save them! This is about my family, not me! Please, I'm *begging* you!"

Rachel began speaking quickly, "She's right. For all we know, Rhydin is after her grandmother. Saarah is an Allyen too after all, but they don't have a chance on their own. It's only safest if we all go together. James is keeping tabs on Rhydin's presence but he is getting *closer* while we sit here *arguing*!"

After that, time froze. I remember grabbing the long, double-edged sword that I had only just begun to wield in the last week. The five of us charged the stairs of the livery basement, bursting through the door. My head filled with the fresh air and sunlight, the first time in a whole month. I could feel the dankness falling off of me, dispelled by the Middle Summer heat.

A few people who happened to be walking by turned to look at us, completely confused to see the missing crown prince and his rumored tiny mistress wielding a sword while dashing out of a local livery. We merely turned and ran toward the pulleys. There was no time.

Fresh oxygen filled my lungs and hurled me forward. I was so focused that I didn't even see Sam as we passed him on his way to visit us. He immediately turned on his heel and followed, six of us now, headed for the Canyonlands.

Headed for Rhydin.

Grandma Saarah's heart stood still when she sensed the dark presence on the horizon. It had been nearly twenty years since she had felt it last, yet it was unmistakable.

Her two granddaughters were cleaning up from supper, the aroma of carrot stew still lingered in the air along with the sound of clanking dishes in the washbasin. Rosetta had really stepped up in Lina's absence, trying her best to keep the house clean, while Keera would help where she could both inside and out.

It had been a month since Saarah moved up to the Canyonlands, and while in the beginning she looked at every shadow twice, she had begun to feel like everything was going to be okay. Yet, in that moment of sensing Rhydin for the first time in two decades, any sense of safety was swept away.

Saarah stood from her chair and cleared her throat, trying to ready herself to no avail. She had little time. Wringing out her fragile, wrinkled hands, Saarah began to focus on the little strength in her chest, building upon it until a small light darted across the cold, wooden door.

Without the locket itself, Saarah's magic wouldn't be strong enough to defeat Rhydin. Knowing this, she mustered every ounce of strength she had left in her elderly body to create an invisible barrier, which fell like a curtain upon the old, rickety house.

Before the curtain fully reached the ground, the shaggy-haired Owens boy slipped through the door so quickly that he startled Rosetta and Keera. Saarah expected him to look frightened for his age of fifteen, but the boy's face was all business as he turned to greet her and her two clueless granddaughters. Saarah allowed herself one small sigh of relief once her barrier was completely sealed.

That was when the rumbling began. It was as if the entire world shook as Rhydin's presence got closer. Rosetta gasped as the tremors caused her to drop the tin plate she was holding. It clanged onto the floor. Grandma swallowed hard as James braced himself, one of his fingers in his ears as he muttered to himself.

At that moment, someone began banging on the door, scaring them all out of their wits. Keera's ice blue eyes penetrated Saarah's, but then a different voice began calling, "Hey, open up! I'm scared. Please let me in!"

Rosetta flung herself toward the door faster than Saarah could process, opening it immediately. "Mikael! Get in here, what are you doing out in an earthquake?"

"It's no earthquake." Mikael said almost inaudibly as he entered the house. The boy was barely seventeen, Saarah knew, but the boy's freckled face seemed older now.

James tried to shut the door after Mikael, but it stopped about six inches from the wall. No matter how hard the boy pushed and shoved, it remained open. His eyes betrayed his true fear as he said, "Allyen Saarah, c-can you get the barrier back down?"

The old woman strained as she lifted her hands, trying with all her might to reestablish the barrier, but it was of no use. Rhydin's magic had found a foothold in those six inches, and before Saarah could think another thought, the black presence became overwhelming. The timeless man himself walked through the doorway, the old wooden door blown off its hinges in his wake.

Saarah's ears barely registered Rosetta and Keera's screams as a final rumble shook them to their knees. Her full attention was on the young sorcerer in front of her. *He has not aged a day*, Saarah thought, *even after all these years.*

A slight, smug grin parted Rhydin's pale lips, his flashing amethyst eyes bright underneath a curtain of hair as black as midnight. His jaw was angular, yet his face was still tinted with roundness, boasting of his youth. Saarah knew better, though. This man was centuries old, and his sorcery was more powerful than all the Royals combined.

Saarah could feel the color draining from her face as she moved in front of the girls, readying herself for anything.

The sorcerer spoke, his voice deep and lightly accented as in the days of old. "Good work, Mikael." He said to the no longer frightened boy before turning to face the old woman. "My, my, Allyen Saarah. How many years has it been?"

Saarah's heart dropped as she turned to where the boy they just "saved" stood. His once terrified expression and voice were no longer, only replaced by loyal eyes and steady words, "Thank you, Master."

Saarah turned back to Rhydin, trying to be as calm as possible as she pleaded vainly, "Nearly twenty years, Rhydin, and it was not long enough. You may have tricked the boy into following you, but you'll gain nothing here. What you're searching for is not here, leave us alone."

Tears began welling up in Rosetta's eyes, her wrist locked firmly in Mikael's grip at this point. She had absolutely no clue what was going on, and yet anyone could tell it was bad. Mikael had betrayed them all. Keera was trembling in the corner next to them, Grandma was doing everything she could to keep a strong face, and this man in front of them seemed to be the utter definition of evil. Rosetta looked up at Mikael, his hold on her becoming painful, confused as to what happened to the boy she had fallen in love with.

Rhydin chuckled menacingly, pulling off his black gloves as he did, revealing thin, pale fingers. "I have no need of the locket today, Saarah." His smirk fell from his face, and his black brows came to a rest over the purple fires in his eyes. His cold voice turned hard as stone. "There are too many Allyens in Nerahdis, and I intend to rid the world of one more. Linaria and Evanarion shall be alone."

Saarah's countenance began to falter. She knew her time was coming, but... As she peered behind her at the inconsolable Rosetta and cowering Keera, thinking of Lina and Evan as well, she knew that she could not leave her grandchildren defenseless. She turned to James now, who had been lurking in the shadows of the room watching Rhydin's every move carefully. She took a deep breath before she spoke. "You told your brother?"

"Yes." James answered, coming out of the shadows to ready himself, his hand tight on his sword as he drew it and assumed the proper stance.

"You." Rhydin glared purple daggers into James, his pointed, pale nose raising into a snarl as if James disgusted him. "You are one of those strange creatures who kept me from stealing Linaria as a child. Tell me why I cannot sense you!"

Saarah seized the moment of Rhydin's temporary distraction to immediately charge the fastest attack spell into her hand and hurl it at the man in the billowing, black cloak, catapulting him out the front door. She turned for a split second, her arms braced in a magic shield for the heavy retaliation that was coming. "*Run girls!*" Saarah screamed, until she saw more figures in black outside in the glaring sun. "James, take the others!"

As Grandma exited the building with her shield in place and her movements strengthened by magic, Keera jerked into action. The twelve-year-old jumped to her feet and grabbed Rosetta's hand as noises as loud as thunder came from outside, the sounds of magic being exchanged. Keera dragged her, unintentionally bringing along Mikael since his hand was like a cuff on Rosetta's wrist, through the house to the bedroom. She released her to open the one meager window since the front door was not a choice for escape.

Keera shoved Rosetta toward the window, and then, she did something she had never done before. She dodged Mikael's punch and kicked him in the pants, causing the boy to grunt and fall while she flew through the window, so that he could not follow. As far as Keera was concerned, it was all Mikael's fault that Rhydin found them. He *made* them open up the door for him, and then they couldn't get it closed again. Keera knew none of them stood a chance against Rhydin, and whatever happened today was all on Mikael's head.

Rosetta was right outside the window when Keera came through, but before Keera could take more than two steps toward the tree line opposite the battle, a woman clad in black appeared in their way. Keera recognized her instantly as the one of Rhydin's people who kept tabs on Evan, just like how

Eli and Terran always seemed to be watching Lina. She was extremely tall with deep blue eyes, bright red lipstick, and a generous bosom. Half of her face was hidden by deep brown hair with blonde highlights, but Keera could not remember her name.

In that moment, as the sounds of the magical duel in front of the house plagued their ears and Keera tried to grab Rosetta to move around this evil woman, Keera felt a deep searing pain enter her side. Rosetta screamed, and it was the ugliest sound Keera had ever heard. Keera gasped as her ribcage continued to burn, falling to her knees, and when she pulled her hand from the area, it was soaked with crimson. It was all Keera could do to drop to her back and try to breathe through failing lungs as she watched helplessly.

"Come Mikael, we must get out of here now if you want this to work!" The evil woman screeched as she tossed her chin at Rosetta, her voice like fingernails on a chalkboard.

Mikael, having come out the same window after recovering, did not dare turn toward Keera, who lay in a mixture of dirt, mud, and blood. He instead reestablished his tight death hold on Rosetta's wrist. "Okay, Kino. Just get on with it and we'll go."

Kino closed her eyes in concentration, but Keera began to fade out of consciousness, the pain in her side becoming too much. The sun was clouding over, and Keera felt a few drops of rain on her cheek. Her breaths became like choking, and she spent her last few seconds hoping with all of her being that Evan and Lina would find each other soon.

# CHAPTER TWELVE

B y the time we reached the Canyonlands, my breaths were ragged, but I didn't care. My lungs were burning, but I didn't care. My legs were numb, but I didn't care. I had tunnel vision on Rhydin because, if we didn't get there soon, my family would be dead before I could do anything about it. If anger alone could kill a person, Rhydin would have been decapitated by now.

Luke and Rachel raced ahead of us, drawing unnatural speed from somewhere. I hoped with all of my being that they were already making a difference and had saved my family. I couldn't have been more wrong.

It was as if an entire battlefield had been spread out in my front yard. On one side, closer to the barn, were James, Luke, and Rachel singlehandedly taking on twice their number in black cloaks. Their swords were drawn with inhuman agility as their opponents fired purple magic at them. Unbelievably, the Owens siblings seemed to be winning against them all.

On the other side of the yard nearer to the house was not

the same story. Two people were dueling in nothing but magic on a bigger scale than I'd ever seen. The noise was deafening. With every attack and every blow, thunder sounded from the immense use and force of magic. I picked out my little old grandmother as one of the duelists with her gray hair hanging loosely around her shoulders, ripped out of its usual bun. Her clothing was scorched in a few places. It was hard to focus on her. She was moving so fast, but if she stayed in any spot too long, she would be killed.

I did not recognize the other duelist, but, as I looked at him longer, I sensed his presence. A shiver shot down my spine as I realized it was Rhydin, clad in black from head to toe adorned with gold. His billowing cloak, which was all I knew of him, lay on the ground in a heap with a broken clasp as if Grandma had blown it off him. I found myself simply staring at him as the thunderous purple and light blasts boomed around me, soaking in his appearance after having talked about him for so long and not knowing what he looked like. He had long black hair and a wiry body, his skin so pale it seemed that he should be dead. His face was angular but rounded as if he were not very old.

In that instant, Rhydin suddenly stopped his offense, raising but a single hand to my grandmother as he blocked every single one of her attacks. I then learned that his most striking characteristic was the amethyst color of his eyes, as he stared me down.

A dark grin spread across his thin face, his voice not much deeper than Sam's, but menacing nonetheless. "Hello, Linaria."

My breath caught in my throat as Frederick and Sam rushed forward to help my grandmother. I willed myself forward, but Mira caught my wrist hard and caused me to swing back toward her. My voice squeaked loudly over another crash like an earthquake. "Mira, what are you doing? I have to help my grandma!"

"Let Frederick and Sam handle it. We need to find your sister and your cousin." The princess explained calmly.

I was about to nod when Mira's expression suddenly changed. Her eyebrows rose into her hairline as she tried to pull me forward with all her strength. As she did, my head turned enough to see what she was seeing. It was Mikael, my sister's crush and the kid who spent all his free time at my house, wielding a dagger aimed for my heart, his freckled face unfeeling.

A scream for help was at my lips when a flash of light blinded us, thunder sounded, and all three of us were thrown to the ground. Instantly, a second round of magic fired a little further away, but we couldn't see anything until the dust settled.

My ears were ringing. The battle had gone silent. Mira and I held on to each other as we tried to get to our feet, a deep chunk of earth missing from just beyond where we were standing. As the dust cleared further, I could see that Mikael had been thrown to the other side of the trench. The front of his clothing was ripped and bloodied, but whoever shot him had clearly missed or had been more focused on simply separating us.

As I recognized the dagger in his hand, my mind refused to focus and connect him to Rhydin. He spent so much time with Rosetta that he was practically family. However, I didn't have long to dwell on it before several of the black cloaked people rushed up and grabbed Mikael, disappearing in a puff of lavender smoke.

I turned in time to see Rhydin grinning dementedly at me.

He was extremely happy about something, and yet that did not seem to bode well for me. He reached out with his hand, and his cloak flew to him like a bird, his eyes glinting with amethyst fire. "Congratulations, Linaria. The Allyen just became a bit rarer!"

As Rhydin disappeared, my heart sank into the pit of my stomach. I failed. I began to run so fast that my feet skidded on some loose gravel, but I regained my footing as I sprinted toward where Frederick and Sam were huddled on the ground. I was crying before I even reached them, hoping that I had misinterpreted Rhydin's words. But I was not so lucky. There, lying in the slightly wet dirt as the rain began to fall, was my unseeing grandmother. A gaping, bloody hole decorated her chest.

My mind does not recall what words began to spill out of my mouth, but someone told me later that I went into shock. I do remember that I begged Grandma not to be dead. I begged her to sit up and come back to me. That I couldn't do this without her. I asked her why. Why did she have to die? Why did she have to see Mikael coming for me and take a precious moment of her focus on Rhydin to fire a shot that likely saved my life? Why did Mikael betray us? Why, after all the times he came over and how in love with my sister he was, did he try to kill me?

When I finally regained control of my mouth, I realized that I had placed both my tiny hands on top of the hole in Grandma's chest, trying in vain to hold the blood in. Trying to push hard enough that maybe her heart would start again. I felt two hands on either side of my waist, but I was too numb to hold back from them. To this day, I don't know who grabbed me and tried to hold me. My guess is either Sam or Rachel.

As I was pulled away, adrenaline surged through me as I

remembered that Mira and I had never gotten the chance to search for Keera and Rosetta. I hardly recognized my own voice when it spilled out. "We need to find the girls! They're not here! Where are they-...?"

Frederick took my bloody hands and steered me to Sam somewhere in the background. His voice was the only calm in my life at the moment, and I was swallowed up into his deep brown eyes. "We'll go look for them. But you need to stay here. You cannot do this right now."

Frederick took Mira and headed toward my house as I slumped into a heap at Sam's feet. He tried to crouch down and console me, but it was of no use. The sight of my house brought tears to my eyes once again. The front door had been wrenched off its hinges, black scorch marks decorated the old wood, and every window had been smashed. Part of the roof was missing because the shingles had danced away with each thunderous wave of battle. My old, normal life had officially been destroyed. To every degree. Beyond recognition.

It seemed like ages before Frederick and Mira came back. I was flat on the ground, staring straight up at the sky because that was the only thing clean. That was the only thing that hadn't changed. It was the only thing that hadn't been destroyed or covered in blood. Sam stared down at me helplessly, facing his own demons that I wouldn't know about until later.

Rachel, Luke, and James collapsed next to us, all breathing hard as they recovered from being outnumbered. James seemed to be in the worst shape since he'd been out here the longest. Rachel held his hand, embracing him like a mother she was so relieved that he was alive. I had to admit that I was glad James was alive, but an angry thought kept me from vocalizing it. Why was he alive when my grandmother wasn't?

I bounded to my feet when I saw Frederick and Mira coming back, my body tired but adrenaline still going strong. "Did you find them? Where are they? Are they alright?" I begged.

Frederick caught me before I could rush off toward where they had come from. "Wait, Lina…"

I could feel my body beginning to break down as I stared up at Frederick's blue eyes, feeling like a child in his grip. My voice began to break, "They're gone too. Aren't they?"

The prince looked at me timidly and bit his lip. He could only nod.

"Where are they?" My voice got louder as I struggled against his grip.

"Lina, I don't think you should see…"

"Frederick, let me go!" I began to teeter on the edge of becoming hysterical, but I swallowed hard and found the right words. "Frederick, I need to see them. Because if I don't… I'm never going to believe they're gone." I stumbled on the last word, another tear tracing its way down my cheek. Yet, even at that moment, I wasn't sure if I was going to be able to handle the sight.

We all went together. I was being solidly supported between Sam and Frederick, my knees in danger of giving out. Rachel was close behind with Luke and James flanking her. Mira chose to stay out front, which I did not blame her for one bit. Frederick led us around to the back of the house, where apparently, the girls had tried to escape.

My heart jumped up into my throat upon sight of the bodies. Keera's eyes were open, staring up at the sky, but I knew she couldn't see it. She had a stab wound in between her ribs, her tiny hand trying to cover it. There were no words this time as a waterfall of tears began to fall down my face. Rosetta lay next to her, but there was no wound that I could see on her.

I kneeled between the two of them, the knees of my trousers and my dress soaking through in the mud made from the rain and Keera's blood. First, I took my hand and gently closed Keera's eyes, brushing her midnight hair out of her face. I made my words as strong as possible. "I am so sorry, Keera... I told you I would protect you. You chose me to come to after you left Evan, and I failed you both." I turned to Rosetta and propped her forward into my arms, her heaviness causing my stomach to churn.

Before I could open my mouth to say something to Rosetta, I was hit with an overwhelming sensation. I was becoming rather adept at sensing Rhydin's magic, and it felt like Rosetta's body had been drowned in it. My body balked at it and wanted to get as far away from her as possible, but I forced myself to hold on. I looked into my sleeping sister's face, and could find no words to express my feelings that wouldn't cause me to fall into a crying fit. So, I only hoped that somehow she could tell what I was thinking and could feel the sisterly love that would never die for her.

I leaned in to kiss Rosetta's forehead as Rachel ducked down to examine her as well, but suddenly her weight was gone in my arms. My sister dissolved into sand, falling through my fingers. My fists dove into the piles, desperate to find something of my little sister to hold on to. *How was this possible?*

I began to hyperventilate as Rachel pulled me in close and said, "I know it won't make it better, but I'm so sorry, Lina. Some death curses do this."

That was it. That was the final straw. In the span of an hour, Rhydin had murdered what was left of my family. My body literally shut down, and I blacked out.

When I came to, night had fallen and we were still on my property, hiding out in the barn. My mind refused to process the memories that I wished were only nightmares. I wondered why we hadn't gone back to the livery, but then I remembered that we had blown our cover there. I pretended to still be unconscious as the group beyond me continued talking.

"James, it's okay. It's not your fault." I heard Rachel's voice from the distance. "Just tell us what happened. We're trying to understand."

Someone took a deep breath, and I heard the most serious James ever. "It all just happened so fast. One minute I was on my rounds like normal, and the next, I sensed Rhydin. I could feel him getting closer, and so I went back to the house. Saarah had known too and so she put down a barrier..."

"If she had gotten a barrier to the ground, no one could have opened it. How did Rhydin draw them out?" A voice interrupted. Probably Frederick.

"See, that's the problem." James continued, "The barrier settled in the walls of the house and the door. That kid who's always with Rosetta came to the door and begged us to open it because he was scared. Of course, Rosetta ran up and opened it, and messed up everything. I tried to shut the door, but it wouldn't close."

"So, it was Mikael in the beginning, too. If he hadn't been there, her family could still be alive." I recognized Sam this time, but his voice was bordering on fury. Mikael was his charge, the boy he had taken in after the Epidemic.

"I don't know about that, but that's how Rhydin got in." James muttered. "Saarah knew I wouldn't last against Rhydin, so she had me take care of the rest of his Followers while she dueled him herself. She told the girls to run, but I don't know what happened to them. Mikael was with them. In the end, I couldn't protect anyone…"

"Hush. If Rhydin was easy to take care of, this would have never happened. You did the best you could." Rachel said, and I knew she was right, even though the fury I was feeling had no name on it.

As the *Alyen nou Clarii*, the group devoted to protecting the Allyen, moved onto a different topic of discussion, I got up slowly, trying not to be noticed. I crept slowly out of the barn, making sure my locket was safely stowed in my sash and my magic feather was still firmly tied around my neck. I rounded the corner to where the barn jutted up against a small hill.

Even in the dark, I could see the shapes of the mounds and grave markers. This was where my family was buried, and there was a tint of nostalgia when I noticed that there were three new additions. Even though my heart was still pained, a small sense of relief came when I realized that they would never be hurt again. By Rhydin or anybody else. But that didn't change the fact that their absences left holes in my heart that could never be filled. Every generation was here, even though the oldest of the graves no longer had markers. This would always be my family's land. My parents and my grandfather were buried here after the Epidemic, and now my sister, grandmother, and cousin had joined them.

There was no one left, I nearly thought, until I remembered Evan. According to Keera, he was my twin brother. The only family I had left in the entire world. On top of that, we had to stand together against Rhydin. I made a mental note to talk to Rachel later about when he and I could meet.

"Hey." Someone came up behind me, but I did not startle since my body was still so tired. It was James, seeming just as weary as he came to join me. "I hope it was okay to put them to rest here."

"It's the perfect place." I said quietly, trying not to cry again. "Thank you."

There were no more words to be said. James left an awkward distance between us, as if he didn't know how I would react, so I closed it and took his hand. Sometimes I forgot how much younger than me he was since he was so much taller than me. Even younger than Rosetta. I put my arm around his back since I couldn't reach his shoulders, as a sister would. Taking a deep breath, I found the last words I needed to say. "I don't blame you, James. You did the best you could."

"Does that mean you're not angry?" James looked at me with pure innocence, his eyes big and blue and precious.

"Not with you, James." I said, my words turning into steel. "Not with you."

# CHAPTER THIRTEEN

T ime melted together. Seconds felt as long as days. It had been a couple weeks now since the deaths, and things looked even bleaker if that were even possible. We *Alyen nou Clarii* were in major trouble. The rumors had started, hedged on by headlines of the daily newspaper, *The Lunakan Moons*.

*Missing Prince and Traitorous Mistress Spotted at Local Livery!*

*SCANDAL: Owens Livery Owner Kidnapped the Prince!*

*This Just In: Princess Mira KNEW!*

*Tragedy Strikes! Local Farm Burned Down; Harvey Family Slaughtered.*

*Mystery Man in Farm Burning: Sources Confirm He's a Rounan! Hide your Children!*

Yeah, that "traitorous mistress"? That would be me. Rachel normally brought home a newspaper whenever she returned to town for food, and so since I was usually the last person of our group who could get their hands on it, I would burn them when I was done. It was rather cathartic.

As the newspaper stories kept coming, our group made some major decisions during the time blur that my memory didn't record too well. Most importantly, we couldn't go back to Luke's livery. From what we heard, Lunakan soldiers had trashed it in search for us on King Adam's orders. Now, we had set up camp in a quieter, thicker section of forest several miles north of Lunaka Castle. There were no towns anywhere in the northeastern section of Lunaka, so we were sure not to have random travelers come across us.

I thought I was miserable in the livery basement. What with having to stay inside all the time and no fresh air, it seemed like the worst situation at the time. But, at least I could hear the people outside. I could hear them talking, hear them on their way to work, hear children running in the street, and the sound of the mines as they sputtered to life every morning and choked to death every evening.

Here, in the forest, it was just us. There was no noise, other than the small noises of chatter and fire that we made ourselves. Don't get me wrong, it was a much prettier hideout than the livery basement. I had never seen such huge trees, ones with trunks so thick that if I wrapped my arms around one my fingers were far from touching. The grass was green, the leaves lush, and the smell of oak thick in the air. The wind wasn't quite as powerful as out on the prairie, but I could catch quite a few breaths between the trees.

Yet, for all its beauty, nature could not shake the misery that gripped my heart like a handcuff. Not only was my family gone, but so was my land. The land of my ancestors. The land that I had worked my tail off trying to prove myself on. The land that had occupied every spare minute of my pre-Allyen mind. Right now, in any normal year, we would be beginning the preparation for harvest. What harvest would there be this year?

My boredom was also worse because Frederick and Mira had chosen to go back to the castle. They decided it would help the rumors die if Frederick popped back up unmarried, and if Mira cleared her name because of her big impending marriage, aka Royal alliance, to Prince Xavier of Mineraltir. With that, all the jokes surrounding Frederick and I's "engagement" finally ceased, the one positive of this move. King Adam thankfully accepted Frederick back into the castle although he was interrogated on my position. He held strong throughout it all.

Unfortunately, our biggest fear was confirmed within a week of Frederick and Mira returning home. Evidence surfaced that King Adam, their father, truly was one of Rhydin's Followers and possibly one of the most dangerous ones at that. Both Mira and Frederick tried their best to use their time at home to see if they could catch word of Rhydin's plans while still protecting their mother, Queen Gloria, and little sister, Princess Cornflower.

They might be going to try and convince the two Royal women to leave the castle. Or, at least, that's what they told me. I didn't understand why we couldn't just go public with the information about Rhydin, make the people see that King Adam was evil, and that he needed to be overthrown. Everyone always shook their heads when I mentioned it. After all, why listen to the grieving girl?

When I tried again to voice that to Rachel, she scoffed at me. "Lina, nobody is going to believe that 'our great king' is working for a sorcerer that nobody believes to exist, who happens to be after a little peasant girl who just discovered she has magic! Even if they did believe it, it'd cause mass panic and make everything worse."

I threw my hands up in the air as Rachel left. Since no one had seen her the day of the deaths, she had been able to keep her maid job at the castle, which was pretty good considering it was now our only income. Luke had sold his livery, unable to tend it after his name was slandered in the papers, and Sam and I were considering our crop – our crop that we had agonizingly tilled and planted and tended – gone. Since the papers had released that my farm was burnt down and my family slaughtered, including myself, there was nothing we could do to save it. Not to mention my goats. Sam's house had also been ransacked because he helped me, which broke my heart.

Sam had been writing letters nonstop ever since it happened a little more than two weeks ago. He explained at one point that all his records of different Rounan families across the continent had disappeared when someone went through all his belongings. These records contained family ancestry, birthdays, ability levels, and most importantly, locations. Therefore, Sam was desperately writing letters to all the Rounans that he could remember to warn them, especially to his sister, Kelsi. Warn them to move, as well as caution them away from his residence. As Kidek, Rounans came to him from across Nerahdis to settle their disputes and seek help from him. Apparently, Rounans didn't recognize the Three Kings. Sam never slept for those few weeks, desperately trying to remember addresses and despairing when, more often than not, he couldn't.

And me? For me, time stopped altogether. I took what little things from my home that hadn't been destroyed in the battle and continued to grieve. Thankfully, my little bag of treasures that I used to hide under my straw tick had been undisturbed, and so I fingered the little rag doll that Rosetta had given me years ago often. I found one of Keera's hair ribbons to tie around it as well.

Lunakan custom was to keep a candle burning for the dead for a whole month after they were gone, but I didn't have one at my disposal out in the forest. I kept the doll and ribbon in the pocket of my black dress instead. I'd even found the myths book that I used to read every day in the livery basement, although a few more pages were now tagged for me to read by Rachel.

Whenever I tried to gravitate to Sam for comfort, he would become angry. I really didn't understand why until I asked him one day. It was late afternoon, the sun shining hazily through the leaves. Sam had mostly finished his letters since he couldn't remember too many addresses outside of the Rounans that he had regular contact with. I came over just to be near him, feeling lonely since my whole family was gone, and he set the last of his letters down angrily, smearing some of the ink.

I swallowed hard, and got up the courage to ask, "Sam… Am I the one who's making you mad?"

He gave a deep sigh, straightening his wrinkled tunic. "No, Lina. I'm not mad *at* you. You just remind me of *who* I'm mad at."

"Oh." I murmured, moving a couple inches away from him to give him some space. "Glad we got that cleared up." I nearly walked away, but Sam stopped me.

"Wait." He said, turning around and looking me in the eye for the first time in two weeks. There were dark smudges underneath his brown eyes, and they were puffy. I hesitated, unsure if I should come close to him or not, but he soon found the right words. "I apologize for not saying it before, but I'm sorry. If I had never taken Mikael in, this would have never happened."

Ah. He was angry with Mikael. I thought for a minute before I responded, wanting to make sure that I chose the correct words since I was still grieving and didn't want to say anything I didn't mean. After all, I blamed James for their deaths initially but came to terms that he had done the best he could. There was someone so much better to blame than James.

I took a deep breath and started slowly. "Sam, I know it's easy to blame yourself, but you couldn't have foreseen that the little boy you took in would do this. I mean, I couldn't have seen this coming. Mikael spent nearly every waking minute at my house with Rosetta. You know that. Remember when we went to the Spring Festival?"

My stomach recoiled. How long had it been since I watched Mikael take my sister to the festival? Her first beau killed her.

Sam threaded his fingers through his hair, rubbing his scalp because his brain couldn't process the information. He stammered, "I-I-It just doesn't make sense. H-He told me that he loved Rosetta, and that he wanted to marry her. And then he *kills* her? He was so happy to live with me after the Epidemic killed his parents. *Rhydin's* Epidemic. And then he joins him?"

My heart began to ache as Sam looked away, struggling to hold back tears. He was my childhood friend of ten years. I had seen him grow from a little boy who wasn't afraid of anything except the dark, to a shy teenager who never knew quite what to say, to a kind, stubborn at times man. Yet, I had never seen him cry. His father abandoned him well before I met him, and his mother died of the Epidemic when he moved to Stellan for a little while, so I never saw him grieve for her.

His sister was older, and so moved away a long time ago when she'd gotten married. Yet, now here he was, his face buried in his hands and completely silent to keep the sobs from coming.

I sat down next to him and just breathed for a second, trying to control my own tears that came so easily nowadays. When I felt in control of my emotions, I wrapped my arm around his shoulders and squeezed tight, resting my head on his arm. My voice was stronger than I would have thought when it came out of my mouth. "I think we both are learning how manipulative Rhydin is. He has been planning all this for the last century, down to the minutest detail. I don't think I realized just how far he's willing to go to destroy us until I saw him that day."

Sam raised his head and looked down at me quietly, his thin cheeks red and his eyes a little glassy as he took in the sight of my head on his arm.

"Blame Mikael all you want." I said firmly, "But Rhydin is the one who tricked him. *Rhydin* is the one who used him to get through the barrier and destroy my family. Did Mikael even know that you were the leader of the Rounans?"

Sam thought for a minute and then shook his head.

"Who do we know in this world that hates all Rounans and would have a motive to ransack your house for your records?"

"Rhydin." Sam said through gritted teeth, "And King Adam. They want to cleanse Nerahdis of Rounans because they believe the Gornish people are the purer race."

"Exactly." I moved my other hand to grip his firmly. "Mikael had no intention of ruining your contact with your people. That was all Rhydin's doing. I know how much you want to protect them." I paused for a minute. "And y'know, Sam, I don't believe this notion that Rounans are somehow 'dirty'. You're a Rounan. I'm Gornish. But to me, we're the same. Two people given magic and responsibilities they never asked for in a world that can't accept it." I smiled timidly.

The first smile I'd seen in a long time spread across Sam's face. His eyes stopped glimmering, but a light blush remained on his face. He squeezed my hand carefully. "Thank you. I appreciate it."

I took a deep breath, and we just sat there silently for some time, letting the sounds of the forest sink in around us. There was the sound of the wind dancing around our little makeshift tents, making flapping noises. There was a squirrel a few feet away that was gnawing on an acorn, but my ears soon fazed that out as I watched the dancing sunspots on the ground when the wind picked up and rustled the trees.

Sam's words broke the silence. "Are you bored?"

I just blinked at him. "Uh, I guess? Why?"

Sam seemed to sense how much I needed to get my mind off of things, so he pulled me over to the campfire. He sat down cross-legged and helped me down next to him. His voice was light. "How about I tell you an old Rounan story?"

I smiled slightly and leaned into him as he began, but I must admit that I didn't pay very much attention. It was more history lesson than story, explaining where the Rounans had come from. It was slightly interesting in the beginning, when the Gornish people traveled to Rounia and made Rounans their slaves after their land died, but when they made it to Nerahdis, slavery was abolished by Emperor Caden.

After that, I found myself losing interest since Sam wasn't the greatest storyteller. By gosh, he was the greatest farmer I knew, but this just was not his gift. Instead, I found myself merely happy to be curled up next to him. It felt totally natural, and I couldn't help but wonder what he thought of me beyond being friends.

I shook the blush from my face and stared up at the sky, wondering where my family was now. The sun was beginning to go down toward the west, sinking beneath the heads of the mountains, and casting a majestic purple color onto their faces. To the east, the twin moons of Lunaka were beginning to rise, one of them slightly ahead with the other in constant pursuit.

They were like Rhydin and I. Up until now, it seemed like he was always chasing me. He was always one step behind me, targeting the people around me until I'd be by myself and vulnerable.

Nearly every day, I thought about going to pick up my sword and practicing with it, but every time I came within a few feet of it, I just couldn't do it. My hand couldn't reach out to take it. I needed some time to recover, but I vowed right then and there that once I was back up to snuff, Rhydin would be the one to find himself with someone constantly behind him. Someone who never let up on coming after him.

And that person would be me.

# CHAPTER FOURTEEN

There was snow. It was falling lightly, little speckles of white crystals playing in the wind until they hit the ground as gravity said they must. There was a wide snowy plain in front of me, as perfect as if someone had dropped a white paint can on the whole kingdom. The wind was nippy, but rather than feeling the gusts of cold that played with the snowflakes around me, my body felt constantly like ice.

As I glanced around, I didn't recognize the scenery until I looked behind me. There, standing tall against the backdrop of beautiful white, was Lunaka Castle, seeming dark and menacing as its spires reached for the heavens. Why was I near the castle? Bad things happened the last time I was here. Frederick and I were nearly killed.

Suddenly, the ground began to shake with such ferocity that my legs could barely keep their balance. My body felt like jelly as loud, cracking noises filled the air. Behind me, one of the oldest sections of the castle crumbled like toast. To the south, a great plume of inky smoke was belched into the air as

I felt the mines begin to collapse beneath my feet. I panicked, my breathing hitching in the icy cold. What was happening? Was the world ending?

The castle bell tower started booming like thunder, over and over and over, not how it typically rings. It *BONG*-ed so loud it reverberated inside my head as cracks yawned wide at the base of the tower. The tower had only done this once before that I knew of, and not even in my own lifetime.

My father told me there was once when he was a boy that the tower rang without end. It was calling the people to the castle because Soläna was in danger. He had heard it during the Quarren War decades ago when Auklia was invading. What was it calling the people to escape from now?

My vision shifted on its own accord, out of my control, and what it focused on caused a jet of heat to race down my spine. It looked almost like a curtain of darkness. A huge blanket of black hung as high up in the sky as anyone could see all the way down to the land below. The curtain draped over the southern wall of Auklia as well as the western wall of Mineraltir. It was rapidly advancing on Lunakan soil, overtaking the mountains as the bell tower roared for the people to come to safety.

There was another shape silhouetted against the midnight curtain. It was long and serpentine in the way it moved through the sky, two crimson red stars for what seemed like eyes...

I sprang forward so fast when I woke up that I smacked my head on a low tree limb. I gasped in pain and began rubbing my temple as I sat back down with my blanket. As my vision cleared, it took me a minute to recognize where I was after such a vivid nightmare. It was dark outside, but with the campfire going, I could see the flickering face of each of the other makeshift tents.

I then noticed that I had worked myself halfway out of my own tent and sighed. I had a knack for moving in my sleep when I had a particularly real dream. I resettled myself to where I had started at the beginning of the night but left the flap to my tent hanging open.

Rachel was also in my tent, sleeping the night away since it was one of her brother's turns to be on watch. Her hair glimmered in the firelight streaming through the open flap. She'd never admit this, but she actually snores lightly. The other two tents housed the Owens brothers and Sam. Lucky him, he got his own tent!

I tried to relax and go back to sleep, but I couldn't. My brain wouldn't quit, kicked into motion by the scary dream. It'd been a month now since my family was killed. My heart still refused to believe that they were truly gone, but my mind had absorbed the shock.

Shortly after Sam and I had our conversation, I found the strength in me to begin practicing again. My sword had grown awkward in my hand after not touching it for a month, but it was easier to get accustomed to it again the second time around. Once I got back to where I had left off, Luke deemed me ready to spar with him one-on-one. It was basically like being pushed into the deep end of the lake with only a basic knowledge of swimming, but I adapted quickly. I even started to learn how to fight with a sword and magic at the same time.

Frederick had visited us once since his return to the castle. During that time, he taught me how to focus a little ball of light in my hand and hold it there until it reached the size I wanted before throwing it at my target. It was pretty simple, but ever since he went back with Mira, I hadn't been able to learn any other attack spells.

The rest of us were trying to give the Royal siblings as much time as possible to glean any information on Rhydin from their father, but it wasn't going well. It was the only hope we had for some sort of lead on what Rhydin's plans were. It seemed that we were in the dark when it came to recent news, here outside of town. Frederick and Mira were even failing to convince the queen and Princess Cornflower to leave for their own safety. Rachel and I were beginning to wonder how much more time we could spare for them.

I didn't see Sam much anymore. He and James found jobs in the mines to supplement Rachel's maid income, and it made me sad. Luke couldn't go, because he was wanted for treason after his livery was seized. He'd made his frustration that he had to stay with me all day very well known. Sometimes I'd see a flicker of red enter his eyes!

Probably adding to his anger was me asking about Evan on nearly a daily basis now. I'd learned that Rachel was communicating with him almost on the hour with some sort of magic that I didn't even know she possessed, but I figured at this point that Frederick had loaned her some, just like Rhydin had loaned some to his non-Royal Followers. Our protectors wanted to keep Evan and I on the exact same page even though we weren't allowed to be together yet. I was so impatient to meet him and get his help, but our combined magical presence would make us way too easy for Rhydin to trace.

A twig snapped and a *whoosh* of wind circled our encampment. Rachel was instantly awake and crept toward the fire, where the sound had come from. Sometimes, I wondered if she had sleeping ninja skills, she could wake so fast. When I looked over, I saw a willowy figure with a purple cloak, but before my mind could even register who she was, I had already sensed her as an aeromage, as well as her meekness and kindness. I knew it was Princess Mira before I'd even glanced in her direction, making me feel pretty good about how my magic was progressing. Maybe I really could do this Allyen thing.

Seeing as I couldn't sleep anyway, I walked over to the campfire with Rachel to meet up with Mira. She seemed distraught and more tired than anything. Rachel asked, "What are you doing here, Your Highness?"

The princess gave a sigh, her face extra pale tonight. "I'm sorry. I summoned one of your brothers to transport me back here. I just needed a break from him..."

"Your father?" I asked, thoughtfully.

Mira only nodded and sank into a heap by the fire. "He's become so overwhelming. He's not even trying to hide his evil anymore. It's become so terrible that I cannot even escape him in my sleep. I have nightmares about him now."

"You're having nightmares too, huh?" I chuckled slightly before I sat down next to her. "I'm glad I'm not the only one. Are yours really vivid? Like it seems completely real?"

Rachel fixed me in her blue death gaze. "Lina. When did you have this real nightmare?"

I shrugged, not thinking anything of it. "Oh, I dunno. My dreams vary in their realness, but I'll tell ya what, the one I had tonight was crazy real. It was freaky, too." I shuddered a bit as I remembered the shaking earth, the black curtain, and the red eyes.

My red-haired friend was down next to me in a flash of lightning, her nose only inches away from mine as she scrutinized every tiny detail of my face. "You need to tell me what happened in it right now."

"Why?" I asked hesitantly, leaning away from her. I was

completely convinced that she had finally gone insane.

"Because!" Rachel began to be frustrated, her tone shooting through the roof. "Allyen dreams sometimes happen in real life! I mean, the only particularly good future-seer is Rhydin, but this could be really important! Future-seeing is a side effect of any magic, but what makes a good user of it is if they can tell it will happen or not."

I wasn't really sure I could believe her, seeing as I couldn't particularly remember any of my other dreams happening in real life, but it was true that my magic hadn't been awakened for too terribly long. Taking a deep breath, I tried to explain the crazy, terrifying nightmare. "To be honest, I'm not sure what happened. I remember there was snow on the ground, and I was standing up by the castle facing away from it. The ground began to shake violently, harder than any other mine collapse I'd ever felt, and when I looked up, there was all this *black*! It's hard to explain. It was almost like Auklia and Mineraltir were still in the nighttime while Lunaka was in daylight. The bell tower was ringing really loud. My father once told me a long time ago that the king would ring it if the people were in danger. And then there were these two red stars in the darkness, almost like eyes!"

"Oh, good grief." Rachel squeezed her eyes shut as if I either just told her the worst news ever, or she couldn't believe the nonsense I was sputtering. I was leaning toward the second option when she spoke again. "Lina, don't you remember that page I tagged for you to read in the myths and legends book?"

As my eyes whirled up to think, I noticed that Luke, James, and Sam had all joined us around the campfire. The first two were listening intently, but it seemed as if Sam was still half-asleep. I knew I had read that whole book cover to cover twice. It was like my school years all over again. In one ear and out the other.

Rachel gasped, flabbergasted with me. "The entry on Duunzer! Remember? The dragon…?"

"Oh, yeah!" I smiled as I remembered, but then immediately frowned. "That's not good, is it?"

"No. No it's not." Rachel smacked herself in the face.

Sam piped up groggily, "I thought Duunzer was just a myth. Like the giants, y'know?"

I noticed an eye roll from both Owens boys.

"It may surprise the *Kidek* and the *Allyen*, but all things considered 'myths' by the general populace are *not* actually mythical!" Rachel grumbled, her sarcasm very evident. Sam and I blushed. "In case you don't remember, Lina, Duunzer was a dragon. Or is, I should say. But not just any dragon, it's a created being. Do you remember what they're called, Lina, from your lesson with Frederick?"

Good grief, it really was like school all over again. Except this time, I remembered the answer. "They're called Einanhis. Frederick explained how Birdie was an Einanhi, a shell created by magic and given life by magic, but it's not real. I remember because Frederick said it was an Old Gornish word for 'puppet'."

I could almost picture Frederick patting my head like a good little student. But Mira's smiling at me would have to do.

"Exactly." Rachel said, "It's a dragon created by Rhydin that commands a special, magical Darkness, which is the living black that you saw in your dream. I wonder if this is what Rhydin has in store for us in the future. You said there was snow on the ground?"

I nodded, but my brow furrowed. "Well, yeah, but what do you mean the Darkness is *living?*"

Rachel didn't seem to know how to answer that question. She raised a finger to her lips, and a few seconds of silence went by before Mira chimed in, her voice almost surprising me. "The Darkness is considered living because it is part of the dragon's conscious. Any person consumed by it disappears, unless Duunzer is defeated."

"How do you know that, Mira? And I don't?" Rachel asked, slightly upset that she hadn't known this information.

A twitch of a grin appeared on Mira's doll-like face. "Growing up as a princess has its few privileges. I have access to histories that the public does not. The reason I know, and the reason Duunzer has an account in the myth book, is because this incident has happened once before. It was back when my ancestor, the first king of Lunaka, King Spenser, was on the throne. The very first Allyen, Nora Soreta, was the one who defeated Rhydin and Duunzer the first time over three hundred years ago."

"So, history has now come full circle." Sam concluded a few minutes after she spoke. "That's how Rhydin is going to make his big entrance all over again."

"But that also means..." Rachel trailed off slowly, and then flicked her eyes up at me.

I swallowed hard. "Let me guess. Just like Nora, the first Allyen, defeated Duunzer, I get to beat it this time? ...Is this open for negotiation?"

Luke's words were like rock, never being the one to show compassion. "You don't 'get to', Lina. You're the only one who has the power to, as well as Evan. If, of course, your dream was accurate and this is what's coming for us."

"Luke, this is the only concrete information we've gotten all month," Rachel retorted. "Yes, it's just a possibility, but it's worth looking into. Besides, we need to work fast to find the arrow now that Saarah is gone so that Rhydin doesn't find it before we do."

"What arrow?" Sam and I said simultaneously. We gave each other a glance before looking back to Mira and Rachel.

"When Nora defeated Duunzer, she crafted a special arrow that could hold the Allyen locket so she could shoot the locket through the dragon." Mira said calmly, her hands folded in her lap. "Allyen magic is made of light, and the dragon is made of Darkness. Nora was very smart to have figured that out in her age. The arrow became an heirloom, passed down to every Allyen just like the locket in case Rhydin ever became able to resurrect Duunzer."

"But Grandma never had a chance to pass it down then… Did she?" I bit my lip to keep my voice from quavering.

Rachel took my hand and squeezed it tight. "It doesn't matter. I'm sure she kept it well hidden in her home, but we need to go find it before Rhydin does. Otherwise, there will be no stopping Duunzer when the snow falls."

"Alrighty then." I said as I rose to my feet, brushing the dust off my behind. "When will we go, then? Tomorrow?"

"Now." The three Owenses said in unison as each of them darted off into a different direction to collect supplies for the trip.

Sam and I were left alone as Mira returned to the castle magically. Sam, who had been nodding off for the first half of the conversation after being sleep deprived for so long, was now fully awake. I could tell just by looking at him that the gears were already moving rapidly in his mind. I wondered what he was thinking about. Duunzer? His people? Rhydin? Me?

I blushed at that last one and knew I was kidding myself. It had been so long since that festival that we had shared. I was sure he had completely forgotten any feelings he could have possibly had. Nonetheless, I gravitated over to him until the siblings came back because it still simply felt right.

I pulled my locket out of its safe spot tucked away in my sash. It was amazing to think I had thought it just a simple heirloom a couple of seasons ago. I looked up at the sky. I could still see the twin moons up high, beginning to sink toward the western horizon. It had to be around two or three o'clock in the morning.

Time was more crucial than I originally thought. Early Autumn had barely begun while snow was falling in my dream, enough to cover all the prairie. If Rhydin had already found the arrow, I didn't want to think about what was coming for us. Even with a season to go, we could already be too late.

Oh, Grandma, I hope you hid it well.

# CHAPTER FIFTEEN

T he sky was still mostly dark by the time we made it to
Soläna. It was that hour of darkness right before the sun's
glow could be visible in the east. We didn't have much time
left if Rachel wanted to be in and out before the sun even
peeked over the horizon.

While we walked, I noticed the earth was beginning to
have that musty smell it takes on after the leaves start to fall
and waste away on the ground. The light covering of fog kept
us from seeing too far ahead of us. It was as if the entire world
had turned gray, seeming rather eerie since I'd never been to
town this early before. All the windows were still black,
empty eyes that watched us as we tiptoed down the edges of
the cobblestone streets.

Once we got closer to Grandma's house, I could feel the
tension rising in my heart. Not only were a few of the
windows around us starting to have lights in them as the early
workers began their day, but I hadn't been to her house since
before she was...before she was killed. The cloak that hid my

identity felt heavier and heavier on my head and shoulders. Sam had chosen to accompany Rachel and I as extra back up while Luke and James were no doubt scouting around to make sure none of Rhydin's people were anywhere close to the house.

As we came around a bend, the house came into view for the first time. I chided myself for not coming to take care of it after the deaths, even if I hadn't really had any choice but to leave town. The door was hanging open, lopsided on its hinges with several long, deep gouges in its wood. Every single window was broken, and the flower boxes had been ripped off, the dead, wilted flowers strewn around the little yard and the road. A towel was hanging out of the one upstairs window, ripped to shreds by the glass.

A lump rose in my throat as I witnessed the sad little house that was no longer a home. I could visualize my grandmother rolling over in her grave. I tried to swallow the lump down the best I could. I knew the inside could only be worse if someone had ransacked it for the arrow.

Once Rachel received word from her brothers that the perimeter was clear, we three entered the house and closed what was left of the door behind us. I took my heavy hood off and tried not to look too hard at the broken dishes in Grandma's cabinet, the upturned table and ripped rug, and the smashed wicker rocking chair that she had rocked every one of her grandchildren on. Rachel and Sam both eyed me carefully, trying to gauge if I was ready for this, but I wouldn't look at them. I began to search, even though I had no real clue what this special arrow looked like.

Wordlessly, we all began sifting through the carnage. Sam and Rachel both attempted to take the messier portions so I wouldn't find so many memories, but when I searched in the beginning, I tried to not look very closely at the things I dug through.

As time went by, it proved to be downright impossible. My eyes noticed every item that was out of place, destroyed, or happened to be in the exact same spot. I'd heard stories about how twisters could come tear apart your house, carrying your belongings for miles, yet still leave something completely untouched. Whenever I came across something that remained neatly tucked into its spot, such as Grandma's biscuit pan safely stowed next to her stove, it reminded me of those stories.

After maybe twenty minutes, I had stuffed several mementos in my pockets, such as my grandfather's watch that Grandma had cherished and my grandmother's journal that was lying on her bedside table as if she was still coming home tonight to write in it. The house was small, so there wasn't much to it, but it amazed me to watch Rachel and Sam search.

Rachel left nothing put together. She mercilessly dumped out vases, dismantled music boxes, and felt for secret compartments inside every one of Grandma's drawers. Sam busied himself with the chimney after thoroughly ransacking the upstairs, prying a few bricks loose before deciding that there was nothing up there. Rachel even took a few of the rods of Grandma's headboard apart to see if something had been stuffed in them. Our precious minutes before daylight ticked on, and we still kept coming up with nothing. No matter how many nooks and crannies we tried.

Rachel straightened her back after leaning under Grandma's old wood stove, dust bunnies caught in her messy hair. "Alright, guys. If it was here, I think we would have found it by now. We're out of time, we need to leave immediately if we don't want to get caught."

My heart sank to the pit of my stomach. It was true. Rhydin beat us to it, or somebody stole it just to pocket the change.

"Does that mean Duunzer really is his plan?" Sam said quietly to Rachel, trying but failing to keep me out of earshot.

Rachel shrugged as if she were at the end of her rope. "I really don't know. It's looking more likely, but it could have been taken by anybody. Saarah could have hid it somewhere different when she moved to take care of Lina's farm. There's a number of possibilities here, but Duunzer definitely isn't eliminated."

Sam took a deep breath. I began to ardently hope that we could come back later and look again, or even search the remains of my own house since she was right. Grandma had lived there for a month before her death. We pulled our cloaks on and waited for a signal from Luke and James before opening the door. Early morning sunlight came streaming through. As we exited the house and tried to turn north, hoping to escape unseen, our plans changed in only a second.

Town was erupting with noise with the coming of the sun. People were beginning to wake up, open up windows, and head out the door to their jobs. Rachel snatched the back of my cloak and pulled me over to a dark alley next to Grandma's house where Sam was standing.

He was flabbergasted as he pulled his hood down lower. "Sheesh, this is the earliest I've ever seen these people up, and I work in the mines every day!"

"And it's all of them." I added as I screened the brown-clad masses moving past us toward the south. "Not just the men. The women and children, too."

As people continued to walk by us, we three simply could not think of a reason why so many families would be heading in the same direction this time of day. It wasn't a market day.

If it was school, it would only be children. It wasn't a holiday either since the annual Harvest Festival wasn't until later in the season. Which I obviously would not be attending this year seeing as Sam and I had no harvest to celebrate. As fewer people began to float on by, it became easier to pick out their words since the roar of footsteps was subsiding.

"I'm so glad they finally got him!"

"Me too... He deserves... Hang."

"That Epidemic was so bad..."

"...My mother died in it, and my brother!"

"...that Parker boy is gonna pay for this!"

Abruptly, it clicked in my head who they were talking about, and I gasped, "Oh, no."

"What?" Rachel looked at me confused. After all, she didn't grow up here. "Who's this Parker kid? Why's he important?"

Sam cleared his throat, crossing his arms quietly. "The Epidemic began in Stellan, twenty miles southeast of here. I lived there with my mother when it began. Mr. and Mrs. Parker were the first to fall sick with it, as well as the first to die of it. The public has blamed their family for it, and this boy has been on the run ever since. Sounds like they finally caught him."

I eyed Sam carefully. "What are you saying, Sam? That boy doesn't deserve this! It's not his fault! It's Rhydin's!" Sam bit his lip, but I kept going, "We need to stop this."

Rachel reached for me like lightning, but I had already turned in to the flow of traffic. If she wanted to stop me now, she'd cause a scene. I held my hood around my face as I walked quickly, slipping between people like water between rocks, trying to get as close to the town square as physically possible. It became more difficult as I caught up with the huge crowd, nearly every citizen in Soläna now. When I looked over my shoulder, Rachel and Sam were following me closely, trying to catch up without looking suspicious as the only hooded figures in the mass.

Once I had sardined my way closer to the center of the square, I got a good look at the stage that had been erected there since the last time I'd been to town. It felt like the air was knocked out of me when I saw the tall wooden beam with a rope necklace hanging from it. It instantly brought back that day when Mama had accidentally taken Rosetta and I to town while one of these was being used. They only hanged the most terrible of criminals in Lunaka, mostly Rounans.

Yet, here standing in front of this noose was a handcuffed ten-year-old kid. Tall for his age and scrawny, like he hadn't had a good meal in ages, a pair of mining goggles strapped to his head. His green eyes were terrified.

My eyes narrowed when I saw who was next to him, King Adam himself. The man seemed to have aged slightly since I'd last seen him at the Spring Festival. His face was etched deeper with lines although not quite wrinkles. Silver curls had appeared at his temples, but his dark eyes were like fire. He was executing this one himself.

I began taking deep breaths as I prepared myself. What was I going to say? What would I do? Would I shoot magic at the rope? I didn't have my sword! How was I going to pull this off without getting myself killed? I needed to work fast or King Adam was going to throw that noose over his head, and it'd be too late. What had I gotten myself into?

Sam reached me as King Adam draped the rope around the poor boy's thin neck. My stomach turned over as I heard the audience around me cheer and chant, hoping for the death of this poor boy simply because his parents died first in the

Epidemic.

I swallowed hard as if it was my own neck about to get pinched, but that was when I noticed the Parker boy doing something strange. He kept trying to use his roped hands to gesture toward King Adam, or at least up towards the noose. A couple times I saw the king's cape move or the boy's own hair rustle as if with an imaginary wind. I squinted at him, trying to figure it out. What was he doing? It was almost like invisible magic...

It hit me almost like lightning. This kid was a Rounan!

Before another thought could even touch my mind, my body was spurred into action. I desperately began shoving through people, finding tiny crevices between them that only my tiny body could fit through. Sam shouted, lost in the roar of the audience, but he was too big to follow me.

"Citizens of Lunaka!" King Adam yelled over the chaos, trying to begin some sort of speech, but I couldn't hear the rest of it. I had a one-track mind, and it was focused solely on the Parker boy. I caused Sam to lose all of his records. I could at least save one of his people.

When people clustered too close together, I knew there was only one way to make them part for me. I scooped a ball of light out of thin air, my magic flowing more freely than it had ever before, and thrust it high above my head where it tripled in size. Everyone in Lunaka was deathly afraid of magic. I knew from experience. Instantly, the people around me turned with enormous eyes of terror. They began scrambling over themselves away from me, inadvertently trampling some of the slow.

As a path to the stage yawned wide, King Adam finally noticed me, his eyes jumping to mine like daggers. "It's the Allyen! Guards, stop her!"

With a boost of magic, I leaped onto the stage, promptly heading for the Parker boy. I didn't get very far before a rock hard hand shot out and knocked me in the head. My vision swirled and my ears roared as I attempted a spell to shove everyone away from me. It sort of worked, considering I made it up and Frederick hadn't actually taught me that yet. As another guard tried to tackle me to the ground, he was thrown away from me by someone else. The screaming instantly stopped as people watched in surprise.

Sam made a gigantic leap, no doubt aided by his magic, to the stage and landed squarely on top of the guard who was trying to take me out. He met my gaze with fierce eyes for a split second before he turned with a flat hand, magically severing the rope that threatened the Parker boy's life. I had never seen him so angry as he shoved King Adam's guards away left and right, catapulting them off the stage with stronger magic than he'd ever led on to have. I found myself kneeling behind him, unsure of what to do.

I felt myself blush. I was so in awe of him. In my defense, I did take out one guard who tried to come up behind him, but I suddenly began to feel like a failure as I watched Sam fight more and more guards. My heart thundered. Nothing could happen to Sam. This was supposed to be me helping Sam, not forcing him to save me.

"Stop!" King Adam bellowed, as I rose to try and help. "You Rounan scum, I hereby order you to *stop*!" He tried to get off a blast of wind magic to knock Sam and I over. As I raised my arms to block, Sam nudged the king's aim too high and then flattened him to the stage with a big, invisible hand. As this happened, a guard rushed up behind Sam, aiming for his head. Sam ducked, but the guard still managed a grip on his hood and yanked it off.

King Adam's eyes grew large once he took in Sam's face and the bandana tied around his head, the gold stars surrounded by blue with a purple border. The colors of his people, Grandma had called it the day he came to take me to the livery after Frederick and I narrowly escaped the Spring Festival at the castle. From his pinned down position, the king sneered, "Kidek Samton Greene is helping the Allyen, eh?"

Sam glared at the king, and his voice was deep, strong, and penetrating. "I will *not* allow you, *or* your master, to murder any more of my people!"

Finally, I made myself useful during everyone's chitchat. I magically rocketed a few more of the guards off of the stage, effectively taking care of the rest of them. Sam turned to me, still angry as he magically held the king down, and took the terrified Parker boy and I by the hands.

The king's eyes widened in fury as he struggled in his pancake position. "*Guards*! Capture them now! Don't let any of them get away!"

Sam hoisted the scrawny boy around his shoulders. I felt him take a huge breath, his magic growing inside him before he turned on his heel, pulling me under his arm and gripping me tight under my ribs. All of this happened within seconds before I abruptly felt my feet leave the ground. We flew through the air in a supersized jump to the edge of the crowd, and I held onto him for dear life. Tears leaked from the corners of my eyes we were moving so fast. Sam kept his balance when the ground came up to meet us, but I stumbled. He mercilessly pulled me forward as we began to sprint away from the square with at least twenty of the guards on our tails.

Time seemed to slow once more as we sprinted at full speed. I couldn't have run faster even if I'd wanted to, and I quickly noticed that the Parker boy had fainted, slung across

Sam's shoulders. I glanced over my shoulder only once to see King Adam's guards yelling and racing towards us. The king himself mustered all his power to try and use the wind to bring us back to him. It was like running against a wall.

As I felt my feet lift the ground yet again, I wondered if he had succeeded. Then I noticed Rachel's tight grip around my middle. In split second, I looked up to see my red-haired friend, whom I had known for years, with colors sprouting from her back that came around and enveloped the four of us. I had no time to look closer at them before the whitest light I had ever experienced filled my head.

It was suddenly completely silent. The silence rang in my ears after being around the noisy crowd and the guards' shouting.

The light disappeared, and, in that same moment, I landed on the ground, hard. My eyes were blinded for a few seconds afterward, but I recognized the now familiar scent of oak and the feel of the soft grass where we landed. Once my vision cleared, I could see our makeshift campsite. I rubbed my eyes hard, and when I saw Sam, he looked just as confused and amazed as I did.

Suddenly, I heard Rachel laughing. "Oh, good grief! *Samton*, really? That's your first name?"

Sam dropped the unconscious boy on the grass, still looking angry. "I really don't see what's so funny about my name!"

"Well, *I* think it's hilarious." Rachel beamed as she went over to talk to her brothers. Luke and James were confused as they kept glancing toward the Parker boy who was still completely unconscious. Rachel seemed to explain the situation further to them. I could just hear Luke's thoughts now, could imagine his grumbling about having another person to babysit all day while the rest of the adults, aside from me, went off to work.

Sam didn't say a word to me, and instead quickly turned around and headed back to his tent after a piercing look.

The boy we saved was waking up as Sam headed away from him, and after a few frantic looks around, he curled into a ball and breathed erratically. I might not have been able to save him on my own, but he definitely needed someone right now. The boy's eyes locked on to me, widening slightly as I crept closer to him. I moved as carefully and slowly as I could, kneeling in the grass still maybe five or six feet away when the poor kid began to whimper.

I held my hands out so he could see they were empty. "It's okay! You don't have to be afraid of us. I promise. We rescued you, remember?

The kid took a raspy breath as he thought, and I began to wonder if he was sick. For being slightly tall for his age, this kid didn't have a speck of meat on him. His arms were so thin they made my stomach churn to look at them, and his neck didn't seem to be big enough to support his head adequately. His clothing was ripped in some places but haphazardly sewn up in others, as if he'd fixed them several times. They were also drenched with coal dust, leading me to believe he'd been hiding in the mines. That assumption matched both his pale skin tone and the big mining goggles strapped to his head. After what seemed like an eternity, the boy barely nodded, a fraction of the fear leaving his eyes.

I grinned a little bit as I sat down cross-legged while inching a little closer to him. "My name is Lina. What's yours?"

The boy looked down and only held his stomach. I reached into the pouch that hung from my waist and dug around until

I found some of the jerky I'd been saving for later. I had hardly offered it to him before he snatched it away and began to nibble on it like a squirrel. It reminded me of the way Rosetta used to eat her jerky when we were little and didn't have as much to go around. It made me teary-eyed.

"Camerron." He whispered.

"Nice to meet you, Camerron." I smiled at him. Once I saw that he had calmed down and was content with his jerky, I rose to go find him some water because I was sure he was thirsty. The Owenses were still off in their corner discussing, although I noticed James had left the huddle. Probably to reassume his lookout post.

When I reached the fire, I noticed somebody was already in the act of boiling water to cleanse it. I lifted the iron kettle off the fire and poured it into my own tin cup that was waiting with everybody else's for whenever our next meal was. I was standing to return to Camerron when I came face to face with a piping hot Sam.

"What are you doing?" Sam's voice was rigid, his arms crossed defensively over his chest.

"I'm taking Camerron some water. I'll add some to your pot later if that's the problem." I replied, a little too edgily. This metal cup was beginning to burn my hands.

Sam balked at me. "Do you have *any* idea what you've done today?"

"I-…" I tried to say, but he cut me off in his anger.

"You have no clue, do you? What being a leader is all about?" Sam's voice continued to rise.

"Sam, I was just trying to save Camerron! After all, he's a-…"

"Lina, you need to understand how much is at stake here!" A pained expression entered Sam's face. "I just got exposed to the entire kingdom in order to save you because you wanted to help *one* boy! I can never go back to Soläna ever again, and my people are in even more danger because of you! I've already lost all of my records and now people have seen me *with* you and *protecting* you, the Allyen! If Rhydin wasn't already after the Rounans, he definitely will be now."

Sam sighed and turned away from me as if the conversation was over, but it definitely was not. I grabbed his arm and pulled him back around to face me, throwing my cup to the ground. "Hey, I didn't *ask* you to jump in and save me okay? I didn't ask you to show yourself off to everyone! I'm sure if you had waited an extra, I don't know, *thirty seconds*? Rachel could have saved me instead. That's their job, if you've forgotten, not yours!"

"Hold up, you're blaming *me* for saving your skin? Lina, a guard was about to tackle you to the ground and likely slit your throat!" Sam shook his head, his eyes becoming like fire and color entering his cheeks. "I don't think you understand that literally *everything* you do affects this whole kingdom, this whole continent. Because if you die, nobody will be here to defeat Duunzer or Rhydin! I know you're still mourning your family, but you need to at least grasp that this is so much bigger than that! I'm an *outlaw* because of you. I lost my farm, my mining job, and all of my records because of you. To top it all off, now all of my people are doomed!"

"Sam, I'm sorry, okay? I never *asked* to be the Allyen!" My words began to slip as my throat developed a lump. I fought back tears hard. "I saved him because-..."

"It doesn't matter!" Sam shouted and then began to shake a finger at me. "I didn't ask to be a Rounan either! I sure as heck never asked to be *Kidek*, Lina, but you know what, life isn't fair! We still have to serve in these roles whether we want to or not!"

"Okay, you know what?" I placed my hands on my hips, trying to ignore the fact that each of his words pierced my heart. "Do you actually want to know *why* I saved Camerron? He's a Rounan! I tried to save him because I get it. It's *my* fault you lost your records. I just thought if I could help you save just one of your people, maybe you would feel better! I guess that's just not good enough for you, is it?"

Sam suddenly looked like I'd slapped him. He peeked over to where Camerron was eyeing us fearfully, having listened to our whole conversation. He swallowed hard as he stomped over to where the boy sat and rolled up the sleeve of his right arm. There was a geometric mark that stretched from the boy's wrist to his elbow, although it was smaller than I would have thought. I remembered how Frederick had explained to me that true Rounans have these marks on their arms, and that they tell you how much magic they have. Sam sighed as he saw it, convicted that I was right as he began to rub his temples. The Parker boy really was a Rounan even if he didn't have much power.

He walked back toward me, his jaw set but his energy gone. "Why didn't you tell me he was a Rounan? I could have helped you."

"Sam, he had a noose around his neck. If I had waited to clear it with you, he might not be here right now." My words were firmer now. "You shouldn't have jumped in. Rachel could have saved me and whisked us far away from there, and you could still have your life!"

"Lina…" Sam looked down, almost embarrassed, shaking his head like something just wouldn't compute. His voice was much quieter. "Lina, I couldn't wait. I couldn't just wait and see what happened. You were in danger."

His change of mood made me quirk my eyebrow. "And it never occurred to you that my three bodyguards could swoop in and save me? That's why they're here, y'know."

"I know. I just…" Sam eyes turned up to the sky, at a loss. "It was something I *had* to do. I didn't even think about it. I just did it. It was…instinct."

"Why?" My voice got louder, getting frustrated with his vague responses.

"Just because. Let's leave it at that." Sam tried to turn away from me again.

"Sam!" I reached out and grabbed his hand. "You can't get all mad at me for jumping in and saving Camerron and causing you to be revealed to the whole kingdom if you can't tell me why you had to save me yourself and not wait for the Owenses!"

Sam sighed, his shoulders slumping. He turned around, swallowing hard and biting his lip rather fiercely before finally looking me in the eye. His expression was almost tortured as the words spilled out. "Because I'm in love with you. I had to save you. I couldn't bear to go one second longer watching you up on that stage. I'm sorry that was such a mistake."

With that, Sam walked away from me. It was as if my heart stopped beating all together. His fingers fell through mine like sand. My mouth fell open, and my arms dropped to my sides limply. I suddenly felt vulnerable as I stared at his back walking away from me. My heart broke as I watched him go, willing him to come back to me so we could continue this conversation.

Had he really said it? Those three tiny, powerful words? He said he was in love with me. After all this time. After he took me to the Spring Festival and after catching me as I fell down the canyon with my magic coming alive. After he came to visit me at the livery every few days, and offered to take care of my farm for me. After I always wondered but always shut it down because I thought it couldn't be possible. Why would he ever love me?

Yet now, I'd lost him. He said he'd made a mistake. He walked away from me before I could even respond. Had he changed his mind?

Of course, it was not until this moment that I discovered how much this idea would hurt. I'd been intertwined with him this whole time and never realized it, even after all the time I spent protecting him at the beginning of the year. All that time, I'd thought I was protecting him because he was my childhood friend. But that wasn't true.

I'd protected him because I loved him. And now, the idea of him somehow hating me was absolutely unbearable.

# CHAPTER SIXTEEN

Frederick and his sister, Mira, arrived in the middle of Sam and Lina's argument. Frederick decided not to get involved. After all, Sam and Lina were each grown adults who could handle themselves responsibly. He truly hoped they could make up and not be at odds with each other anymore. Anybody with two eyes could tell that they were in love with each other. Although, to be honest, Frederick hadn't quite picked up on it until Rachel told him. It was not his gift, he had been told by Cassandra, his own soon-to-be wife.

When he reached the Owenses, he noticed Luke and James on either side of Rachel, as if they had to hold her back while Sam and Lina had their argument. Frederick knew that Rachel was fiercely protective of Lina and had been so ever since she began her assignment in Lunaka a few years ago. He was glad Lina had such a good friend during this time.

Frederick cleared his throat, and the three Owenses looked at him. He grinned slightly. "So, I suppose you're the reason they got out of there so quickly?"

Rachel nodded, straightening her posture as if she'd never gotten riled up. "Yes. Unfortunately, I had to show them my magic, but there was no other way. If I hadn't, we would all be in prison right now facing our own nooses."

"It's a handy skill." Frederick said, not angry at all. "It's convenient that you and your brothers possess it since the only other person who can use transportation magic in the world is Rhydin. One of these days, we will need to explain what you three are to Lina and Sam. They deserve to know."

"She hasn't had time to ask about it yet. But when she does, I'll be referring her to you." Rachel winked at him.

Mira stepped forward, her pale, stoic face seeming more of a mask today. "Are there any updates that we should be aware of?"

Rachel answered first. "Oh, let's see. We couldn't find the arrow at Saarah's, but we've decided to go look for it again when we can. The house was trashed pretty badly, so we're not sure if a regular thief stole it, one of Rhydin's people took it, or if we just didn't look in the right place. Sam revealed himself to your father to save that little Rounan boy over there, which makes things a lot more complicated."

"I saw Eli and Terran today on my rounds," Luke added. "They walked into the forest a couple miles, but then they turned around and disappeared magically. I'm not sure what they were doing, but we'll make sure to watch that area closer."

Rachel grumbled, "Oooo, I hate them. I want to smash Eli's glasses."

"So, what are you doing here, Your Highness?" James piped up, always the curious one.

"Well, I won't beat around the bush. We're going to Mineraltir in a week," Frederick said plainly.

"What? Why?" Rachel gasped, "We're safer here in Lunaka. We have more reinforcements nearby if we need them! We've been in constant communication to get Evan here as quickly as possible if Rhydin really does plan on using Duunzer."

"I agree with all of that." Frederick conceded, remembering the lessons he'd had in etiquette. Always appease the angry person first, then continue. "But a rare opportunity has been presented to us." He nodded to his sister.

Mira took a deep breath, her fingers fluttering awkwardly. "Officially, my father and I are traveling to Mineraltir to meet with…Prince Xavier. My father wants to create the marriage agreement and all the political liaisons that go along with it."

"I believe that a few of us should tag along in order to meet with Xavier ourselves." Frederick resumed since Mira still found it uncomfortable to talk about her engagement. "We've sent multiple letters to Xavier over the past several seasons, trying to figure out if he is on our side or not, and we've never received a response. It's possible the courier is never getting through since his stepmother is rather torturous. This would be as good an opportunity as ever to speak with him in person. I already know that King Daniel of Auklia is on my side, but we need to know if Xavier is on board against Rhydin."

"Well, it will be easy for me to sneak along, I'm Mira's maid," Rachel said. "You're right. We're running out of time, and the next three rulers of the kingdoms *need* to be on the same side in order to defeat Rhydin."

"Here's the real question. Do we take Lina?" Luke added, always knowing that he was the main caretaker of her since Rachel worked at the castle and James at the mines. If she was going, he would likely be the one assigned to her.

"I think she should for two reasons. One, she can meet

Xavier properly, since we will need to be a team against Rhydin in the future. I doubt he will go down with Duunzer even if we can somehow defeat it. The second is that she and Sam need a break from each other." Frederick's voice grew quieter as he went on, eyeballing the diminutive woman by the campfire. He truly cared about Lina, and it made him sad that she was so upset. A break would do them good.

Rachel's expression fell, worried for her friend.

"Then it's decided." James said, "Rachel will ride along with Princess Mira and King Adam. Luke will take Lina separately so nobody knows she's there, and I will stay here with Sam and the Parker boy. I can help them figure out what to do with the boy while you're gone and be here to wait for Evan."

Frederick nodded. "Sounds logical to me. Rachel, Mira will be in touch on the departure time, and we can plan from there. I will remain at the castle to have more time to convince my mother and sister, Cornflower, that my father isn't who he says he is."

The five of them shared knowing glances. Things would get much more complicated as soon as they split apart, but it had to be done. James used his magic to transport Frederick and Mira back to the castle, but as they went their separate ways, they couldn't help but worry. What would happen if they reached Mineraltir only to discover that Xavier was helping Rhydin? At this point, anything could go wrong.

When Rachel announced that most of us were going to Mineraltir in a week, I wasn't sure what to think. Not only was I apprehensive, seeing as I'd never been outside of Lunaka before, but I felt uncomfortable to be leaving Sam back at the base. We weren't speaking at the moment, but there was still that part of me deep inside that couldn't help but feel strange about leaving my childhood friend alone with James. I hoped that Rhydin wouldn't take advantage of this separation of our group. Surely, since most of us were wearing those crystallized feathers, he won't be able to sense any difference.

I tried to work up the courage to talk to Sam a couple times, but I wasn't ready. He thought it was a mistake to be in love with me. He never gave me a chance to tell him my feelings that had been suppressed for so long. I couldn't help but think that if I had held back my feelings all year, I could do it again. Therefore, I was determined to keep my space from him until I could say the same.

I threw myself into my new training with Luke. It focused on bow and arrow skills since if Duunzer really was coming, I needed to learn how to shoot. He started me off on a light bow with a target not too far away, which was smart since it took forever to figure out how to aim. It was a skill I'd never needed to know when I was an average farmer. Just like the sword.

As the days stretched on, it became easier and the bow became more familiar and comfortable in my grip just as the sword had become. I nearly had to start all over when they gave me a full-sized bow, the one I would actually need to shoot the special arrow. Luke even attempted to teach me a sort of magic that would help me aim, when usually that was Frederick's job. Luke was actually a pretty understanding teacher during this time, which was a nice change from the pressure-filled lessons from before. Normally, he and his siblings were gung-ho hardcore, almost downright militaristic, but with this, he went slowly with me. Why, I had no clue, but I appreciated it.

In my spare moments, I would sometimes reach into my pocket and finger my grandmother's journal that I had taken from her house while we looked for the arrow. I hadn't worked up the courage to actually open it and read it yet, but it was still an item of comfort when I returned to our tent at the end of a long day of training. On this night in particular, two days before our journey would begin, I found the bravery to at least read the first page, snuggled up with my one moth-eaten blanket in the corner of our otherwise empty abode.

Apparently, Grandma inherited this journal from her father, Jordaan Rodgers. She wrote about how she was so excited to be trusted with the Allyen journal and the things he had written. This didn't make much sense, as hers was the only writing inside. But, it was fun to read the first entry. After all, I definitely couldn't imagine my wrinkled, wonderful grandmother as a spunky sixteen-year-old who loved life. She was also thrilled by discovering that she was an Allyen, and at that, I had to close the journal.

Previously, I had come to recognize that maybe being an Allyen could be really great. But, ever since the argument, I decided it was the most terrible job in the world. I wished with all of my being that I had asked her what she thought of being an Allyen once she actually got some practice. But now, I would never know.

At that moment, Rachel stooped into the tent, clad with a whole bunch of gear. It was getting dark outside, and since she began to unstrap her swords, I knew it was either Luke or James' turn to watch the camp. I wondered if they ever grew tired of the night shifts, aside from James who only needed three hours of sleep. When Rachel noticed me stuffed into a corner, she smiled. "Well, hello there. What are you doing?"

"Nothing really." I responded, taking a deep breath to forget my thoughts. "What did you do today?"

"Oh, y'know, the usual. Counting trees and specks of dirt." The redhead chuckled, "Watch is boring, but it's better than sitting around watching your lessons."

"Hey! I'm actually getting quite a bit better if you could believe it! I've gotten used to holding the heavier bow. I've just got to work on my aim." I defended myself, slyly putting Grandma's journal into my pocket before Rachel could notice it. I was keeping it hidden because I didn't want the others to think I was weak simply for being nostalgic.

"Good! I'm happy for you." Rachel sighed as she finally collapsed onto her blanket next to me, the shadows under her eyes screaming for sleep.

"Hey, Rachel? Can I ask you something?"

"Sure."

"Back when we saved Camerron from King Adam, something weird happened with you. When you transported us away from there, it almost looked like you had these things coming out of your back. Like big, colorful *wings* or something." I said, finally asking the question that had been bugging me all week and trying to remember that hurried moment of action in vain. "What were they?"

"I'll let Frederick explain that one." Rachel winked at me. "All that matters is that we got away, and they can't trace us to the forest."

I nodded, not totally satisfied with that answer, but it'd have to do for now. I expected her to go right to sleep, but she didn't. Rachel lay there with her eyes open, staring at the ceiling of the tent with an arm casually behind her head. When it seemed that she was sleeping with her eyes open, I nearly pulled the journal back out read more, but she suddenly spoke.

"Lina, can I ask you something now?"

"Of course. What about?" I hid the journal again.

"Sam?"

I screwed up my face and then puffed my cheeks out. "Do we have to?"

"I'd like to." Rachel's eyes met mine. "Do you still love him?"

"Rachel..."

"I know I've given you plenty of jokes about it over the years, but seriously. Do you love him?"

I threw my hands up in the air as I fell backwards onto my blanket, preferring not to look at her as I thought. As soon as my thoughts started making no sense, I began to think out loud. "Honestly, it's really confusing... All this time he has been such a big part of my life, and I never even allowed myself to hope that he had feelings for me because his friendship was so important to me. Now, suddenly he tells me he's in love with me, and it woke me up to what had been really going on between us. But he also said it must have been a mistake and never gave me a chance to answer."

"Yes or no question, Lina." Rachel rolled over and propped her head up on her fist to look at me. It was hard to read her face. I could barely see it in the dim firelight that fell through the open flap to our tent. It seemed somewhere between impatient and the desire to know the true answer.

I breathed in. I breathed out. "...Yes."

"I knew it." Rachel cracked a grin.

I rolled over to fix her with one of my looks. "Rachel, you haven't given me any time to get over him. That argument happened like five days ago! Give me some more time. Give me the trip to Mineraltir to forget my feelings and just go back to being friends."

"Honey, I don't want you to 'get over him', as you say." The smile worked its way into Rachel's eyes. "Sam was angry five days ago. He may have said some things he didn't mean, but he was upset. He's only human, Lina, even you know that. He isn't Mr. Perfect. I highly doubt he actually meant that he thought he'd made a mistake in loving you. Love is complicated. Trust me, I get it."

"You've got a guy?" A grin crept onto my face without my even knowing it as I scooted closer to her.

Rachel laughed and gave me one of her serious blue eyeballs. "Don't change the subject. All I'm saying, is that you should at least give yourselves a chance to talk about it. You've been avoiding him all week. I can't guarantee what he'll say to you, but you need to at least give him a chance."

My smile died, and I lay back down on my blanket, drawing it around me. I curled into a tight little ball, raising my elbow to use it as a pillow. My body was weary after the long day, and I could feel myself slipping off to sleep easily as Rachel blew out the lantern.

"You've got until we leave for Mineraltir. Don't leave anything unsaid. You could regret it later. Don't forget, Rhydin is still out there waiting for us."

"Good night, Rachel."

"Good night" was a joke. I lay awake all night considering what Rachel had said. Sure, I had two days till we left for Mineraltir. However, that window was slowly decreasing as the night stretched on, and my brain could not stop whirring at top speed.

Really, I needed to talk to Sam tomorrow. Would he even talk to me after how long I'd avoided him? I hoped with my entire being that we could come to some sort of conclusion and that we could just go back to being friends. After all, both of our old lives were completely destroyed, and we would make great partners in crime against Rhydin when he came with Duunzer. What were the odds of that? I mean, he walked away after he said it was a mistake. Did he hate me?

And yet, I was still in love with him. How could I not be? I'd known him since he was a little boy. He was always looking out for me, and he was so kind. I couldn't lie. He was pretty attractive, too...

*Oh, Lina, you're just digging yourself deeper.*

I sighed rather loudly but then caught myself, realizing that it had to be around three in the morning and most sane people were asleep. Rachel's snoring remained constant, so I knew I was in the clear. As I rolled over to find a new comfortable position on the rocky ground underneath our tent, I continued to think, trying to come up with some sort of speech.

Would I tell him I was still in love with him? No, maybe not... If he'd changed his mind, then we could simply be friends. What would I say then? Should I apologize for anything? I kind of already did... This was ridiculous, why was I even doing this?

*You know why you're doing this, Lina. Love or not, you want your friend back. You need to at least apologize for avoiding him for the last several days. Start there. See where it goes. Good plan.*

Regardless of getting around three hours of sleep, I ended up wide awake at first light. Rachel was already up and gone with her gear, a staunch believer in making sure she relieved the watch on time. How that woman and her brothers didn't fall over out of sheer exhaustion was beyond me, but I knew what I needed to do this morning before anything else. I needed to cleanse myself of this anxiety. Technically, I had all day to talk to him, but I couldn't bear it any longer. I needed to get this off my shoulders. I dressed quickly, pulling on my tunic, my trousers, and then my dress. I hadn't been wearing my dress the last few days due to all the training, but it was chilly this morning.

Middle Autumn was in full swing now. I could see my breath coming out in little wisps as I pushed the flap open and entered the land of dew and white sky. Most of the leaves had fallen from the trees, turning the ground from green to reds and yellows and browns. It scared me because it made it seem like we were more out in the open without all the lush foliage we had started with back at the end of Late Summer.

I saw at least three squirrels as I crossed the small clearing to Sam's tent. They were rapidly rushing around to find nuts and stuffing them in their cheeks until they were bulging like the bread that used to rise in our wood stove at home. This was the season when Papa became extremely busy with the farm, but he could always find time for Rosetta and I. Sam and I would have been running around like chickens with our heads cut off if this was a normal year. It made me sad to think that last year had been our last harvest.

I ducked down as I opened the flap to his tent, but a quick glance around the piles of blankets and writing paper told me he wasn't there. Rubbing my arms to keep warm, I began to walk away from camp when I saw that he wasn't anywhere in the clearing either. He couldn't have gone too far. The Owens siblings would never have allowed it. After they sighted Eli and Terran, they made stricter rules on how far out we could venture.

I began to focus on the region in my chest where I knew my magic resided, trying to send out feelers to sense his presence. It didn't take long to find it, as it was a presence that I knew very well. It was the same presence, too. It hadn't changed for me after our argument. It still felt warm, kind, and smelled of freshly tilled Lunakan soil. He wasn't very far away from camp, just out of sight to the north, so I started walking.

Sure enough, it didn't take long to find him. He was looking away from me out into the distance, sitting next to a rather large rock. As I came closer, my ears began to pick out bubbling sounds, and soon a little creek came into view. I wondered how long he'd known about it, how many times he had come to sit here all by himself. The creek was decorated with small stones along either side, each of them perfectly smooth and rounded after centuries of being washed over. Leaves, also, were trailing down the center of the creek, spinning slowly as they were carried along in a current they could not control. I could smell the water, slightly mossy, but it smelled clean, clearing my head.

"I can feel you sensing me." Sam said just loud enough for me to hear although his eyes remained trained on the creek.

I looked down, surprised. Frederick hadn't mentioned if people could tell if you were sensing them. Maybe it was a Rounan thing. As I came up closer, he still didn't look at me, so I sat down on a rock a few feet away from him. "I'm sorry, I wasn't trying to sneak up on you. Um, I wanted to talk to you."

He turned to face me. I took in the brown pools of his eyes and the shadows underneath them. He looked as if he hadn't slept at all last night either, and his face was becoming increasingly unshaven, something he normally never allowed to happen. I felt a blush creeping to my face at the eye contact, and so glanced away to stop it.

His voice was gravelly. "What do you want to talk about?"

I took a deep breath. "I just wanted to apologize. For

avoiding you, I mean."

"It's okay." Sam said as he looked back to the creek. "Things got complicated the last time we talked."

For a few minutes, the two of us were silent. We watched the creek as it bubbled eternally, carrying little twigs and leaves downstream like tiny boats for ants. We watched as the eastern sky turned pink and the sun peeked over the horizon, making every blade of grass shine as the dew began to evaporate.

When Sam continued to remain silent, I wondered if that meant he had nothing else to say. My original plan had been to merely apologize for avoiding him, but it seemed lacking. I struggled for a few minutes to try and figure out if I should say something else but came up with nothing. I rose quietly, hoping to disappear without disturbing him, so I could tell Rachel I had completed my homework.

"Did you ever know I was in love with you?" His voice broke the silence abruptly. He twirled a little rock in his fingers, smoothed by the water.

Great. The exact subject I'd been hoping to avoid.

I settled myself back down on my rock, my hands clenching together. I hadn't planned on bringing up this topic. My voice was quavering as I mumbled, "Um... To be honest, I'm not really sure. Not really, I guess. I kind of hoped a couple times, but I didn't want to lose your friendship because I didn't know if you did for sure. It all happened at the same time as when I was keeping the Allyen thing a secret."

Sam barely nodded, tucking his lips between his teeth briefly, before meeting my eyes again. "Why did you keep it a secret from me?" Sam's eyes were pleading as he turned more of his body to face me rather than the creek. His hand was gripping the stone now.

"Because I didn't want you to be in danger. I didn't want your life to be ruined because of me. You can see how far I got with that." I shrugged as my voice began to morph by the lump in my throat. I looked at him slowly, "I tried really hard, Sam. I really do care about you. I'm sorry you think loving me was a mistake."

He turned back to the creek and then out toward the sunrise. His hand reached up and tugged at his bandana, and then his forehead cracked between his eyebrows as they rose. He sighed eventually, and looked at me again. Meanwhile, I felt my heart wanting to thunder right out of my chest. He spoke slowly, "I never was able to apologize for not listening to you about Camerron. You tried to tell me so many times in that conversation, but I wouldn't listen."

My heart trembled, and my eyes squeezed shut. That wasn't the response I was yearning for.

Sam reached over and gripped my hand hard. "Lina, I am truly sorry. I was angry and I… I don't know what came over me. I, of all people, the Kidek, should understand being given a job that I never asked for. I promise to help you from now on to be the Allyen. And I've never thought loving you was a mistake. I was upset that you couldn't see that I loved you."

I nodded promptly, trying desperately to listen to him and not cry.

"I never gave you the chance to respond when I told you I loved you for the first time." He ducked his head a little lower to be able to see my eyes, the chattering of the creek roaring in my ears. "Do you love me?"

I couldn't handle this. I should be happy with his apology, but my heart still felt pain. I was afraid if I said yes, he would change his mind, and if I said no, I would kill off the chance of anything starting up again. I swallowed hard. I knew what

I needed to say, or I would be miserable for the rest of my life. The words squeaked out, clutched by fear. "I do... I do love you. I always have." The floodgates broke, and tears streamed down my face.

"Lina." Sam breathed as he pulled me to my feet by my hands. The world around us slowly grew quiet. His eyes dove into mine as he released my hands and closed the distance between us to embrace me, my head settling perfectly under his chin. "It's only ever been you, Lina. It can only be you."

I threw my arms around his neck and gripped his shoulders tightly as he whispered the three little words I ached to hear. Present tense, nothing added to it. "I love you."

The sun began to warm the world around us and shed light on us as Sam's fingers found my chin. He lifted it to meet his own, pressing the very first kiss onto my lips. It was surreal, but it was sweet. It was everything I'd ever wanted. It was as if I had finally found myself after searching for it for so long without even knowing it.

"So, I will proudly take full credit for this one, boys. Pay up."

Sam and I jumped although his arms kept me close. On the opposite bank of the creek stood the three freckled Owens children, each with their respective big grin, small smile, and slight scowl. Rachel seemed especially excited as both Luke and James reached into their pockets to withdraw a few copper pieces and hand them to her.

"Nice doing business with you, my brothers!" Rachel gleamed, checking out all the money in her hands.

"I am so glad you woke me up for this." Luke spat, though there was no denying the slight smile on his face as he turned to return to camp.

"*Rachel!*" My voice shot up two octaves as I glared at her, but Sam didn't seem to care. He was on top of one of the moons right now.

Rachel shrugged innocently and put a hand to her mouth in an effort to hide her huge grin. "I'm so very happy for you, Lina!"

I glared at her, but there was no denying the joy on my face. Sam pulled my face back for another warm kiss, and Rachel's giggling melted away into the gurgle of the creek along with everything else. Even Rhydin was swallowed up as the new day began, and I ardently hoped that somehow Grandma, Rosetta, and Keera could see this.

# CHAPTER SEVENTEEN

Before I knew it, it was the morning of our departure to Mineraltir. After Sam and I's early morning conversation yesterday, I found myself in a heated training session with both Frederick, who had come to visit, and Sam. They were working hard to familiarize me with the different types of magic as well as how to use it to your advantage in a fight. Most importantly, how to use it defensively.

Frederick was becoming a little easy to spar with, in that I could always sense when he was getting ready to use his power. I could always see it coming. Sam, however, was impossible to predict. He could shove me over, pick me up, and squish me to the ground all with a flick of his hand. On top of that, I could never tell which one he was going to do because of the invisible movements. Sheesh, no wonder people didn't like Rounans!

"Okay, hang on." Sam halted the session for a second, giving me a chance to breathe. "Lina, you're going about this all wrong."

"Thanks." I gasped, stabbing my sword into the ground.

"No, it's just you need to learn to be sensing at all times. Eventually, you *will* be able to sense when I'll use magic, even if you're not quite sure what I'll do with it. At least then you'll know what direction it's coming from." Sam explained, handing me a canteen of clean water that had been sitting on the sidelines in the cool earth, beginning to freeze. "You're actually doing really well."

I scoffed at him between gulps of water. "I would hope so! Y'know, I've been doing this for nearly two and a half seasons now!"

"Well, you also have an unfair advantage." Frederick chimed in, smiling as he leaned on his spear. "The magic you were given is much more powerful than most."

"Uh huh." I rolled my eyes as I turned around and tossed the canteen a safe distance away. Experience outweighed power in my opinion.

Once we resumed, I did try really hard to sense when Sam was going to use magic. I discovered that I could sense it if he was going to do something huge, such as do a super-sized jump the way he had at Camerron's near hanging, but if it was something that only required a slight movement of hand, I was at a loss. He was always careful with me if I was caught off guard, his smile big and his face pink as he watched me dangle mid-air. It made me dread leaving him for Mineraltir the next day. However, the highlight of training was that Frederick officially taught me how to successfully complete the maneuver that thrust away anybody standing in the vicinity of me that I had attempted at Camerron's hanging.

After a long day of practice, Frederick and Rachel left together. Rachel would set out in a few hours with Princess Mira and King Adam in the Royal coach. Her job as Mira's maid was becoming handier and handier. As I packed, I wondered how my own journey would go, as they had planned for me to travel separately with Luke Owens. I'd gotten to know him a little better with all this time in hiding. He was particular about his food, and he didn't seem to care for jokes. He was my constant bodyguard now that he couldn't return to work at his livery, but he'd never actually talked at length to me. This trip would definitely be interesting. The fact that I had to leave Sam behind with James and Camerron made my stomach roll over. I ardently hoped that nothing would happen to them while we were gone.

The morning we were to depart was calm, before the breath of Lunaka's wind had come to ravage the countryside. It was growing colder with every hour, and I could see the wisps of warm air condensate around my mouth as I gathered my few, meager possessions. The trees had dropped all of their leaves by now, and it made our little campsite feel even more open than it had before. I stared up at the crystal clear sky and wondered why it seemed so pure in the autumn, unlike the rest of the year.

Sam took my hand then, pulling my attention back down to earth. As I faced him, his expression seemed carefully controlled. His smile said he was fine. His eyes told me he was worried as he cleared his throat. "So, are you all ready to go then?"

"I think so." I beamed back at him, trying to make him feel better. "I'm glad Luke and I will have a shorter journey. I feel bad for Mira and Rachel to be stuck in a coach with King Adam for a whole week! I'd really love to know how the Owenses can use transportation magic. I keep forgetting to ask Frederick about it."

Sam chuckled, stroking a lock of my hair behind my ear.

"Keep in mind, you can only get so far as the mountains. You'll actually have to walk through those before you can transport the rest of the way to Demora. That's where the Mineraltin castle is."

"Really?" I looked at him quizzically. "Why? How do you know that?"

"Perks of being a leader of people all across the continent." Sam winked. "I don't know the actual details because I've never traveled there, but I've been told that magic doesn't work in the mountains that surround Lunaka."

"Huh. I wonder why that is..." I murmured, staring off into the distance where I could barely see the hazy faces of the mountains that always served as nothing more than a border for my view.

"Lina." Sam took my hand again. "That also means you really need to be careful. In the mountains, I mean. Your magic isn't going to work there. You won't be able to defend yourself."

"Oh, I'll have my sword. And Luke. We won't be totally defenseless or anything." I shrugged, beginning to walk toward the campfire where I could see Luke was semi-impatiently waiting for me. "It's going to be fine, Sam. I wish I could send you a letter or something when we get there, but we don't exactly have an address."

Sam took a deep breath and looked down at my fingers in his hand. "It's okay. We can't really do anything about it. I'm sure the Owenses have some sort of communication between them. It'll just be a long week or so."

Someone made a throat clearing noise, and the two of us turned to see Luke standing with James and Frederick. His arms were crossed with his bag already slung over his shoulders, he eyes staring me down impatiently. It was time to go, yet I didn't feel quite ready. We walked together over to the campfire where they stood.

Luke's voice was stagnant. "Rachel and Princess Mira have nearly reached Lun. We need to leave quickly to begin our trek through the mountains, or they will overtake us with their carriage. We cannot be seen."

"I understand." I met him in the eyes, which suddenly seemed awkward to him. I lifted my pack over my shoulder and gave James and Camerron a quick hug. Camerron likely wouldn't be here by the time we returned. Sam planned to transport him to some northern settlements where he often sent Rounans for safety, along with the information that they were not to seek the Kidek at the moment. Lastly, I turned to Frederick.

He seemed solemn as he reached out and squeezed my shoulder. "Look after my sister for me. And tell Xavier hello."

I nodded. "Keep yourselves safe while we're gone."

Turning to Sam, I tried to hold it together as he folded me into an embrace. Abruptly, he whispered into my ear fiercely but undetectable to anyone else. "Don't trust anyone."

He pulled away and gave me a quick kiss, leaving me wondering what he meant as I turned to see Luke offering his arm. I took it gingerly, not really knowing what to expect. The last time I transported with one of the Owenses, it had been rather impromptu. I really wanted to pay attention to how it worked this time.

To my dismay, Luke rotated me on his arm so that I was facing Frederick, James, Camerron, and Sam. This prevented me from fully seeing what those same colors were that had come out of Rachel's back. Luke's arm grew very warm in my grasp, and we were enveloped in that same blinding light, blocking my view of our entourage along with everything else. My ears began to ring as it became deafeningly quiet. My feet never left the ground this time, and then out of nowhere the whiteness and silence disappeared.

I blinked my eyes several times to regain my sight, letting go of Luke's arm to rub them. The mountains were beautiful! I had never seen them so close before. We stood only ten feet away from where the higher rocky faces rose out of the foothills, reaching up to touch the sky with snow-capped peaks. The oaky smell I had become so used to at our campsite had vanished and was replaced with some of the prairie scents that I had grown up with, along with an indescribably clean smell that I felt could only emanate from these great stone masses in front of me. They were so much bigger here than I could ever have imagined from looking at them from so far away. They seemed more enormous than my mind could compute, and I realized how daunting of a task this was going to be to traipse over them on foot. I instantly was very jealous of Rachel in King Adam's carriage.

At that moment, Luke snatched my arm and pulled me behind a rock without a word, his hand clamped over my mouth. I struggled a little before noticing what he had seen. King Adam's carriage was hurtling toward the mountains only a few miles down the road. I guessed they hadn't stopped in Lun because they were making excellent time. As they skirted to the north of us towards the one mountain pass that was traversable by carriage, Luke released me and stood back up.

He looked up at the mountains, and, once he found the tiny navigable path he was searching for, he sighed. "Well. It's not getting any shorter. The sooner we can get over these, the sooner we can use magic for the rest of the way."

"Alright then." I straightened my pack and started after Luke as he picked his way through the rocks.

Almost immediately upon stepping foot on the stones, I felt a change. Instantly, the little lump inside my chest that I had learned to depend on was gone. It was as if something began to sap my energy, and my mind became a little muddled. I shook my head to clear it and took a deep breath. I had no idea that I'd depended on my magic so much just for everyday life. I hadn't even had it that long. How long had I depended on it like this and never knew? What was it about these mountains that did this?

When I looked up, I saw Luke eyeballing me over his shoulder, as if he knew my thoughts, but I put my head down and focused on my footing. Definitely jealous of the carriage.

The hours stretched on as the sun stretched across the sky. It made its appearance in the east, blinding us as it shed its beautiful pink hues across the mountain tops, slowly traveling overhead to turn the sky a brilliant blue. The journey had come to the point where I was becoming afraid to look behind me, astonished at how high we had already traveled.

Lunaka was transformed into a giant scroll of prairie laid out behind us. You could see the divides of land between farmers, the rivers as they wound their way between the subtle hills, and the little towns huddled together, especially Lun since it was the closest. Once we got even higher, if you really squinted and tried your best to focus, you could barely make out the canyon where Soläna rested, a short black line in the distance.

Luke was angling us between two of the smaller peaks, hoping to do as little climbing as possible, which I appreciated in my debilitated state. My legs were beginning to numb and freeze after so long, the temperature falling at a steady rate. My bodyguard spun around abruptly, seeming to be totally fine and not deteriorating like I was. He eyed me carefully, his blue eyes intense in this sunshine. "I have a question for you, Lina."

I looked up at him, trying not to feel totally out of breath as I stretched my legs at the unexpected break. "Oh yeah? What's that?"

"A few weeks ago when we were talking about Duunzer, Sam mentioned some sort of 'giants'. I was wondering if you could tell me what they were."

My eyebrow quirked since that was not a question I had expected from him, much less any sort of conversation since he was a quiet guy. I racked my brain back to when I had read that entire myths and legends book during my hideout in the livery basement. I shrugged, "I don't remember exactly. I think they were just mythical creatures who live in rural Lunaka and the mountains."

"But why are they called *giants*?" Luke crossed his arms as a red tinge entered his eyes.

I began to walk along the path again, getting closer to him. "Because they're supposed to be really tall, I think. Nobody's really seen one. After all, they are mythical creatures...right?"

"Yeah." Luke grumbled as he turned around, beginning to climb again.

"Hey!" I called, trying to catch up. "So, why do you and Rachel and James have magic? It doesn't make sense, especially since you can transport and nobody else can. I know it's impossible, but do you think you can try and teach-...?"

Time stopped as the rock underneath my foot gave way. My body lost its sense of gravity and balance. I could feel myself tipping over back toward Lunaka and my vision threatening to black out when, like lightning, Luke was next to me with firm grips on both my arm and belt. He hauled me back over hard, causing me to do some sort of somersault onto the rocky path. My head connected with stone, and when I looked back at Luke, his eyes were a fierce yellow color. It seemed so real, and yet, I wondered if I had a concussion.

I coughed as I tried to talk, "I'm sorry. Um, thank you. Why-...?"

"Enough of your questions. I do not have the patience to explain it right now. Our priority is to arrive in Mineraltir on time." Luke turned from me instantly and began to walk again.

Sniffling like a little kid, I rose and brushed myself off, noticing a nice scrape on my leg. No magic to heal it right now. I checked to ensure I still had my locket secured in my bag and my feather around my neck before following Rachel's brother in silence.

The hours passed on again, the sun warming our faces as it fell toward the western ocean, lighting up the sky in purples and reds. All I could smell was mountain now. It seemed so clean, yet my nose was beginning to repulse it. I wanted out of these forsaken mountains. Luke hadn't said a word to me since the mishap, which I figured was halfway warranted. It still made for a dull journey.

When we came around another bend, I finally saw it. Mineraltir. My first impression was simply this: *green.*

As we got closer, I began to make out a ruffled appearance to this green. Then, I could make out individual tops of trees that dominated the ground. Earth could not be seen there were so many trees. The leaves and needles were all mixed in together. All completely green even though all the leaves in Lunaka had long colored and dropped dead. They were all a type of tree I had never seen before. They seemed so wide from far away. I knew that if I was up close, there would be no way that less than five people could join hands and create a ring all the way around one of the ancient trunks.

The forest was so beautiful and strange compared to what I knew, and I realized that this world held many things I'd never encountered before. At the Spring Festival as Sam and I sat eating our little Mineraltin dish, I never dreamed I would be in Mineraltir less than a year later. Now that I was an Allyen, my world was expanding by leaps and bounds, in good ways as well as bad.

Night began to fall. By the time we neared the bottom of the mountains, about to touch down on earth rather than these cursed rocks, the trees had come to tower above us. They weren't as tall as the mountains, but they dwarfed Lunakan trees. They had to be at least a mile high! If I hadn't seen the sun disappear above the tree line, I would have thought the leaves were blocking out the daylight, the foliage was so thick and the dark they created so deep a shade.

Luke kept on ever forward ahead of me. This guy was a workhorse. We hadn't so much as taken a break at all! My knees were aching, and my lungs burned, glad for some thicker air now that we were at a lower altitude. I wanted more than anything to jump the last fifty feet or so, ready to feel my magic coursing through my veins again, but I knew that would probably result in at least one broken bone. No need for that right now.

I stopped mid-step. Something seemed off. Luke kept going ahead of me, but instead of continuing to follow, I couldn't help but strain my ears for the smallest sound. My magic hadn't come back yet, so I knew there was no way I was sensing anything. But I could not shake the feeling that there was a pair of eyes on my back.

I only heard Luke's steps slapping the rocks, and the rustle of the leaves in the weakening wind, nothing else. I couldn't make my feet move, and yet I couldn't find the courage to turn around. Ice slid down my spine.

My guardian noticed that I wasn't following him anymore, and when he turned around, his reaction told me everything I needed to know. Instantaneously, his reprimanding look became one filled with adrenaline. His eyes widened and flashed several colors before he sprang into action, sprinting toward me. Luke moved like lightning, yet his energy spurred me to turn at last and see what was making me so fearful.

Not twenty feet away from me, perched on a rock with his leg up like some great conqueror was the very man who frequented my nightmares. Rhydin. His cloak billowed in the wind, obscuring his form for the most part, his black hair caught in the breeze. His amethyst eyes burned like fire deep into my soul, but it was the smirk holding his pale lips and the flare of his nostrils that were emblazoned onto my memory before the whole world went white.

When my vision cleared, I found myself sprawled in the grass between two massive tree roots thicker than my own shoulders. As soon as I gained my bearings, I was on my feet, the adrenaline still pumping from seeing Rhydin. Yet, after a quick look around, I found myself alone. My breaths went from loud and heavy to small and quiet.

I reached for my locket and found it still safely tucked away in my pouch, but my breathing quickly gained energy again as my thoughts took flight. Rhydin saw us. He saw Luke and I traveling to Mineraltir. He knew now that we left some people behind. That we split up. Nothing good could come from this!

"Look at that. She awakes." A voice sounded, slightly irritated.

My head snapped in that direction, afraid to see Rhydin,

but only seeing Luke bearing a bundle of firewood. I reached for my head, beginning to feel it pound. "Where are we? What happened with Rhydin-...?"

Luke cut me off as he dropped his load next to a smoldering campfire that I had yet to notice. "We're in Demora, Mineraltir. I had to transport us away rather abruptly, so I couldn't control where we landed very well. You got knocked out by a tree trunk. Sorry 'bout that."

I let that sink in for a minute before responding, "Were we off the mountains? I thought nobody could use magic on the mountains and I'm pretty sure we were still several feet up."

The young man shrugged, his eyes focused on the fire. "Sometimes magic is more powerful when you're in danger. We were close enough. Anyway, you've been out for a couple days so the Royal carriage should be here any minute. Don't get too comfortable here."

At that, I looked around. The trees were even more impressive up close than they had been from the top of the mountains. They were giant umbrellas, stretching miles tall and miles wide with their leafy canopies. The bark of the trees was the richest brown I had ever seen. Nothing could even compare to it back in Lunaka, and the huge roots spread out in every direction, tangled into knots bigger than my wagon back home. There were so many, it seemed that you were walking on more roots than dirt.

I'd had a faint idea of what Mineraltir smelled like from the stand that was always at the Spring Festival, but that little booth couldn't even compare to the real deal. The air was laden with scents of a million different herb varieties and the heavy odor of this new species of tree that was both coniferous and deciduous. The scent was like oak and pine had reproduced, which was the best way I could possibly describe it. The sun peeked through the foliage miles above our heads creating spotted patterns on the ground while the wind made it sparkle. This country was gorgeous.

Apparently, Luke was watching my breath being taken away. He called out to me from a knoll several feet away. "Hey. Want to see something truly amazing?"

I nodded and bounded over to him like I was a child again. Following Luke's gesture, I saw what I had initially missed from behind a giant tree. A few miles away was Mineraltir Castle, an enormous structure formed from a myriad of stones and woods. It seemed to be as large as Lunaka Castle; however, it appeared more grand and wonderful because it was if the castle had been built around the trees that were there first. Some of the spires hugged massive trunks as they reached for the sky, but only the main tower actually achieved the same height as the canopy. Two isolated trees rose out of the courtyard, and another supported the drawbridge over a small moat that encircled the expansive hodge-podge building. With lights burning in most of the windows, it seemed a very cozy place despite its size and stature.

At that moment, the comparatively tiny Royal carriage pulled up to the drawbridge, its Lunakan crest emblazoned door swinging open to reveal King Adam. He rubbed his goatee as he stared up at the castle himself. Luke put his hand on mine, and I knew it was time to move.

The gigantic wooden drawbridge began to lower slowly at the sight of King Adam, and Luke and I crept ever so carefully, but promptly, over the gigantic roots that threatened to trip us at every turn. There was one knot that Luke stealthily helped me down because it was nearly the size of my house back home.

With an echoing *thud*, the bridge landed in the mossy

overgrowth in front of the carriage. Servants began unloading, among them I could see Rachel with her bright red hair, but as soon as the bridge was secured, the nearly empty carriage jetted inside, leaving Rachel and the others to carry in the Royals' luggage.

As we reached the last line of bushes before crossing into the road, Luke turned to me and grunted quietly. "Put your hood up, we need to wait for Rachel's signal."

I did as I was told, watching carefully as the servants divvyed up their loads and began to carry them on foot across the bridge. Rachel purposely took longer with Princess Mira's trunk so that she was the last to leave the area where the carriage had unloaded. As soon as the rest of the other servants began to stride across the bridge, she reached up and gave a hard pull to her ear. Needless to say, I didn't need Luke to tell me that was the signal.

We strode rapidly over to her, keeping Mira's baggage between us and the castle. Luke spoke first, "How was the trip?"

Rachel scoffed and rolled her eyes. "You owe me one, to be stuck in that carriage with *him* for a week!" She slammed the trunk shut and proceeded to lift it all by herself, not showing much strain. "Hurry, we need to get across before the bridge closes."

The three of us promptly shuffled across the bridge, trying to be fast yet inconspicuous at the same time. When we reached the stone mouth of the castle, Rachel put down Mira's trunk beside the small side door to the servant's entrance. She then moved us toward the main courtyard where King Adam and Mira had disappeared with their carriage.

I pulled my hood farther over my head and nearly squealed as I whispered to her. "Rachel, what are you doing? We'll get caught if we go that way!"

Rachel's blue dress swished the ground as she turned back to me. "We might not be too late to see how the king greets Queen Jasmine. It might give us a clue if she's working with him for Rhydin or not!"

Luke and I glanced at each other for a split second before following Rachel through the carefully manicured courtyard. Aside from the two giant trees, everything else had been painstakingly sculpted for optimum elegance. The roots had been buried in feet of soil in an attempt to make it look like real ground with normal grass. Pink flowers dotted the outer rim of the yard and the trees. Thankfully, the main door into the hall of the castle was still open a crack because, from the look of the ancient wood, there would have been no way to open it without letting out a screaming groan.

One by one, we slid through the thin opening and hid behind a big marble pillar that looked as if it had once been covered with ivy. The floor was checkerboard, black and white every few feet, and at the far end of the room, I saw the thrones and all the people. There were four thrones, all made from carved wood although bedazzled with gold trimmings and many gems. The largest throne in the center was speckled with emeralds and peridots, all gleaming green, the Mineraltin Royal color.

Sitting upon its cushion, however, was not a man, but a woman. She was tall with black, curly hair pulled back in an unruly ponytail. Rather unlike the few parts of the castle I had seen, her immaculate dress was completely covered in gold. Gold beads, gold tassels, gold coins, and gold drops. The crown she wore was also gold, although it also sported the only green on her person. It didn't make sense. Who was this woman?

King Adam bowed like the gentleman he wasn't before this golden woman and proceeded to present her with a gift. Mira seemed to be trying not to throw up as the woman accepted the parcel. King Adam spoke elegantly, "Your Majesty. It is an honor to be in your kingdom once again."

The woman chuckled. "Thank you, Your Majesty. I am glad to see you and your daughter have arrived safely. I am sure Xavier will be here momentarily."

King Adam elbowed Mira in the ribs. She sputtered slightly, "Thank you, Queen Jasmine. It is nice to see you again."

*Queen*? This lady was Queen Jasmine? I'd heard of her, and had even seen her at the Spring Festival, but I had never paid much attention. She looked greedy what with all the gold glued to her from head to toe. Where was King Morris? Why was she sitting in his throne?

Jasmine rose from the wooden throne, looking completely out of place in her golden attire. "I apologize for my husband's absence. As you know, he does not get out much anymore. Only for very special occasions." A queer smile was on her heart-shaped face.

"I understand perfectly." King Adam replied, matching her eyes as he walked to her and offered his arm. She took it, and they began to exit the room with Mira trailing them.

"What was that all about?" I whispered to Luke and Rachel. "It doesn't seem right."

"Jasmine mostly controls the kingdom." Rachel breathed back. "King Morris hasn't been the same ever since his first wife died, Xavier's mother. He probably doesn't even have a clue who Rhydin is."

"Seems like they get along pretty well. Think she's working for Rhydin, too?" I whispered again as I watched the two disappear behind giant wooden doors.

A new voice responded, "I say, the Allyen must be pretty desperate to get killed in order to wind up in my castle."

My heart hammered right through my chest as Rachel immediately pushed me behind her and Luke drew his long sword.

There, standing in the shadows, was a young man. He was dressed primly in an emerald green suit coat, his sleeves trimmed in the politically correct amount of gold while a leaf pattern was etched onto his shirt pocket. His face was wide and angled, his skin very pale and dotted with freckles, adding a boyish quality to his grown-up features. His eyes were a brilliant blue as they stared intently at us from underneath a swath of the reddest hair I'd ever witnessed, even redder than Rachel's, pulled back in a stout ponytail at the base of his neck.

Stupidly, I stammered, "Who are you?"

The red-haired man chuckled, a small rat-like grin appearing on his freckled face. "Xavier Rollins. Crown Prince of Mineraltir."

# CHAPTER EIGHTEEN

I stared at Prince Xavier wide-eyed, unsure of whether to run or spill all my guts. Rachel quickly intervened, her voice calm and mystifying. "My apologies, Your Highness. We are merely servants of the Lunakan princess." She added in a deep curtsy for effect.

The Mineraltin man's red eyebrow quirked sharply, and then his white teeth appeared again in that crooked grin that made him look like a rodent. He lifted his hands to his hips as he spoke. "If you think I'll believe that, you must think me an unobservant fool. I see things nobody else sees in this palace, but even an idiot could see that you three didn't come in with the rest of the servants."

Luke and Rachel peeked at each other hurriedly. I might have missed it if I wasn't desperately penetrating them each with my eyes for a clue as to what I should be doing right now.

Xavier cleared his throat. "Now. If my assumption is correct as to *why* you have risked your lives into coming here, I believe it best if we find somewhere more *private*, to converse. Madam Allyen?" The prince turned to me and offered me his green-clad elbow, bowing to me.

This was either really good, or really bad. When I turned to Rachel in question, another smart remark reached my ears.

"You can make your own decisions, Allyen. Do not forget. They serve *you*."

I gulped hard and fought the urge to look at Rachel or Luke once more. It suddenly occurred to me that he was right. I was soon to be given the responsibility of saving the entire continent. I needed to start acting like it.

Xavier paused patiently, looking down at me from his height of perhaps six feet. His eyes grew dark under his red hair, yet his long arm remained outstretched in front of me. He was waiting for me to decide if I was going to trust him or not.

Remembering Sam's fierce words not to trust anyone, I was hesitant. Yet, I closed my eyes and reached deep down inside of myself as I allowed my magic to flow freely. Xavier's presence was quite different from ones I had sensed and read in the past. I could feel a fiery strength in him, perhaps a temper, and a frightening amount of boldness.

However, as I searched deeper, my senses became overwhelmed with the feeling of loss. It was as if Xavier's presence was sitting in a black hole, eternally waiting. Waiting for someone to reach out to him where he had been isolated for so long. There was no evil in this man. Just heartbreak. Sam would understand.

When I opened my eyes again, he was still in the exact same position, possibly even evaluating me as well with those piercing blue eyes of his. Without hesitation, I took his arm, leading Luke and Rachel to both drop their jaws. I smiled slightly at their reaction and then turned to my escort. "We have matters to discuss, Your Highness. Please, lead the way."

Xavier nodded, and I could tell that he was slightly surprised that I had chosen to trust him. He hid it rather well though, as he walked us away from the throne room. The interior of the castle mirrored the exterior, in that it was just as jumbled up. There were sections of wall and hallway that were made of rectangular rock carefully sectioned together, ancient wood that decorated the space with spirals and rings, and cobblestone that lent a variety of colors and textures to the areas we walked through.

I saw several tapestries as well of the Mineraltin Royal family and their ancestors. Most of them depicted Queen Jasmine, making my stomach churn in apprehension. This woman became a Royal by marriage. Why was she so heavily present in these portraits? There was another young woman that featured highly in them, who looked to be a much younger version of the queen. Instead of gold, she was bedecked in every shade of my least favorite color. Pink.

As more and more pictures of her floated by in one particular hallway, I piped up in a quiet voice in case someone else was nearby. "Your Highness, who is this girl that I keep seeing?"

"Ren," Xavier said barely above a whisper. "My half-sister."

I let that soak in as Xavier led us to a small door at the end of our long hallway. It seemed to be a door built for someone more of my stature than someone of Xavier's. Or any normal human being for that matter. It seemed to be an average looking door that I would have guessed was some sort of servant's entrance rather than the passage to a prince's set of rooms. The only thing that seemed different about it was there was no doorknob. In its place was instead a small, metal panel etched with old, faint leaf designs.

The prince dropped my arm to retrieve a large, antique key from around his neck. It appeared to have rusted thoroughly a long time ago, but the emeralds in the end were unmistakable, shining brightly from what I assumed to be use. Xavier stole a quick glance behind him to assure the hallway we'd traveled through was clear, and inserted the key into the ancient lock with his left hand while placing his right hand against the metal plate above it.

Immediately, I felt the heat radiate from Xavier's hand and the metal underneath it. The little plate began to turn red, then orange. And then, a yellow from a brilliant sunset, yet his hand seemed unharmed. As the very edges of the metal visible beyond Xavier's hand began to turn scalding white, the prince turned the key with his other hand. I heard an audible click as the cogs of the lock groaned, and Xavier pulled the door open in front of us as the metal was still molten and glued to his hand.

He bowed and gestured to me. "Ladies first."

I stared at him hesitantly, not necessarily fearful of his power but definitely curious, before pivoting to face the tower of old wooden stairs that stood before us through the tiny doorway.

"Wait a minute." Luke whispered just loudly enough for us all to hear.

When we turned to him, he held one solitary finger up to his mouth and rotated around to the hallway we'd come down. A feeling of nervousness arose inside of me until I realized that Luke had not drawn his sword, and then I knew that whatever he was hearing was not someone who posed a threat. I tuned into any presences that could be near us, beginning to be very comfortable with this kind of magic.

I immediately felt the familiar presence of Princess Mira. I had sensed her before, and so it was her name that occurred to me first rather than the different components of her presence like usual. It made me excited to think I was starting to become experienced with this sensing ability.

As if on cue, Mira ducked out from under yet another tapestry covered with Queen Jasmine and Princess Ren. Her violet eyes seemed happy to see us until they glazed over at the sight of our princely companion. She crossed her arms tightly and one of her hips jutted out, suddenly reminding me that this girl really was only eighteen even if most of the time she acted twice that age. Her doll-like face crimped into an unbecoming frown, before dipping into a shallow curtsy. "Your Highness. A pleasure, as always." Her words dripped with hatred.

Prince Xavier's eyebrow quirked, and that street rat grin of his came back. He gave her a fancy bow. "My alabaster rose. My heart is warmed at the sight of you." If Mira's words were dripping, Xavier's were flooded.

"Ah, lovely. The lovebirds are reunited." Luke's eyes rolled, his words loud enough for Rachel's ears alone although I overheard.

She stifled a giggle as she reached out with her exceptionally wide arm span to herd us all toward the tiny door. "Now that we're all here, I think it best that we continue this conversation upstairs."

Xavier chuckled and offered his arm to Mira, who turned up her nose and headed into the tower of stairs on her own. The rejection rolled off Xavier like butter, and without even a blink, he turned and offered the same arm to me.

Although I knew I could climb those stairs perfectly well on my own, I could feel Rachel's eyes boring into the back of my head. I was learning fast on this trip that, judging from the looks of Xavier and Mira's disdain for each other, we would have to negotiate more than we had planned. Those two had much more of a history than I had known before, but nothing could go wrong. So, no matter how little it seemed, I took his arm and allowed him to lead me up the stairs.

They were that old-fashioned type of stairs, which seemed to be twice as high as they were long. My tiny foot could barely fit comfortably on the squeaky wood while I was sure my boots were the smallest in this party. I watched Xavier's feet in particular since he was right next to me, the corridor barely wide enough for us both. Only the balls of his feet could fit on these stairs.

As we went on, I began to get winded because of the height of each step. While everyone else seemed to trek up them just fine, each stair came up to the middle of my shins due to my tiny legs. Everyone else was just above their ankle, so while they were still taller than normal steps, they weren't as out of the ordinary for them.

I tried not to let my huffing and puffing come to Xavier's attention, but by the time we reached the top of the tower, I had given up. I was gasping for air when Xavier used his antique, rusted out key on the door at the top as well. This door was equally, awkwardly undecorated for housing the rooms of a prince. At least this one had a normal doorknob.

When the door opened, my eyes became like sponges to everything inside. It was not a suite of rooms as Prince Frederick or Princess Mira had. It was one small room. The walls were so filled with different decorations and knick-knacks that one could barely see the collaborative mix of building material underneath. There was a tiny bed in one corner. The same size as the cot I had occupied while hiding out in the livery even though the comforter was of a thick, rich green material.

There were books of every type littered around the room, on the floor, on shelves, and on the one small desk. Drawings of different lines and angles were strewn across the desk along with a couple of plants, one scorched to a crisp. It was now only a limp, blackened skeleton of what was once a Mineraltin nut plant. I recognized the intact chocolate colored nuts on the living plant next to it as ones that used to find their way to Lunaka, though they were always out of my price range.

As my eyes registered the ashy leaves, they began to pick out similar scorch marks around the room. A round one next to one of the book shelves maybe four feet off the ground. Another one just above his tiny bed. A third one was spread into several black dots along the wooden shutter for the single window. A long, burnt slash stretched from the ceiling to the floor behind us as I turned to look around. It finally hit me. Prince Xavier was a pyromage. Fire magic.

Right next to that slash, untouched, was a tapestry with people I hadn't seen yet while traveling through the castle. There was a man, a woman, and a child in the center, surrounded by beautiful, embroidered trees. They all wore crowns of green and gold on their red-haired heads. The man was tall with his hair pulled back while a long beard stretched beyond his collarbones. A tiny smile was on the man's lips, and there were slight wrinkles at the edges of his blue eyes.

The woman looked as if she could be half his age, barely old enough to be holding the small child in her arms. The way her bangs spread across her forehead reminded me of Xavier, along with the freckles on her cheeks that the tapestries' creator had painstakingly put in. She looked so happy with her big grin. The child showed no emotion as he stared back at me with gigantic blue eyes, probably still at that age where he had no idea what was going on.

Ever the cat, because curiosity constantly got me in trouble, I had to ask, "Your Highness. Who are these people?"

"Lina..." Mira tried to intervene, but a pale white hand came up to silence her.

Xavier looked at me with daggers for eyes, and a small fire appeared in his hand as he brought it back from shushing Mira. He played with it using his fingers for a few moments before he spoke again. "None of your business."

I couldn't quite restrain the gulp that leaped down my throat as Rachel moved forward. She looked at Xavier carefully, her eyes threatening, until the little fire in his hand was extinguished. She cleared her throat as she sat in a chair that had lost its back from a previous fireball, and pursed her lips like a polished speaker. "Prince Xavier. Have you, or have you not, received any messengers from Prince Frederick of Lunaka?"

A grin cracked the prince's face as he flopped onto his bed like the teenager he was. "That depends."

"On what?" Rachel's eyebrow rose, sounding unimpressed.

"Things."

Luke rolled his eyes hard and whispered into his sister's ear, "I say we do this at sword point."

Rachel gave him a good glare and then turned to Xavier again. "Prince Frederick has been trying to contact you on the subject of Rhydin. Do you know who he is?"

"Maybe I do, maybe I don't." Xavier laughed. I was sure that, if his legs were far shorter, he would be swaying them back and forth like a child as he lounged on the bed.

Rachel's poker face was impressive, a trait that Luke did

not inherit. Her words continued to be calm. "Has anyone approached you about joining Rhydin? Have Queen Jasmine or Princess Ren mentioned his name at all?"

Xavier sighed mischievously as he drew circles on his blanket. "Oh, I don't know. One such as me can only hear whispers through these dry hallways. After all, what could I possibly know?"

"You are such a child!" Mira hissed, angrier than I'd ever seen her before. "You haven't changed a *bit* since we were kids!"

Xavier leaned forward quickly, his eyes like blue fire. "Do you really think me to be so stupid that I don't know who Rhydin is? Of *course,* I know who he is! He's the biggest threat this continent has ever faced time and time again! What I need from you, *Princess*, is to tell me that your little Allyen here isn't going to be just as bad!"

Mira was instantly within a few feet of Xavier's red face, her countenance all but gone. I wondered if Frederick would even recognize his sister if he were present. "We are not out to make you into an idiot! You are doing a fine job of that yourself with all these sideways answers. You're right. Rhydin *is* the biggest threat this world has ever seen, and we need to work together if we're ever going to defeat him. Both my brother and King Daniel of Auklia have sworn allegiances to the Allyen. Where do your loyalties lie, Xavier?"

The prince looked at her calmly, the harsh color faded from his face but not too much so. A smile spread across his face that didn't seem like a rat at all. More like the smiles in the tapestry that I had dared ask about. "Here I've thought all this time you were a twit."

"Huh?" Mira was caught completely off guard, stumbling away from him with a crimson blush on her face. Xavier then proceeded to wink at her, effectively silencing her for the rest of the conversation.

"As I was saying…" Rachel tried to pick up whatever threads of her interrogation were left. They continued to banter back and forth, but to every question Rachel asked, Xavier had another snippy remark or smoothly somehow turned the question back around on us.

As Rachel and Luke kept their attentions solely on Xavier, I watched Mira for a few moments as she wrung out and folded her little silk handkerchief time and time again. The coloring in her cheeks had faded slightly but was still noticeable.

No matter how hard Rachel tried, Xavier continued to give dead ends. Luke had lost his patience with him ages ago, and Mira had reduced herself to a lump of nerves. After an hour, even Rachel seemed to be losing steam, as Xavier once again declared "I don't trust you!"

At those words, I felt my thoughts suddenly speed up to a mile per minute. I turned in my seat to view the mystery tapestry once again. The bearded man with the sweet smile, the young woman with the brilliant grin who resembled Xavier greatly, and the small boy child that she held. I finally recognized the man as King Morris. Xavier had called Princess Ren his half-sister as we traveled here, and she looked exactly like Queen Jasmine in all the portraits. Rachel had mentioned briefly that Jasmine ruled the kingdom because King Morris became a hermit…

Because his first wife died! That was what Rachel had said! I'd bet anything that the young woman in that tapestry was his first wife. She was Xavier's mother and she had died. Putting that with how terribly lonely Xavier's presence felt, and this guy had some pretty serious demons that he was dealing with. He'd lost his mother a long time ago and now had lost his father to his grief.

On top of everything, his stepmother was running his kingdom likely right into Rhydin's grasp with her familiar greeting of King Adam. It was then that it hit me hard that talking to him like a politician was simply not going to work. Everyone else in his entire life talked to him like he was the prince of Mineraltir. Someone needed to talk to him like he was a person.

When Rachel paused to consider a new route to get through to Xavier, I stepped forward. Feeling my color rise as I interrupted them, I tried my best to keep my words steady but soothing. "Your Highness... Um, can I just call you, Xavier?"

The prince quirked his eyebrow and brought one of his hands to his mouth. His interest was piqued. "Why would you want to call me that?"

Here was the hard part. I tried my hardest to swallow my fear. "Because I suspect that no one really does, and I would like to be your friend."

I had Xavier's full attention now. He didn't know how to react he had been caught so off guard.

"Um, we haven't been properly introduced. My name is Lina." I said, trying to smile as I reached toward him.

Instead of shaking my hand, he simply stared at it as if he didn't even know what it was. He gave me a hard look instead.

I cleared my throat as I retracted my hand, trying to continue awkwardly. This was the first time I'd ever spoken to a Royal I wasn't at least somewhat familiar with. "You're right. I am an Allyen. I'm kind of still in the middle of figuring out what all of that means, but I've learned a lot in the last year! I'm getting pretty good at this magic thing, although I'm sure you could beat me pretty badly."

Xavier grinned slightly. I had no clue if he could beat me or not with how well I was doing, but it didn't hurt to stroke the redhead's ego.

"Um, I can promise you that I'm not going to take over the continent like Rhydin wants to. I grew up as a simple farm girl who thought magic was a thing for Royals to kill us with. It didn't become my problem until I figured out who Rhydin was, and that he killed my parents." A lump rose in my throat. I thought this was about showing Xavier he wasn't alone, and now I was the one who was beginning to get emotional. "I started my training with these three's help" – I gestured to Rachel, Luke, and Mira – "Along with Frederick. They've all taught me so much, but I still wasn't strong enough to save the rest of my family. Just a season ago, Rhydin killed my grandmother, my sister, and my little cousin. So, trust me when I say that I know what you're going through."

It was then that Xavier realized what I was doing. He stared up at me in shock, his blue eyes wide, and then he stared down the room at the tapestry that depicted his family when it was whole. He was the little child in the picture. Xavier was completely silent as he looked at his hands, unsure of what to say.

I squatted down in front of him as he sat on the bed like I used to do when Rosetta was younger. It would make us sisters on the same level, but it made me much shorter than Xavier's sitting position where I could see his face. I tried to smile as I talked. "When we first met you downstairs just a couple hours ago, you offered me your arm and told me to make my own decisions. I took your arm because I decided that you were all bark and no bite, and that I could trust you. Can you trust me now? Trust us?"

Xavier rose from the bed, causing me to stumble backwards into a standing position as well. Now, he towered a good foot or more over my head, about the same height as Sam. He met each of us in the eyes as he spoke, his voice sounding different. It was genuine. "You all must understand that I have no control over my kingdom. The queen made sure of that when she entered my father's life."

"We do." Rachel reentered the conversation. "But we also understand that most of the people of Mineraltir's loyalty is with you. The rightful heir. Not her. They see her as a usurper."

Xavier nodded slightly. "Then you have my allegiance. And my trust." He looked to me on the last part. I glowed with happiness. He glanced at Rachel solemnly, "To answer your question, both the queen and Ren have tried to recruit me for Rhydin's cause. I refused, because I want nothing to do with those witches."

"Well, that tells us what we needed to know. I will happily report to Prince Frederick that you have joined him and King Daniel, as well as the news of the queen and princess." Rachel smiled her politician's smile. "Rhydin had better look out. The future Three Kings are in unification against him now."

When Rachel said those words, I actually felt a glimmer of hope. After all, I had done my first great deed as an Allyen nearly all by myself! I was the one to convince Prince Xavier to align himself with us. I knew regardless of his mischief, he would remain loyal, not just to Frederick and King Daniel of Auklia, but to *me*. And that was *huge*. That was when I first began to feel the power of my position. Rachel's words made me feel so confident, as if defeating Rhydin was now going to be an easy task and would happen soon.

Even years later, I cannot believe how naive I was.

Our original plan had been to escape to the safety of the Lunakan woods as soon as we had Xavier on our side and had discerned whether Queen Jasmine was working with Rhydin or not. However, that quickly changed when King Adam decided to spontaneously move up Mira and Xavier's nuptials to later in the week.

Rachel and Luke were still in communication with James, who was back at our camp via some magic I still didn't understand how they possessed. Frederick was livid that the king would do this so out of the blue. He was fearful that something would happen to his sister in Mineraltir, so we were commanded not to leave the kingdom without her. Rachel and Luke kept their eyes peeled at every moment for a chance to steal Mira away to safety while I remained sequestered in Xavier's room, unassailable to anyone who wasn't a pyromage.

The chance never presented itself.

The Kingdom of Mineraltir absolutely exploded at the thought of a Royal wedding. The marriage of the heir to the throne no less! Almost overnight, Xavier and Mira's faces were plastered on every wall of the kingdom along with whatever decorations one could find in the increasingly colder outdoors. I knew at home, winter would have set in. I could imagine the beautiful snow beginning to take over the landscape until nothing could be seen except for pristine white. But here in Mineraltir, everything looked the same with all the pine trees, although many of them generously donated a multitude of their branches to the wedding cause.

Suddenly, anything from pine bough table centerpieces to a huge, elaborate archway could be seen within the castle courtyard as the people prepared for their heir's wedding. Xavier and Mira's dramatic and romantic "love story" dominated every news article, and one could even buy a miniature of the Mineraltin Prince and Lunakan Princess at the quaint peddler shop on the corner.

Even though I was forced to hide in Xavier's tower throughout the days and nights, I was spared no detail of the preparations from Rachel. Mira and Xavier were constantly under the supervision of King Adam and Queen Jasmine, and she said she wouldn't be surprised if they were chained together at the ankles with how often they were forced to be together now. He was only released from her once while Queen Jasmine saw to fitting Mira with her wedding gown.

"You should have seen her face!" Rachel laughed, but then put on a pitiful grimace. "The poor girl though. The queen is imposing her own style upon her, so you can imagine how layered with gold she is. I say, any more and it might snap her poor little figure!"

Regardless of the insanity, Rachel also proved herself to be very perceptive. While Luke remained diligently by my side, his sister was able to spend every moment with Mira and Xavier. She told me how Mira's animosity toward him seemed to have vaporized. Her hatred was gone, and while Xavier still found the energy to joke with her, his quips seemed more lighthearted. They didn't seem to be quite as opposed to this union as they had been.

Even with their changing feelings, every night when Xavier returned to his room he was like a ghost. His blue eyes were empty when he settled down to the little cot he'd come to sleeping on since we came to visit. He would collapse in a heap of long limbs and red hair, not even bothering to take his green suitcoat off. This prince had been raised into an introvert, and suddenly everyone needed a little part of him every day.

Xavier gave up his bed for me, and I never could quite wrap my head around the idea that I was sleeping in an heir to a throne's bed even if it was tiny. Just before my eyes closed for the night, my mind always wandered back to those woods in Lunaka to Sam. Was he still even at the same campsite? It had only been a couple of weeks, and yet it felt like eternity. Did he still remember me? My thoughts were always silenced by the heaviness of sleep.

Three days passed with the entire kingdom enthralled with wedding planning. Flowers poured in from the humid sections of Auklia, bolts of the finest cloth arrived on wagon trains every day from the desert to the south, which wasn't owned by any kingdom. Even new exotic cuisine was brought in on ships from the small island republic of Caark on the other side of the world that everyone usually forgot existed.

However, none of that remained on my mind when I was jerked forcibly awake in the middle of the night. I had been in a deep sleep, and, even with the ferocity of the shaking, it took a minute for my brain to register what I was hearing.

"*Wake up!*" I heard someone scream at me again, "All of them are gone, you need to get out of here now!"

As my vision cleared, I saw Xavier fly away from me and begin to shake Rachel and Luke, both laying on the hard floor. They had taken to sleeping while in Xavier's impregnable chambers, feeling no need to keep watch. He was shouting at them so hard, his voice began to be hoarse. They were on their feet within seconds as they never were ones to be light sleepers.

Luke's hand went instantly to the hilt of his sword as he asked, "What is it? Is someone attacking?"

"No, you idiot! They're all gone, it's coming!" Xavier's eyes looked nearly mad as he made to grab Luke's collar in order to shove him toward the door.

"Who's gone?" Rachel squealed as she strapped her bag over her shoulder and hurriedly pulled me out of bed.

"King Adam, the queen... Even Ren! All of Rhydin's people have disappeared!" Xavier gasped for breath as Luke pushed him off. "I thought I heard something downstairs so I went to go look. Everyone is gone! The blasted front gate of the castle is hanging open!"

With one look between Luke and Rachel, the latter disappeared in a flash of white light. I was finally up and moving, quickly dressing and grabbing my bag. When Rachel vanished, my voice came out staggering, "Where did she go? What's the plan?"

"She went to retrieve Princess Mira. We're getting out of here. Now." Luke said harshly as he breached the distance between us in only two strides. He grabbed my arm tightly and spun me into him so that he was in core contact with me, which brought back images of the livery basement before we had our feather charms. He was keeping Rhydin from sensing me, even though I still wore my feather.

A strange expression crossed Luke's face as he looked back across the room to Xavier. "Your Highness...what is your plan of escape? I can only transport one with me."

My eyes widened, and I nearly gave myself whiplash as I turned to look at Xavier. My voice screeched with how hard the adrenaline was pumping through my body. "Xavier, you have to come with us! We don't know what's coming. You could die!"

The red-haired prince cracked that crooked grin that made him look slightly rodent-like, as if this was all a joke to him. He chuckled, "Don't worry about me, Madam Allyen. I'll hold whatever it is off to give you more time. Just get Mira out of here." With that, a menacing fireball burned into the palm of Xavier's hand, casting eerie shadows onto the face of its creator.

"No!" I screamed as Luke tried to restrain me. "You have to come! We need you!"

The smirk disappeared from his face, and that empty look filled his eyes once more. "It's okay. I'm not worth it."

"*Xavier!*" My voice was drowned out as I was blinded by that all too familiar white light.

It was a rougher trip this time. In the past, it always seemed so smooth, almost transition-less. Now, I clung to Luke for dear life as it felt like we were being rocked in an ocean or storm without mercy. All I could hear were the sounds of my own heart beating and my own lungs gasping for breath in the void, repeating over and over.

Luke and I landed hard on rocky grass, which jutted into my shoulders so bad that I cried out. Immediately, Luke scooped me up and began sprinting slightly uphill, faster than even the speediest of messenger boys at home.

When I could see again, I recognized the stone faces in the distance that we had trekked over two weeks earlier. The mountains. Their rugged cliffs were beginning to quake, rocks sliding down their slopes. It was then I noticed the sky was growing darker than night, and it felt as if the wind was trying to suck us backwards.

Luke continued his dead run higher and higher into the foothills. I noticed Rachel in a similar predicament with a white-faced Mira in her arms a few yards away, equally as fast as her brother. I thrust my head over Luke's shoulder to see what it was that we were running from, and I felt all the blood drain from my face.

Behind us, consuming the beautiful forests of Mineraltir,

was a wall of black smoke that towered into the sky higher than any of those giant trees. It was like a huge thunderstorm that reached from the ground to the heavens, taller than any human could see, and it was not long before the most horrible stench filled my nostrils. It smelled like a thousand different campfires along with the reek of sulfur all mixed together, enough to knock anyone over. Seconds passed before it clicked in my mind from the story I had read in the livery.

It was the Darkness. Duunzer's Darkness. The dragon really was Rhydin's plan, and it was coming *now*.

Luke was yelling with exhaustion, desperately willing his legs to keep going forward and to use the oxygen tainted with lung-burning ash. The Darkness was overtaking us, traveling at an unimaginable speed. A hundred horses put together would never dream of running that fast.

Just as Luke and Rachel were steps away from hauling Mira and I onto the stone of the mountains, the Darkness overcame us. I swallowed hard, squeezing my eyes shut as tight as possible as I gripped Luke so fiercely my fingers tore his clothing.

Nothing happened. I looked up barely in time to see the Darkness hesitate, for lack of a better word, for less than ten seconds. It was the time Luke and Rachel needed to give one last burst of dying energy to fling us over the foothills onto the actual mountainside.

The four of us skidded our separate ways upon landing. I winced as I felt my skin shredded from my body along the rock. When I found my bearings, I expected to see the Darkness take us for real this time. Yet, to my complete shock and horror, it was as if it had slammed into a glass wall. The murky smoke poured into it with intensity but did not, could not, come an inch closer. The Darkness flooded upward against the imaginary boundary, and rapidly blocked out any speck of light from the entire kingdom of Mineraltir.

"It's the mountains!" I mumbled loudly through my pain, remembering how magic was impossible here. "It can't get through the mountains' magic barrier!"

"You're…right…" Rachel heaved for air. Even her hair was drenched with sweat as it trickled down her freckled nose, light blood seeping from her cheeks.

Mira was trembling a few feet away from me, her doll face the same shade as her formerly clean nightgown. "What happened? Why did it stop for those few seconds when it could have gotten us like Rhydin wanted? Where's Xavier?"

"I know why." Luke said as he caught his breath, flung out on the ground just as we were. His eyes remained trained on the night sky as he spoke. "It was Xavier. He held it off for us as long as he could."

That hesitation I had noticed. It hadn't been even ten seconds, but it made all the difference. Mira's eyes began to fill with tears, and I knew in my bones that Rachel had been right. Mira had fallen for him indeed, and soon it was her wail of despair that flooded my ears. My heart belonged to Sam, but that didn't stop my own tears from tracing their way down my cheeks.

# CHAPTER NINETEEN

Our bodies were beaten and broken. Our hearts were distraught and despaired. But somehow, we made it back over those mountains. We never stopped once, not a word spoken. I simply could not wrap my mind around the fact that Xavier was gone. It had happened so quickly... I found myself mourning someone I had barely known while Mira silently wept the whole way back to camp.

As soon as we stepped foot off of the mountain rock, Luke and Rachel transported the princess and I back to rural, northern Lunaka. Once we returned, I found that my body repulsed the new landscape. Every time I turned around, I expected to see the same old skyline that I'd known my entire life. The same old mountains tinged with blue because they were so far away. The same old mountains that caught the sun in its fall every evening.

Now, it was as if a curtain of midnight had been hung to the west, where Mineraltir had once been. We would be there too if it hadn't been for Xavier.

The sun was beginning to rise in the east as we approached camp, sending its light across the sky to illuminate the clouds, but unable to penetrate the Darkness on the opposite side of the kingdom. I was right. Winter had definitely set in for the long haul here in Lunaka. Snow crunched under my feet with every step, and the air felt like crystals as I breathed it in. I was freezing, but my body was already numb anyway. You could tell which direction the last snow storm had come from, as all the trees now wore a coat of white on only the northern side. They stood like bare skeletons against the blue-white sky.

Flakes were falling from the sky even now, but I knew better. These were not the light, airy diamonds of snow falling gracefully. These were dirty. These flakes were gray and fell heavily to the ground. They smelled of burning, and if they touched your skin, they did not melt into a cool drop like snow. They simply clung there and left marks when you tried to remove them. They were death.

"Lina!"

I heard that all too familiar voice ring out through the dead trees. When I looked up from the somber footsteps in front of me left behind by Luke, I saw Sam perched on a small knoll outside of our camp. He was bundled tightly in his thickest cloak although it was moth-eaten, and a scarf was pulled over his nose and mouth as if he had been sitting there for centuries.

My eyes filled with frigid tears at the sight of him. Just seeing him was enough to push me over the edge because we had lost someone again. He took this all in stride as he reached me within seconds, throwing his arms around me. I felt myself numbly reach up and take big fistfuls of his cloak, clinging to him for dear life just as I had done with Luke as we escaped from Mineraltir. It was then, feeling his warmth pouring into me, that I realized how freezing it was, and I clung to him tighter.

"What happened?" Sam bellowed, his words bouncing off of the hollow trees through the quiet wilderness. Then he turned to begin hollering behind him, but Frederick had already appeared, likely sensing our arrival. He also wore several layers and came toting a blanket, immediately throwing it around his stricken sister. Her face was porcelain again now. White, but unchanging. Before Frederick could repeat Sam's question, the Owenses jumped in.

"I don't know how to break this lightly, so I'm just going to say it and explain later." Rachel said fiercely, her blue eyes like fire. "Rhydin has launched Duunzer's Darkness on the Kingdom of Mineraltir. We barely escaped with our lives."

"You are sure?" Frederick mumbled as if in disbelief.

"Extremely. There's nothing else it could be. We wondered at the possibility of Rhydin using Duunzer as he did centuries ago, and the dragon cannot stand light. As the legends say, the entire continent must be in the Darkness for it to attack. This is just the beginning for Mineraltir to be taken." Luke responded this time as he twiddled with the hilt of his sword. He cleared his throat as if it was even hard for him, one who showed few emotions. "We were warned in the middle of the night by Prince Xavier. He noticed that all of Rhydin's people had evacuated."

Frederick swallowed hard. "What became of Xavier?"

"He held it off and allowed us to escape, Your Highness."

Mira's eyes closed in Frederick's embrace. I saw the blond man try to put on his regal, politician's face, but he didn't quite succeed. "Lunaka will remember his service for eternity. Do we know where the Darkness will strike next?"

"Not for certain." Rachel's eyes were downcast. "But I

imagine Lunaka will be one of the last. That way Duunzer itself can attack where Lina is. Rhydin wants to be rid of all of us at once. The Allyens, their helpers, and the Rounans. We have people scouting the Darkness, and it has begun a slow sweep through the Great Desert south of Mineraltir. We need to contact Evan immediately so he can escape from Auklia with King Daniel and Queen Lily to help Lina fight the dragon."

"Well then. That is your first task, Rachel." Frederick's voice choked slightly, and then he turned to me half-hidden in Sam's embrace. "I suggest that you find that arrow as quickly as possible, Allyen Linaria."

I stared at him warily as he began to guide his broken sister back to camp. I had never seen Frederick so emotional before, and his words had kicked my adrenaline into gear all over again. Duunzer was coming. The brother I had never met now had to run for his life just as we had. We didn't have much time left. And I wasn't ready.

Rachel left to go to our tent, likely for her contacting business. Luke was motionless as James ultimately headed over the hill to join us, his hair nearly long enough to reach his shoulders now. The two brothers talked for a while and caught each other up as I vainly tried to warm my fingers in Sam's hands. They felt like wooden ice cubes and I could barely bend them.

Luke scoffed slightly, bringing Sam and I's attention back to the brothers. "You're joking!"

"What?" I mumbled, my voice cracking from disuse.

"The people of Soläna have seen the Darkness, and they turned into a frightened mob, paralyzed with fear." James explained, his eyes hard. "King Adam has told them that Mineraltir had a very large forest fire because of all the ash in the air. He's proclaimed that both Xavier and Mira are dead, and then moved on to planning the annual masquerade Winter Ball as tribute to their memories in a couple weeks. I saw it all when I went to town to quit my job at the mine."

Bile flowed up my throat. King Adam had been disgusting before, but this was a new, ultimate low. This man vowed to protect the people of Lunaka the day his father died and handed him the crown. Now, he was trying to pass off the most dangerous threat to the world's safety as a simple forest fire? He was willing to sacrifice his own daughter for this, and feel no remorse? This man had an ugly heart, and I knew that if his was ugly, Rhydin's was distorted beyond recognition. I knew what I needed to do.

I pulled myself away from Sam and faced the boys. "Luke. James. We need to go back to my grandmother's house to search for the arrow again."

"Now?" James whimpered, eyeing the daylight warily.

"My people are in danger, and nobody else is going to protect them." My voice was stronger than it had been in a long time. "Didn't Mira say that if I can defeat Duunzer, the people who disappeared will come back?"

"I respect your resolve, Lina, but we will wait until night falls. The last thing we need is for you to be imprisoned or someone else to get hurt." Luke said quietly, "It's possible, but keep in mind, this happened the first time three hundred years ago. We do not know how accurate the stories are. We will leave at dusk. We have traveled all night. Get some sleep now."

The rest of the daytime passed rapidly for me, considering I walked back to the tent I shared with Rachel and pretty much collapsed out of sheer exhaustion. To be honest, I didn't even remember parting from Sam or ducking into the tiny fabric dwelling. When I awoke, my last memory was Luke's promise, and I bounded out of my blankets with new vigor. This time, we *were* finding that arrow, no matter what. If there was even the slightest chance that Xavier and the other innocent Mineraltins could be recovered, I was going to make it happen.

Rachel stayed behind with Frederick and Mira, who were both dealing with their grief in different ways. It seemed strange to watch them, like an outsider peering through a window, when I had just been through the same ordeal myself when Rhydin murdered my family. After all, they had spent summers with Xavier as children, I learned. Frederick was quiet, but I could tell by looking at him that his entire presence had shifted. He used to be so on top of things and so in control. It was one of the things that made me sure he was going to be a great king, but he seemed scatterbrained and fearful now. Mira kept up her stone-face charade whenever people were around, yet her sadness was palpable.

My personal ache for Xavier had dulled now that I was focused on finding the arrow. But, every so often, I would remember how he truly believed himself worthless, and it got me all over again. I was determined to save him. Save everyone from Rhydin.

Luke and James transported Sam and I to the outer edges of Soläna, careful to avoid most of the people in the very end of the canyon. When Sam volunteered to go with us, I could really tell that he was getting tired of being left behind. I wanted nothing more than to be able to simply talk to him about everything going on in my head, but we hadn't gotten the chance yet. Now was certainly not the time as we lurked our way through the dark town, the Lamp Master already having doused most of the street lights.

Winter Ball decorations were beginning to be hung, and while as a child I had always squealed with delight at the sight of them, they now only made my stomach churn because of King Adam's heartlessness. There were a few pine boughs wrapped with blue ribbon hanging from the lights, as well as golden bells and silver stars intertwined along windows and doors.

An ardent ache for Rosetta bloomed in my chest. This was always her favorite holiday, as well as my own. I looked to Sam next to me, both of us cloaked and hooded, and his eyes locked onto mine. He gave me a small grin, not saying a word, and I reached for his hand and squeezed it tightly. Three times. I. Love. You. It was an old Lunakan custom, and when he returned it, his brown eyes warm, I began to feel a lot better.

When the four of us turned onto Grandma's street, I began to prepare myself for the sight of her upturned and ransacked home. It was difficult to see all of her precious belongings strewn about or missing. I gripped Sam's hand tighter as we came closer on the cobblestone road covered with snow. Before we quite made it to her little yard, another cloaked figure came out of her front door.

I couldn't see any discerning features, but one of his hands was pulling his hood on and in the other was a long, thin object. My magic immediately sensed something in this person that I had never sensed before. A powerful light that felt familiar to me. It felt just like my own Allyen magic, however, it seemed faintly tainted by something that reminded me of Rhydin's ancient, cold presence.

I naively ignored that tiny detail, chalking it up to Duunzer's Darkness that was constantly encroaching on the area, and realized that this was an Allyen standing in front of me. It had to be Evan! Rachel just contacted him to get out of

Auklia and come meet us in Lunaka so that he could help me against Duunzer. This had to be him, and he found the arrow we'd been searching for!

I grew excited to meet this new brother of mine who had saved our tails and took a few quick steps forward. "Evan!"

The hooded man whirled around, his face obscured by the light in the distance, but his angry glare unmistakable. As both Luke and James reached forward to grab and shush me, the man let out a scream of rage and snapped the thin object over his knee before vanishing in a flash of purple light. This registered to me as undeniably Rhydin's magic. It could be nothing else.

After he disappeared, the four of us rushed forward to the spot. There, lying on the snowy cobblestones was the shaft of an arrow, the head missing, splintered into two pieces. My heart sank as my knees simultaneously sank to the ground. I fingered the wood of it in disbelief. "This is it, isn't it? What now?"

Luke picked up the end of the arrow that should have had an arrowhead attached to it. He rubbed the end with his thumb, very carefully and painstakingly looking over it. "Good news and bad news. The arrow shaft is ruined, but the actual head has not been attached in years. Rhydin's Follower never found it, which is probably why he was angry. If we can find the arrowhead, we may still have a chance."

I let out a breath I hadn't known I was holding and stood back up. I said to Luke fiercely, "So, who was that then? I sensed him as an Allyen."

Luke gave me a grim stare, nothing more. Even James looked sheepish.

"I thought the only Allyens were me, Evan, and Grandma?"

"He was one of Rhydin's Followers. Nothing more." Luke turned away from me to enter the house, James close on his tail, but I wasn't convinced. "Allyen Saarah must have hidden the arrowhead well to protect it even from Rhydin. We will have to double our efforts."

Sam seemed as skeptical as I was when I turned to face him, but he shrugged his shoulders. "It felt like an Allyen to me too. Like it was you standing in front of me, but different. A lot of Rhydin's magic was mixed in there. The Owenses have never steered us wrong before."

"I guess." I grumbled, beginning to get fed up with what seemed to be a lot of secrets as we headed into the house to search a second time.

Our precious midnight hours stretched on. The two Lunakan moons long passed their zenith and slowly plummeting toward the western horizon that no longer existed because of the Darkness. It was somewhat easier to look through Grandma's meager possessions this time because of the goal at hand, but I couldn't stop myself from dawdling over certain precious objects. Her reading glasses, still stowed safely in her bedside drawer. Dried flowers from occasions that no one remembered now, somehow still intact after the initial upturning of her home. Even pieces of quilts that she had been slowly working on over the years, ones that I could never know their purpose now. These quilt squares were littered around the house, nearly one in each of the three rooms, which I did not remember from our first search. It made me wonder how many people had come to this house searching for something. How many of them were looking for our special Allyen arrowhead?

As dawn began to light Grandma's shattered windows like rainbows, James gave a loud groan, pushing over what remained of the chimney. "Is there anywhere we have not checked yet? It feels like we have inspected every speck of dust! Lina, are you *sure* you have no idea where it could be?"

I sighed heavily, my body tired from searching all night, my fingers full of splinters from combing the rafters. For the record, I had to sit on Sam's shoulders to accomplish this. I hated being short. "I really don't know. I feel like I had to have seen it at one point, but it's just been too long! I don't remember."

I numbly reached into my pocket where I stored Grandma's journal, which I hadn't read since the day we'd saved Camerron, and began to flip through it. It seemed that this was the only way I could get help from my grandmother herself.

Luke and James magically transported us back to the woods from Grandma's living room. Just before the white light consumed me, my eyes glanced around everything I could see. Even if it was broken, this would probably be the last time I'd see this room. Our search had failed, and the house would likely be claimed by the town to be sold off. The magic came too soon, and when the snowy woods appeared once again in front of me, I began to scour every page of the journal. The outside world became invisible to me, even as my legs continued to carry me forward to follow my companions.

Its contents stretched across decades, from when Grandma discovered she was an Allyen at the age of sixteen to just before her death near sixty years old. I flew through it, barely absorbing anything that didn't say "arrowhead". Grandma's marriage to her husband, my grandfather, Rix Harvey. The births of her sons, Keera's father and my father. Even the births of her grandchildren.

I slowed down when it detailed my own birth, and about the decision to separate Evan and I. It had been Grandma's apparently, against my mother's wishes. Grandma knew how powerful our presence would be together, even without either of us possessing active magic. She knew that we needed to be taken far away to keep Rhydin from finding us. I wondered how my mother could choose. Who to keep with her, who to send to Auklia with my aunt and uncle. It was mindboggling to me.

"…on Lina. Perhaps, it is worth a shot?"

We were gathered around our meager, barely lukewarm campfire when my attention was snapped back to the present. Frederick and Mira were huddled closely, listening to every detail that Luke and James seemed to be relaying to them. Rachel sat next to me on our old log bench with Sam on the other side, his arm protectively draped around my shoulder at Luke's words.

I scoured Luke's blue eyes carefully, and then glanced up at Sam. "What about me?"

Sam looked unsure as he looked down at me. His wary eyes gave him away. "Luke thinks I should try the Rounan memory spell on you."

My eyebrow rose. Hadn't heard of that one yet! "What would that do?"

"Well, if you really have seen that arrow, I could guide you back to that memory. It could possibly give us a clue as to where it is now." Sam's eyes slid to the side and his big hand clenched into a fist.

"That sounds great! What's the problem?"

"It can be, er… Rather unpredictable, at best. The spell sorta has a mind of its own." Sam grimaced slightly. "To be honest, I don't use it often. The few times I did it, the person always seemed to be in pain."

I turned so that I was facing him, gripping his hands with my tiny ones and trying to look as sincere as possible. "It's okay, I want you to do it. This could save everyone!"

Sam met my eyes for several seconds, and I could almost see the gears in his mind moving, trying to decide if he was willing to do this. While I was beginning to reinforce my argument, he rotated in his seat to face me as well, mumbling the simple agreement. "Fine."

He began to roll up his heavy cloak sleeve, and then the thin sleeve of his tunic, which revealed the long, geometrical mark on the inside of his wrist and forearm. The mark that made him a Rounan. It was mostly a diamond shape on top of a square with a long point extending toward his elbow. Sam told me once that the square was how much magic a Rounan possessed while the diamond indicated how much of it they had access to, which didn't make a ton of sense to me. Then again, Rounan magic was entirely different than Gornish magic, like mine. Sam's diamond and square seemed to be equally represented, which was logical because he was the Kidek. The leader. He needed to be able to use all of his power.

He reached toward me and pressed his marked forearm against the side of my head, lightly brushing my ear. Sam's gaze was intense until his eyes fluttered closed. His voice was nearly inaudible as he whispered words that were like harsh grunts, ones I couldn't understand.

The scenery around me melted into whites, browns, and yellows. A dull headache began in my head, the same side where Sam had placed his arm, but he disappeared. The world morphed, the trees transforming into walls with flowered paper, the snow transitioning into hardwood floors and rag rugs, the logs around our campfire into white wicker furniture that I recognized immediately. I looked down at my hands and found that they had shrunk into those of a child's, chubby palms and short fingers.

"Lina, would you please fetch my eyeglasses for me? These stitches are so tiny I can barely see them!"

That voice. It was hers. The dull ache in my head began to deepen into a slight throb as I whirled around to see my grandmother, perhaps ten years younger, sitting in her rocking chair quilting away. Her gray hair was still pulled neatly into a bun, not ripped free by the rough battle with Rhydin. Her sweet, wrinkled face was clean, not stained by blood. Her eyes were open with life, not closed with death. A lump rose in my throat, but the memory continued to pull me forward. I heard my tiny, child voice say, "Yes, Grandma!"

The child Lina of the memory rushed away from my grandmother, to my disappointment, into the other room. It was Grandma's bedroom, and I hopped over to the bedside table and pulled out the drawer. Inside were several things: doilies, a couple books, her journal, her eyeglasses, and another object. It was metal and larger than I had envisioned. It was an arrowhead, carefully crafted with immaculate designs all over it, except in the very center. There was an empty space in the shape of a perfect circle, where I knew my locket must go. My tiny hands quickly grabbed the eyeglasses, paying the arrowhead no attention, and bounded back into the other room right up to Grandma's quilt-covered lap.

"Here, Grandma! Um, Grandma, what's that pointy thing in your drawer?"

"What pointy thing, sweetie?" She looked at me, and my heart felt like it was going to stop. My head was really starting to throb now with more intensity.

"I dunno what it was. It looked like a triangle and a circle had a baby."

"Oh, so that's where I put that!" Grandma laid her sewing aside and pushed herself forward. I noticed that she could move rather well without her cane ten years ago. "It's something of an heirloom actually. Someday, it'll be yours when you're ready. I've been meaning to find a safe place for it."

I followed her back into the bedroom and asked, "Why? What's wrong with the drawer?"

Grandma turned to me and chuckled, bending down to tickle me. "Well, it's rather valuable, dear, believe it or not! I would never forgive myself if I lost it."

My temple began to sear with pain as I watched my grandmother pull open the drawer, pull her journal out, and then place the two items on top of each other on her bedside table.

As the throbbing began to become unbearable, the world began to melt again. My eyes threatened tears as the walls and shelves lost their shape and began to turn into barren trees covered with snow coats. My body became cold again. I watched my grandmother fade away in front of me, and it was like losing her all over again because I knew it would truly be the last time I'd ever see her.

As Sam materialized in front of me, I could tell from his expression that he had witnessed the memory as well. He was quiet, his brown eyes thoughtful, as I wiped my tears away as quickly as I could. Time to be strong now. Rhydin couldn't see me cry.

"Well?" I heard Luke from across the blurry campfire.

I was about to open my mouth to answer, trying my best to swallow any lumps in my throat, but Sam beat me to the punch. He took my hand quietly, I squeezed it hard, and he turned to the three expectant Owens siblings. "Lina saw it when she was a child, but it was a long time ago. Her grandmother mentioned finding a better hiding place for it, but that was it. She put it on the bedside table."

"I'd say she found a pretty amazing spot for it because we already checked that table at least four times. It was empty, except for that journal Lina took." Rachel sighed, working her mouth in frustration as she turned and walked away, headed for her normal guard duty spot.

Slowly, one by one, everyone else disappeared. Luke headed for his own scouting location while James retired to his tent, his long legs hanging out of the flap. Frederick bid a quiet, heartfelt farewell to Mira when he returned to the castle with the help of Luke. She had to remain out here in the forest with us now that the world thought she and Xavier had been killed in Mineraltir's "wild fire", aka Duunzer.

It still killed me inside how clueless King Adam was keeping the people. I knew this was going to be hard for Mira too, since she'd likely never roughed it in her entire life. I must admit, the look on her face was priceless when Rachel showed her to our own little makeshift tent. No bed, just a measly blanket and a mattress of hard, cold earth. Her fragile doll face was whiter than snow. Soon, it was only Sam and I who remained by the campfire.

He let go of my hand and wrapped his long, wiry arm around my shoulders, pulling me closer. "First moment of silence in a while, huh?"

"Yeah." I said tiredly, thinking of all the things that happened. My heart shuddered for the millionth time thinking of Grandma, Rosetta, Keera, and Xavier. "Just think, wintertime is usually the dead season for us farmers, and it seems like things just keep getting busier and crazier."

Sam chuckled, "First winter for magic and dragons and lunatic kings, that's for sure. First winter for this, too." He leaned down and fit his lips perfectly to mine. When he came away, his breath sprang forth in cloudy wisps, a small smile on his face. "I'm okay with that one."

A smile broke my face. It had been so long. "I am too."

# CHAPTER TWENTY

A gust of wind whizzed past my shoulder as an invisible shove attempted to knock me to my knees. I dug my heels straight into the snow to prevent Sam from succeeding before I answered his blow with a magical blast of light. My aim was true, but he simply smiled at me.

With a nudge of his elbow, my shot was sent flying to the left, straight into the little campfire audience. Princess Mira shrieked, caught off guard, but Rachel was pretty savvy with a frying pan, whacking it into the dirt where it singed out of existence.

I realized I'd watched too long as a sword swiped through the air above my head, nearly cutting a couple inches off of my brown hair. I dropped low and rolled to where I could get my sword around to face Luke. His eyes fiercely glared me down. All of this always seemed more real to the Owenses than it seemed for me, but I was proud of my progress.

I knocked him out of the way with a little help from my magic and then withdrew my bow, nocking an arrow onto the string in only a couple of seconds. Probably a new personal record, I thought, as I smoothly stretched the string back to my anchor, the corner of my mouth, and let the arrow fly.

James had kindly etched a poor rendition of a dragon on a nice, thick tree, which I had been using for target practice. I preferred to think of it as Rhydin instead. Every arrow I sunk deep into that bark was plunging into Rhydin's heart. I was so ready to rid the world of him that I practiced my magic nearly every minute of every day to the point it was easy to forget that I had once been terrified of it. I had once believed magic was only a scare tactic that Royals used, an especially effective one at that, and that the world would be better off without it.

Now, my eyes had been opened to the benefits of magic and how it could be used to protect people. I truly believed that being an Allyen was a good thing and not a curse. It had turned my previous life of a simple farmer upside down, and, for the first time, it might actually feel worth it to save people. I felt ready to face this Einanhi dragon of Darkness.

"Nicely done, Lina." Frederick quit his onslaughts of wind and clapped as he smiled lightly. "You've come far since your magic awakened and saved you from falling to your death."

Sam grinned while I grimaced, remembering my near collision with the canyon floor. By now, I knew at least ten spells that could prevent that from ever happening. "Oh shush, Frederick. Whose fault was it that we were running for our lives in the first place?"

The prince blushed and promptly backpedaled off of my dignity. "I am well aware, Lina. Thank you." He smiled again before turning back to the campfire to find one of the Owenses to take him home for the day.

"Wait, Frederick," I called after him, and once he turned

toward me with an expectant look, I added, "Shouldn't Evan have come by now?"

Frederick's expression became conflicted. "If I could have my choice, he would have been here a week ago. However, Luke has informed me that Evan refuses to leave Auklia without King Daniel and his queen. Apparently, Daniel does not want to abandon his kingdom until he absolutely must."

"Isn't that dangerous? Does he know how fast that Darkness can move?" I asked, shuddering at the memory of Luke and Rachel speeding with their magic as fast as they possibly could and still nearly not making it. If it hadn't been for Xavier's assistance, we wouldn't be here.

"He has been made aware." Frederick stared hard at the ground. "I send him messages almost daily. If he does not arrive in a few days, I will be headed to Auklia myself to retrieve the three of them if necessary."

"Hmm," I grunted absentmindedly. Sounded like we just needed to go get them today, but Frederick still trumped me on the totem pole of discussion making.

I took my bow and leaned it against my punctured dragon tree, noticing that the sun was nearing the new western horizon. Now that Mineraltir was taken by the Darkness, the sun set a good three hours earlier than it used to, which was really throwing me off. As a farmer, I lived by the sun. It was my constant companion as I worked through the fields, and I only had to take note of the shadows on the ground to figure out what time it was or what part of the season it was. It kept me on my toes then, and now, whenever it abruptly set beyond the curtain of Darkness to the west, it made my very body shudder. It was just plain wrong.

Now that the Great Desert was being swallowed up, more of the sky was becoming incrementally black. It made me wonder how much longer King Adam was going to be able to convince the people of Lunaka that it was simply a forest fire. After all, that had happened weeks ago, and there were no trees in the Great Desert.

Sam walked over to me and lightly brushed my arm, his thick woolen gloves catching at the tiny snags on my warmest cloak. His cheeks were red, stung by the icy air. "You did really well today. I think you've finally figured out how to sense my moves before they come?"

I laughed and rolled my eyes as I pulled my hood over my head. "Yes, good grief. That took me forever to figure out! It was really hard, but now I can finally feel when you're about to do something with your magic. Although, I figured out a much easier way to do it now that doesn't require magic at all!"

"Oh really?" Sam looked skeptical. "And what is that?"

"Every time you're getting ready to use magic, you squint your eyes and raise one of your eyebrows." I tried to keep myself from giggling.

Sam's eyes widened in surprise, but before he could get any words out, he tried doing magic slowly to see if he really did it. After squinting his eyes and quirking his eyebrow, he looked at me warily. "No, I don't!"

I eyed him slyly and crossed my arms, "Ask anybody else in this camp, and they'll say the *exact* same thing. I promise." I winked at him.

Sam pouted slightly and then offered me his arm. We began to walk the short distance back to my tent. He decided to change the subject as he saw me fingering the feather charm around my neck absent-mindedly. He cleared his throat. "So... Uh, can you believe it's already time for the Winter Ball again?"

The ground reached up and handcuffed my ankles. There was no way. I looked up at Sam in shock. "It's today?"

The grin fell off of Sam's face. "Yeah, I thought you knew that. What's wrong?"

Something like a river crashed into me, an entire wave of memories and feelings. It was time for the Winter Ball. This time last year, Rosetta and I had been huddled around our little tiny lantern as we journeyed to town. It had two slightly dented copper bells on it. I'd saved money all year so that we could have bells for it. Those bells were still at our house somewhere, if they hadn't been stolen, yet there was no one to use them this year.

Every year there was a Winter Ball at the castle and what we called the farmer version in town. My parents used to take Rosetta and I to the one in town, and I can remember it from my earliest memories because of all the gorgeous decorations. I had been looking forward to taking Keera to it for the first time this year...

"Lina?" Sam stopped. Both his hands were on mine now as he stared at me.

I swallowed back the coming tears as best as I could, my voice coming out slightly distorted. "It's nothing. I just can't believe nearly a year has gone by. It was less than a season after the last Winter Ball that I figured out I was an Allyen. It feels more like a hundred years with how many things have happened."

"I know." Sam said quietly. "Remember them, Lina, but don't dwell on them. I know it's hard, but dwell on the happy things." He squeezed my hand tightly.

I tried my hardest to start coming up with good things that had happened this year, but to my dismay, it never quite worked. My nightmarish memories could never be forgotten, seemingly intertwined with the good memories for eternity. I got to bring Keera home with me. She was killed by Rhydin. I became friends with Frederick and Mira. I lost Grandma and Rosetta. I was finally with Sam and excited for our future. I lost my parents' farm. I became an Allyen. I became an Allyen… I sighed and gave him a small smile. "If you say so."

Sam's expression quickly changed from one of concern to one I hadn't seen on his face since we were children. His brown eyes lightened, and his lips drew back into that lopsided grin I loved. Excitement was almost dripping from his body.

"What?" I asked, beginning to fear for his sanity.

"We're going to the ball."

"Wha-…?"

"Just hear me out!" One of Sam's giant hands clapped over my mouth. "We need a break from all this seriousness, and I would like to take you. After all, I never did get that dance back in the spring." He smiled, looking at me warmly.

"But there'll be people everywhere! Everyone knows that I'm the Allyen, and you're the Kidek. There's no way we can go and not be recognized!" I shrieked, my voice becoming higher with every syllable.

"You got that right."

My hair suddenly stood on end as Sam and I turned to see Rachel, solidly in the middle of our path with her hands on her hips. I began to feel like a guilty child because I actually really wanted to go. I just knew it was impossible. My voice was quiet. "Rachel, I-…!"

Sam stepped forward. "Rachel, we're twenty-one and twenty years old, I think we can make our own decisions! It's a masquerade ball this year, so no one will recognize our faces, and these feathers that you gave us hide our presences, don't they?"

Rachel eyed Sam with her blue daggers before suddenly seeming off guard for a second. She tried to look angry, and then sighed the deepest sigh I had heard in a long time. "Well, if you're going, then you can't go like that!"

"Huh?" I merely blinked at her, my mind unable to process her words.

The redhead walked forward and waved her hands in Sam's direction. "Shoo boy, I have work to do."

Sam smiled so much it seemed like his face might crack, but he did as he was told and hustled away toward the campfire. Rachel turned to me with her chin in the crook of her finger, silently judging me from my head to my toes. She reached forward and grabbed my hand. "I'm going to need help."

A couple hours later, when the sun had fully sunk and set the night sky in its rotation above, I stood in front of Rachel and Princess Mira feeling like a doll. I had never been much of a girly person, and right now, my skin felt foreign to me. I immediately objected to the dress that they used, seeing as we were just going to the little ball in town, but Mira then informed me that it had been cancelled a few days ago.

Apparently, people were no longer interested in heading out of doors with their growing speculation that the Darkness wasn't a forest fire but, instead, something deep, dark, and magical that truly was a threat. This meant that not only were we going out in public, but we were headed to the castle of all places. My anxiety skyrocketed, yet Rachel and Mira endeavored to convince me that it would be okay with all the masks and feathers.

Rachel used her immaculate sewing skills to size down one of Mira's nicer frocks that Frederick had fetched for her from the castle. Mira was taller than me by six or so inches and built like a willow tree. I, on the other hand, was not only short but "petite and well-built at the same time" as they called it. I'd always known I was small, but the second attribute was a new one. Must be from all the sword practices.

The dress was a cream color with a long flowing design and the tiniest of seed pearls embedded in the bodice. I was sure that while it was one of Mira's more common dresses, it was the richest thing I could ever hope to wear. Rachel also took the time to crisscross my head with mud-colored braids. Mira insisted on naming my hair color "brunette", but to me, it was the color of mud and always would be.

Before I knew it, I actually felt like a girl for the first time in a long time. A girl who was newly twenty and who was expected to marry soon or would be considered an old maid as far as Lunakan customs were concerned. To complete the costume was a matching mask that Rachel created from leftover fabric. The only article on my body that didn't change was my beautiful amethyst feather charm, still hiding my presence from Rhydin every minute of every day. My anxiety and excitement began to parallel as each escalated.

Mira clasped her hands together, her grief beginning to disappear for the first time. "This is so exciting!"

I smiled hesitantly, feeling as if I was on display. I didn't like it. "I just hope this isn't a big mistake."

Behind Mira, Rachel was handling my sword and a scarlet sash before a bright light flashed. The sword dove into the simple fabric. No rip or hole appeared, but there was no sword anymore either.

Rachel turned to me and tied it tightly around my waist. "This is for you, to protect you. Just take the sash off, ball it into your hand, and your sword will spring forth with a little bit of magic. Trouble or no trouble, my brothers and I will be watching. As always." She smiled her beautiful motherly smile, her freckles squeezing together as she handed me my locket to stuff into my corset. She had exasperated me for years with her hints that Sam and I were destined to be together. This truly was a holiday for her.

"How do I look?"

I turned to the source of Sam's voice and felt my cheeks grow hot. There, standing before me, was my beau, yet I could barely believe it was him. Instead of the Sam I was accustomed to, who wore old clothes that were the victims of the farmer's curse of never coming clean with his blue, purple, and gold bandana, I saw a handsome man in trimmings that looked more like they had once belonged to Prince Frederick. Sam was taller than Frederick, so I assumed Rachel's skills had gotten a thorough workout tonight. He held a plain black mask in his fidgety hands. Sam's eyes were warm, and his reddish-brown head looked bare without its normal covering. I bit my lip. I couldn't keep the smile off of my face. I joked, "You look like a Royal, Mr. Greene."

Sam grinned, his brown eyes dancing as he looked me up and down. "As do you, Miss Harvey."

And suddenly, it was as if nothing had ever changed. I never became an Allyen. Rhydin never existed. We had reverted to our old joke from when we were kids, addressing each other that way.

My anxiety abruptly vanished as I donned my mask, and Sam kneeled and kissed my hand as if we really were Royals. I pulled on Mira's violet cloak, and Rachel took my hand. Luke and James appeared out of the shadows to take Sam's arms as well, and, after double-checking that Sam had his orange feather, there was a flash of blinding light.

We were dropped off toward the farther edge of the canyon, up on the plains already, so the magic wouldn't get any attention. Rachel, Luke, and James made themselves scarce even though I was sure that they weren't more than a mile away, their eyes firmly on the two of us. Snow was beginning to fall lightly, its crystalline flakes gently swaying to the ground. It truly felt like the two of us were alone in the longest time.

Sam grinned, looking down at me as he clasped my hand tightly. "Are you ready?"

"Yes!" I couldn't keep myself from beaming. I tugged on his pretty collar to coax his head down a foot to where I could kiss him, and then we were on our way to the castle!

As we grew closer to where the pulley systems lifted people up out of the canyon, the booths began to appear. Normally, they were down in the square where the common people's ball was, but they must have moved them up to the plains this year to get the nobles and other people traveling to the Winter Ball.

The stalls were well decorated with silver and gold with stars shining amongst the garlands. The color blue was everywhere. All the stands were painted a beautiful navy, as were many of the things for sale. Little Winter Ball trinkets that the peddlers usually made half their yearly salary on and some Lunakan delicacies made up their wares, such as five grain bread, buttered chicken, and coal cake. It was named for the chocolate powder decoration, not actual coal, I promise.

I looked over my shoulder to the canyon and could barely see the town below. It was completely empty. No one was straying from their homes after dark tonight. I shuddered. It was so joltingly opposite of the norm for this night. Around me, more and more nobles joined our little migration to the castle or broke off to purchase something from the booths. The notion that something was off this night was tangible.

While the children were happy and merry, the adults were having a hard time covering their fear with masks of gaiety. Some scolded their children a little too harshly. Some spoke a little too tersely to one of the booth people. Some continued to look over their shoulders to the southwest where the dark curtain was ever growing. King Adam's lie wasn't going to work much longer.

Sam seemed to notice the same thing but only shrugged his shoulders at me as he grabbed a pole with a big globe lantern on it. These were a tradition at every Winter Ball, both at the castle and down in the square. It symbolized everyone coming together in the dark, led by the lights, to celebrate the holiday together. Last year, I had carried it as we trekked from our house to town with Rosetta and Grandma flanking me.

I struck up a random conversation with Sam to fill the time as we walked to the castle, crunching through the falling snow. It ranged from farming to various memories that we had from our childhood, including the one time I had thrown a wadded-up paper ball at his head in school because he fell asleep and was an easy target. My feet quickly became soaked through the little flat shoes that Rachel made for me, and I wondered how Mira managed to wear these all the time. They really were not functional whatsoever. I missed my boots.

As we entered the towering castle gates, Sam and I made sure to remain within the flow people and not break apart. A huge tapestry of Prince Xavier and Princess Mira welcomed us into the courtyard, surrounded by candles, and I remembered how this event was supposed to memorialize them. I still thought it was ridiculous, but that feeling was forgotten when we entered the ballroom.

Queen Gloria's decorations blew the town's decorations out of this century. It was like comparing an intricate, porcelain doll with a detailed, painted face to the corn husk dolls that Papa would make Rosetta and I every year during harvest. It was always his way of making up for that time of year where we barely saw him because he was up before and after the sun with no breaks.

Instead of simple paper streamers hanging from lampposts, there were huge, silken drapes that gave every marble pillar a deep navy or sparkling silver outfit. There were massive collections of pine boughs speckled with silver paint for the centerpiece of every table. The delicate lace tablecloths could have been mistaken for snowflakes. Gigantic gold and silver stars were hung around the very top of the room.

As my eyes shifted downward to the people in the ballroom, I saw at least a hundred of them twirling around the marble floor in long, elegant gowns and prim suits. I was suddenly glad for Mira's dress that I wore because, while it was probably the plainest in the room, it was far better than sticking out like a sore thumb in my best cotton dress at the Spring Festival.

The queen herself sat by her despicable husband up on the thrones along the northern wall. Only the two gold thrones remained, the extra silver ones I'd seen at the Spring Festival had been removed. Queen Gloria's face shone radiantly upon her people, her golden curls tumbling down onto a dress of ermine fur and sapphire accents. The king beside her was no more dressed up than his normal, an embroidered vest with Lunaka's seal of twin moons shining over a sea of wheat. King Adam's piercing eyes analyzed the room yet seemed to see nothing. His mind was definitely elsewhere.

In front of them, their young daughter, Cornflower, danced

with the son of a nobleman. She was only eleven, the very picture of the queen, yet I wondered how long it would be before King Adam auctioned her off to the highest bidder.

"Hey, look it's Fre-... I mean, the prince!" Sam caught himself, since we were still in a string of nobles, and then nodded with his head toward the other side of the ballroom.

I followed his gaze to see the twenty-year-old Frederick dressed in his princely best, actually looking his age for once, rather than ten years older. The shadows under his eyes and the lines that usually creased his forehead vanished as he danced with a shapely, midnight-haired young woman with a red rayna flower in her hair.

I stared at her for a moment until I recognized her as one of my old friends from school, Cassandra Gale. She was a nobleman's daughter, yet her mother had sent her to school with the common people to keep her from becoming a brat. Needless to say, it worked. She was very nice, but I hadn't seen her in years. She and I used to be best of friends in our school going days. I actually had been returning from her house when Rhydin apparently tried to kidnap me. Now, she and Frederick wore that certain expression of absolute happiness on their faces. The same kind of happiness bloomed in my chest. Frederick deserved this after everything he had been through.

"They're betrothed," I said, the edges of my mouth drawing upward into a smile as I remembered Frederick mentioning that he had chosen her as his wife.

"I thought King Adam was planning to betroth him to Princess Ren?" Sam looked at me quizzically, quoting one of the recent newspaper headlines.

"Ugh." I wrinkled my nose, remembering that fowl, pink-obsessed Mineraltin princess who happened to be one of

Rhydin's Followers. "I hope he gets out of that one. He looks so happy with Cassandra."

"Yeah." Sam muttered, his eyes trained on something other than Frederick. Then, he cleared his throat rather unsuccessfully as he led me over to one of the navy blue laden columns, not too far away from the crowd, but enough that we could speak freely. He paused, as he looked me in the eyes, a nervous smile on his face. "May I have your locket?"

I felt my face fall. It was ingrained into my very bones to protect this little hunk of metal now. It was the only thing standing between Rhydin and total power over Nerahdis. Evan and I were the only ones who could stop him, but I trusted Sam and his intentions.

I took a deep breath as I turned away from Sam and to fish the locket out of my corset. It sure was annoying to carry around ever since Birdie destroyed my shoelace. Its silver gleamed in the light; the intricate etching swirled around the tiny amber jewels. I cautiously handed it over to Sam, slightly embarrassed at how warm the metal was after being so near my body.

Almost instantly after my fingertips left the locket, it was like someone laid a heavy coat on my shoulders. My body felt heavy, tired, but not quite as exhausted as the mountains had left me. Frederick once told me that the reason Rhydin wanted my locket was because it was an amplifier. It strengthened the magic of the person who wore it, although most powerfully for the Allyen. My entire life, I had kept the locket on my body to keep it safe, even when I slept. Letting go of it completely for the first time was far more draining than I'd ever imagined.

Sam scooped my locket up into his palm, his cufflinks flashing in the light, and he smiled that lopsided grin of his before he pointed his finger to the floor and made a circular motion.

I puffed tiredly. Really? He wanted me to hand my strength to him and then turn around to where I couldn't see what he was doing? I turned and drummed my fingers impatiently against my arm, feeling much like an anxious child.

At the very moment when I felt as if I couldn't wait a second longer, I saw my locket appear over my head, along a strong, glittering chain. Sam's work-hardened and scarred hands followed the chain as he strained to get his big fingers around the clasp. He got it after a couple seconds, which I thought was impressive.

After taking a second to appreciate my restored energy, my fingertips rose to brush the chain, which kept my locket securely on my breastbone. I turned in shock to him, my voice clamored uncertainly, "Sam, I... I love it. But what is it for?"

"Happy extremely late birthday. Now you can wear your locket like a real Allyen." Sam chuckled, looking right pleased with himself.

My forehead crinkled as my eyebrows rose. My birthday was Middle Autumn 27th, nearly a full season ago. It had passed without much ado, as it did every year due to harvest time, so I hadn't thought much of it. I turned twenty. A whole two decades old. I began to stutter, "But I didn't get you anything for your birthday."

"Easy. It feels like I've been waiting decades for a single dance with you, Miss Harvey!" Sam laughed, raising his arms to the stance of a dance. I grinned mischievously and fit myself into his frame, one of my hands on his shoulder and the other in his right hand as his left came around my waist.

The music began to fill my ears, a light, airy Lunakan number. So, I would like to put in here that we did this beautiful, awesome dance that only nobility ever dances and that we got every step right because we're just that great, but I can't. We stepped on each other's feet all the way around the room, tripped over my dress a couple times, and never were quite in time with the rhythm. Thankfully, even though we did get some judgmental stares, nobody could place who we were.

When the epic failure of a noble dance came to an end, a new, faster tune began to play. We did much better with that one once we transposed it in our heads to the jig-like melodies that we were accustomed to in town. The world became only a blur of navy and silver. Sam was the only thing I saw though my mask, and I was okay with that.

The musicians stopped far too soon for my liking, and, as the audience began to clap for them, Sam leaned down and planted a kiss on my forehead, looking happier than I'd ever seen him before. But as I gazed back up at him, something caught the corner of my eye.

King Adam stepped down from his gilded throne, worked his way through the masses of beautifully clothed people, and tapped the shoulder of his one and only son. I watched as he tried to persuade Frederick to follow him. After a few more words, which we were too far away to hear, the prince reluctantly gave a couple quick words to Cassandra and trailed after his father out of the ballroom.

"Did you see that?" I asked Sam, still looking at the door to see if Frederick came back.

Sam wore a skeptical look on his face, though he looked slightly disappointed that our moment was over. "I did. And I don't like it."

Rather than beginning another dance, Sam took my hand securely and led me through the globs of people weaving around the marble floor to Cassandra, who now stood by herself next to a silvery column. Her sparkling blue eyes lit up at the sight of the two of us, the masks no use against her. Her voice was sweet. "Lina! Sam! It's so good to see you! Why are you here at the castle?" She looked genuinely confused.

"It's really good to see you too, Cassandra. It's been too long." I said, clasping her outreached hands. "But where did Prince Frederick go?"

"Oh, yes." Cassandra wilted slightly in disappointment, "His father came and demanded his presence so they could discuss something. He said he would return in a few minutes."

Sam glanced at me, and I knew he was feeling it too. The desire to think it was nothing, yet not being able to. What could King Adam possibly want to talk to Frederick about in the middle of the Winter Ball? Sam turned to Cassandra and put on his best fake, reassuring smile. "It's great to see you again, Cassandra, but we actually should probably be going."

"Okay! Have a wonderful Winter Ball!" Cassandra beamed as she waved, her red rayna flower nearly falling out of her hair.

Sam and I walked as briskly as possible without looking conspicuous toward the same door that we had seen King Adam disappear with Frederick. It opened to a dark hallway. When Sam closed the big, stone door to the lights, laughter, and music behind us, we were enclosed in a cold, muffled silence.

Immediately, something felt off. The air itself turned strange, and the hairs on the back of my neck stood on end as my magic kicked into gear trying to sense any sort of presence. Absentmindedly, I began to unwrap my sash and ball it into my hand as I sensed what I'd been dreading. A flash of purple magic down the hall confirmed my thinking. Rhydin's Followers.

I drew my sword from my sash and noticed that Sam too

was now armed with his own sword. Without a word, we both began to run toward the opposite end of the hallway where the magic had come from, where the dark presences were.

Before we could make it, the very castle itself began to shake, rumbling the two of us to the floor. Sets of armor crashed down into pieces and tapestries fell off their hooks. I hung tight to Sam for a split second until I realized the tremors weren't going to stop. Then, we helped each other stumble upright to continue our rush to the end of the hallway.

A man's scream of pain edged me on faster, and I wondered if we were too late.

# CHAPTER TWENTY-ONE

The quaking stopped by the time Sam and I peered through the doors at the end of the hallway. The sight we beheld made my stomach churn. The doors opened up into a rather large, curved balcony with waist-high railings made of marble. There were several people in black, instantly sending my adrenaline levels through the roof.

I recognized Eli, the one who had held me at dagger point at the Spring Festival. There was also a woman with a long ponytail as well as Terran, the red-haired Mineraltin man, and several masked bodyguards. These I could sense were absolutely drenched in magic, meaning they were likely Einanhis, created beings. King Adam was with them, but in the middle of it all was Frederick, lying on the ground, looking like the tar had been beaten out of him. Rhydin's Followers were trying to push his motionless body over the balcony railing.

"This will be the end of you, Frederick. You have stood in the master's way for far too long!" Eli yelled as he kicked the barely conscious prince in the ribs, resulting in a grunt and another few inches toward the edge. "Nobody will ever know that you didn't throw yourself off willingly after the death of your sister! Kino, help me!"

The woman joined his tirade as she helped, covering up some sort of weak rebuttal Frederick was trying to give. "The Allyens *will* be alone when they face Duunzer!"

"Stop!" I found my voice as Sam and I burst through the door. Rhydin's Followers appeared confused until I ripped my mask off to free up my vision. Their eyes went wide at the sight of me, and then back down into deadly glares. By now, I was far too angry to mince words with these people. I could feel my magic boiling up inside of me, and I chose to unleash it on the person I hated the most at the moment other than Rhydin – King Adam.

I knew from the start that I wouldn't be able to fight in this cumbersome dress, so I reached down and tore the length of it off jaggedly, before charging at the evil king. I was so completely fed up with everything he was doing to my homeland. He seemed surprised when he discovered he was my target, his golden crown even fell off his black, curly head, but he recovered quickly.

Our swords clashed, and I fired magic at him mercilessly, as well as against any Einanhis who moved forward to try and stop me. I didn't feel too bad about smacking them off the balcony since they weren't real people. King Adam tried to defend himself with his wind magic, being an aeromage just like Frederick, but it was no use. I had the upper hand. After all, I had the element of surprise, was half his age, and was twice as powerful.

"So, she's got a piece of dirt helping her, huh?" I heard Terran laugh behind me. "This should be easy. You should know, Rounan, that we have destroyed hundreds of your people after we got ahold of your records!"

In the midst of my duel, I didn't get a very good look, but I saw an expression come over Sam's face that I had never seen before. He was a quiet man, a kind man. He was always so tender with his crops and his livestock. But now, words could not even describe the kind of grief, hatred, and ferocity that overcame him. His hands lifted in front of him, and, as they did, Terran and one of the last couple Einanhis began to float.

The two struggled in midair like bugs about to be swatted as Sam swung them over to the very edge of the balcony where they had been aiming to toss Frederick. The Mineraltin hurled more insults at Rounans along with a couple wimpy, magical fireballs, but Sam's invisible grip did not budge. As he released, Terran vanished in a puff of violet smoke, Rhydin's magic, but the Einanhi plunged to the depths below.

King Adam gasped for breath as I never let up on him, blow on blow, sword on sword, magic on magic. This was what the Owenses and Frederick had been training me for all year long, and I felt like I was making them proud. At last, I cornered the Lunakan king against the castle's stone wall. A trail of blood ran down his cheek into his peppered goatee, as I had nicked him with my sword. I held my blade up against his throat, my voice a twist of scream and snarl. "You're destroying your kingdom and your family! How could you do such despicable things?"

The king smirked, his wrinkled face only a few inches away from mine. I realized, in that moment, that a year ago I would have been scared to death to even imagine this. I had changed a lot after becoming an Allyen.

His voice was raspy and out of breath as he grinned

menacingly at me. "My country is corrupt. My family is broken. Master Rhydin is the only one who can heal it all." – His body abruptly disappeared in purple smoke as his last words were thrown over my shoulder to Eli and Kino – "Kill the Rounan and get that locket!"

After King Adam dissipated in front of me, leaving nothing but a spot of blood on my silver sword, I turned to regroup with Sam, who was actively holding back the only two people left. As I leapt to join him, Eli revealed that he was an aguamage, like many of the Auklian nobility were. Torrents of water soaked us, pounding us backward and burning our skin every time. I had never fought an aguamage before, and I found myself faltering. Kino kept firing shots of wind at us, which meant she was Lunakan, too. With that and the water, Sam and I were having a difficult time. Where were the Owenses? We were getting annihilated!

As we were both blasted off of our feet by more of Eli's water, Kino let out a rippling laugh as if this was child's play. "Master Rhydin doesn't believe we should kill you, but if we were to bring him your locket, he could hardly scold us!" She swirled her hands together and aimed a gusty gale right at me. Combined with the water spilled all over the marble floor, I found myself sliding away faster than any river.

There was nothing to reach out and grab on to in the middle of the balcony. My fingers clawed at tiny edges in the stone as I sailed, unable to grasp anything. Suddenly, I felt my back crash into something solid, which immediately gave way to the point where there was nothing underneath me at all! As I fell, by some happenstance, my hand finally found a hold on a tiny piece of iron from within the shattered marble floor. When I looked down, I found myself hanging off the balcony with only grassland some hundred feet down below me.

"*Lina!*" I heard Sam bellow as my hand became numb. I tried to pull myself up, but I couldn't get my other hand to the iron. My shoulder felt like it was coming apart, sinew by sinew, because my weight was too much for one arm to bear. My head started reeling with every possible spell I knew, but none of them could save me. As I was about to let go, my hand screaming with pain and Sam's shouts becoming muffled as he fought for his life, I suddenly felt arms come up and around me. The tension in my arm was alleviated as we rose up together.

I looked behind me to see my best friend in the entire world. Rachel. She returned the smile, especially as my wide eyes took in the things on her back. They were the same colorful objects that I had seen the day we saved Camerron. Now, I got a real look at them as Rachel floated gently upwards and landed on the balcony. They *were* wings. I was right! They were shining shades of glittering purple, green, and brilliant orange, the same colors as Sam and I's feathers! They were like shards of glass, not fluffy or feathery like a real bird's wings, just like my little feather charm.

Luke and James promptly flew up on either side of Rachel with wings that mirrored hers, and made lightning fast work with Eli and Kino. They moved faster than any human, and while I always figured they were in good shape in the past, I knew now that they could move that fast because they *weren't* human. Sam and I had struggled hard against those two Followers, and in less than thirty seconds, Luke and James sent them packing in purple smoke.

Rachel set me down, and I stared at them slightly agape. She looked down at the dress that she had so carefully sewn and altered for me, the bottom of it torn unevenly so I could fight. She giggled, "You know, I kind of like it better that way!"

Sam ran forward, limping slightly from the fight, and grabbed me with both arms, holding me tight. No words were said, but I clung to him. That was definitely too close for comfort. After a couple of minutes, when Sam finally released me, I turned to Rachel and her brothers, whose wings had disappeared by now. "Alright, you three need to 'fess up. You've been keeping me in the dark on something else, haven't you?"

Luke was the one to shrug and actually flash a rare grin. "Remember our conversation about giants on the way to Mineraltir?"

My eyes probably grew as large as orbs. "Yes?"

"The world calls us giants." Luke said, glancing at James as if they thought it was hilarious. "We call ourselves Ranguvariians."

"Rang-goo-var-ee-ens?" I tried to say it, but gave up till later when I could practice. "But you guys don't look like giants! You look normal size!"

"Compared to Lina, everybody is a giant." James whispered behind his hand to his brother, his other hand leveled out at a little under five feet above ground to show my height. They both laughed heartily.

"But-...!" I exclaimed, hurt that no one was paying attention to me.

Rachel moved past us to the unconscious Frederick. She withdrew another feather charm from her pocket, the one of a brilliant green that Frederick had worn while we were in the livery basement. She waved it over his body, and I saw his wounds close up before my very eyes. His expression ceased to be pain-filled and relaxed into sleep while Rachel put the feather around his neck to hide his presence.

She turned around to me as she hefted the fully-grown man over her shoulder, far heavier than I ever imagined she was able to lift before. Her voice was light, not strained at all. "I would love to answer all your questions, Lina, but we're not in a good place for that right now. Frederick isn't going to die, but I still need to tend to the rest of his injuries. Rhydin's magic is difficult for me to heal."

The shaggy-haired James came forward to take my hand, smiling innocently, while Luke put his hand on Sam's shoulder. I reached up to feel my locket and its warmth to make sure it was still there after the fight and near fall. Their elegant, shard wings appeared once again, not trying to hide them anymore, and the familiar bright light flashed.

Instantly, we were back at our pitiful campfire in the small, snowy, uninhabited woods of Lunaka. The cold had really settled in now, but I didn't feel it as I remained intent on finding out more about this Ranguvariian business. Luke and James moved one of our makeshift tents closer to the fire for Rachel to tend to Frederick as much out of the cold and snow as possible. I followed them around like a little child, waiting until they had finished their work so I could ask the myriad of questions floating around in my head.

Mira came flying out of her tent as soon as she awoke from our noise, reminding me of the hour. It was definitely a few hours past midnight. Her porcelain face was screwed up with worry for her brother as she scrambled to his side. She turned her violet eyes up to James as Rachel continued her healing process, her hands stretched out over Frederick's ribcage while she hummed a strange tune. Mira's voice was on the edge of frantic as she spoke, "What happened to him?"

"King Adam tried to kill him and fake his suicide." James said hesitantly, his eyes sad. "I apologize. It happened so quickly and subtly in the big crowd. We truly didn't think Frederick was in danger, being the heir to the throne."

Mira nodded slowly, her eyes glancing back and forth until they looked up at the horizon. "I hope you know that we have an even bigger problem." She pointed south.

Granted, it was nighttime. But with both moons full tonight along with the shining stars, the sky was decently lit. However, there was no mistaking that the great curtain of Darkness had expanded. It not only covered the west, Mineraltir, and southwest, the Great Desert, but now it had conquered the entire south as well. My heart dove into my stomach.

Auklia. Auklia was to the south of Lunaka. Auklia was where my brother was. North and east of us were only ocean along with the distant island of Caark, likely too far away. Lunaka was the only kingdom left.

My voice shook, and my hands began to tremble. "Rachel, please tell me Evan got out of the country before the Darkness came…"

Rachel hardly heard me, her eyes staring out in front of her as if she had been dealt a brutal blow. Luke placed a hand on her shoulder as it began to quake, stilling her instantly. She didn't look to me but whispered something that I couldn't hear, her words tinged with emotion.

Luke faced me then, his face wiped clean of any sort of feeling. "We can't get any sort of response from the Ranguvariians that are protecting Evan."

My eyes unwillingly closed as I desperately avoided being pulled to the depths of my anxiety. Evan wasn't coming. He was gone. He couldn't help me against Duunzer. I had to do this by myself now, and the thought was completely overwhelming. We hadn't even found the arrowhead yet! I began to stutter, "Surely... Surely, he got out! I mean, we were able to get out of Mineraltir!"

"Yes, because Xavier figured out it was coming and held it off for as long as he could! If he hadn't, we would have been sleeping when the Darkness came. Just like Auklia." Luke's words became firmer, but his eyes were soft, turning more blue than normal.

I turned to find Sam behind me and gripped his arm hard for support. He was my calm in the storm, and he stared deeply into my eyes, trying to anchor me to him. His voice was low but audible. "You won't be alone, Lina. Don't forget, I have magic, too."

I nodded dumbly, swallowing hard as I allowed the thin wave of consolation to wash over me.

As Rachel returned to healing Frederick, Luke cleared his throat, motioning for us all to sit on our logs around the campfire. "Now. I am sure you have questions, Lina. Go ahead and shoot."

My head whirled as Sam sat with me, trying to remember what my questions were, and where I should even start.

Sam took control at that moment, apparently being just as curious as me for once. "You said you're called Ranguvariians, but we call you giants. How much of our little giant story is true?"

James grinned, and Luke revealed a sly smile. "Very little unfortunately, aside from the fact that we live in the mountains. You humans really are quite clueless."

My eyes widened as I found my voice. "If you're not humans, why do you look like them?"

"An excellent question." Luke remarked, seeming much happier than I'd ever seen him before. "We are part human. Our grandfather, the Clariion or leader of our people, married a human woman, a princess from the Mineraltin Royal family. Our mother looks about like we do, mostly human with some Ranguvariian qualities."

I peeked at Rachel for a split second, because I had always wondered where she had inherited her red hair. It certainly wasn't a Lunakan trait. She had Mineraltin Royalty in her blood.

Luke seemed to foresee our next question, so he picked up again. "We are able to perform the Ranguvariian flying spell, or have wings as you call them, as well as the strength and agility of a Ranguvariian. A full-blooded Ranguvariian can be around eight or nine feet tall with eyes that change color with their feelings and pointed ears. James, here, inherited the ears while Rachel received a rather disproportionate height. I was the lucky one who got the eyes."

I looked at Luke closely, realizing that I had already noticed his eyes. Always only for an instant, like on the way to Mineraltir when I'd thought they'd flashed to yellow when I nearly fell off the mountain. Normally, I thought of Luke as a very quiet and expressionless person. What if he did that to hide his eyes changing color with his feelings? I eagerly responded, "Is that why you're always so dull?"

Luke smiled happily, the first time I'd ever seen such a smile from him. His eyes turned a bright pink. "You are more observant than I thought."

I couldn't help the grin that spread across my face as I turned to James. "And that's why James always needs a haircut. His shaggy hair hides the ears?"

James grinned and shoved as much hair as possible to the side, revealing an ear much larger than a human's with jutting points. It was a wonder his hair could even hide them.

I turned to Rachel now, unable to see how she was

different. She had been listening to the conversation and grinned slightly as she rose, but her freckled expression was still filled with worry. To any stranger, she probably looked fine, but I had known Rachel for nearly three years now. I knew when she was trying not to look worried to others, but it always failed on me.

She motioned for me to stand before she knelt to the ground. For the first time, I noticed that this made her the same height as me. "Look at our waists," she said quietly. "They're in the same place even though I'm kneeling right now. I inherited the long legs of a Ranguvariian, so I always have to wear dresses with low waists to make me look normal. Tall for a woman, but normal proportions at least."

I gaped at her, slightly freaked out by the length of her legs at the moment, which ultimately reminded me of how short I was. Rachel rose from her kneeling position and returned to Frederick, obviously not very interested in talking at the moment. I turned back to Luke, who seemed content, but I wasn't done. "I still have two more questions. Are these feathers you gave us taken from your wings? And, you once told me that you consider yourselves part of a group called the *Alyen nou Clarii*. Where does that fit in?"

"What we told you about the *Alyen nou Clarii* is still true. It is still a group devoted to protecting the Allyen. In Ranguvariian, it means 'the Allyen's soldiers'. Our grandfather, Arii, founded it three hundred years ago when Nora became the first Allyen. Our father was one as well, but he was killed by Rhydin when he tried to kidnap you as a child." Luke's eyes dipped downward, turning a mix of orange and blue.

My brow furrowed, and I shot him a confused glance. His words were tugging on my memory, but they led to nothing.

They had told me before that Rhydin tried to kidnap me, but it was linked to the blacked-out memory in my mind. Rhydin erased it with magic, they'd told me back when I first learned I was an Allyen. The first thing I remembered afterward was waking up in the middle of the small wood on the way to Auklia and seeing Sam. I was nine and he was ten at the time.

It used to bother me that I couldn't remember, but once Rachel told me that the memory had been forcibly erased, I hadn't thought about it really at all. In fact, I realized with a jolt, I had never even asked for the details. My words were hesitant. "I have no memory of that night. Would you tell me what happened?"

Luke looked downward. "You were very young, walking home from your friend Cassandra's house. Rhydin intercepted you, but you were so tired from playing and walking that you were pretty much delirious. He picked you up and headed to Auklia to get Evan. My father and his group were able to sneak up on Rhydin because he cannot sense Ranguvariians. The fight was pretty brutal from what I've been told since it's hard for us to be around his magic. After some time around Rhydin, we lose quite a bit of our strength. My father was the last one standing, but even he was no match for Rhydin…"

"How did Rhydin not get away with me?" I asked carefully.

"He couldn't sense us, but he could hear more Ranguvariians coming. So, he wiped your memory and left you there." Luke said solemnly. "As for the feather charms, they do come from our flying spell wings. They have healing properties, which is what Rachel is doing right now to Frederick. They also give ordinary people the same presence hiding capability that Ranguvariians have. When you wear our feathers, you become like us and Rhydin can't sense you."

293

I reached absentmindedly for my neck, feeling my locket, but I snapped to my senses when my fingers could not find the cool, smooth shard of feather. I looked down and nearly screamed, "My feather is gone!"

Before my mind could even process this, something hard collided with my chest, and I flew backward off the log. My head smashed into the snow, and, when my eyes finally cleared, I saw Luke above me. His nose was inches from my face as he moved to grip me securely around my middle.

Sam was on his feet in seconds, looking unsure as he stared at the two of us in the snow. He said slowly, "Is that really necessary?"

James raised his finger. "Core contact with a Ranguvariian does the same thing as a feather. Remember when I had to sit with Frederick and Rachel with Lina down in the livery? That hides presences, too, just much less convenient."

Rachel came out of the tent followed by a rather weary Frederick. He had a few bruises still, but he looked far better than he had moments ago. His Royal voice was definitely unharmed. "Since we don't know how long Lina has been without her feather, I believe it safe to say that Rhydin knows where she is. Duunzer's coming is imminent."

I gasped as I tried to get air in through Luke's tight hold, and the idea gripped me. "What do we do? We don't have the arrowhead!"

Frederick looked at me with his clear blue eyes, and they betrayed his fear. "All we can do now is head to the castle. It's the only potentially safe place left and much easier to defend than out here in the middle of nowhere. Perhaps, we will have time to search Saarah's house one last time on the way."

Everyone nodded, and it abruptly felt like time was sliding through our fingers. It took an hour to break camp and another to begin heading toward Soläna. We left our tents where they were. After all, we didn't need them anymore. I tried to ignore the sense of finality this gave me.

I tied the sash with my sword around my waist and filled my quiver as full as possible with arrows, all with Luke keeping core contact with me. There were only three Ranguvariians to the four of us humans, so we had to travel the old-fashioned way. Luke ended up carrying me most of the way since walking was pretty much impossible.

By dawn, we reached town, which was quiet and barren. The sun was only barely beginning to rise over the eastern ocean, its rays illuminating Lunaka alone. Only mineworkers were daring to stray from their homes because the churning goliath in the heart of Lunaka stopped for nothing.

Now that Auklia was taken, I was sure that the people would turn on King Adam. There was no way they'd believe it was a forest fire now. After all, Auklia was a marshland. Fire was generally unheard of there. Plus, what were the odds of all Nerahdis being consumed by fire? Not good, and it showed. Normally people would already be up and about, doing shopping or heading to work or taking children to school. Now, Soläna was merely a ghost town.

The seven of us quickly made our way to Grandma's house so we wouldn't look out of place, but nothing could have prepared me for what we found. Instead of a quaint white house with blue shutters, we found nothing but the bare canyon wall, crumbling to pieces.

My jaw dropped. The cobblestone road butted up to nothing but dirt. Even the flowers had been reduced to ashes. The yard was filled with the gray stuff, only the barest of outlines left to show where walls once stood. My mind could not fathom it. Her house was simply gone with only some ashes to tell its tale.

Rachel spoke slowly, "There was nothing from that memory that hinted where it could be?"

I sighed loudly and one of my hands ripped through my hair as I began to pace. This was totally unexpected. If I didn't find this arrowhead, we were all going to die, and now the only place where it could be was burnt to the ground!

As I continued pacing, the boys started shuffling through the ash and dirt, out of lack of anything else to do. Rachel took Luke's place hugging my back. She watched me for a couple minutes before giving a huff and fingering her sash with one hand.

In the memory, I had asked Grandma what the arrowhead was. While she hadn't exactly told me, she did say she wanted to find a better place to hide it. A better place than her bedroom nightstand. Where could have been safer than that? We never found it in her house, and it was obvious that Rhydin hadn't found it either since his Follower snapped the arrow shaft in half. Grandma must have used magic to conceal it somewhere, otherwise we would have found it months ago.

Luke kicked something hard. I watched him duck down and inspect a little kettle, then untie his sash, ball it up into his hand, and his sword sprang forth from it. It was the same trick that Rachel taught me to do with my own sash only last night at the Winter Ball. When the kettle turned out to be nothing, I returned to my thoughts.

Grandma wanted the arrowhead somewhere safe. Somewhere likely protected by magic. She wouldn't have put it in just anything though. She would have put it in something important. The very last thing I had seen in the memory was Grandma pulling the arrowhead out of her bedside drawer and setting it on top of her journal.

What would she think was important? That no one would accidentally throw away, like an old sash. She didn't own anything of considerable value. We weren't Royals after all. It couldn't be important to just anyone either, otherwise it would have been stolen by a common thief. It could be important only... Only to me! Grandma was going to hand it down to Evan and I! So, she wouldn't put it in anything a thief would find desirable, only her grandchildren!

My knees sank to the ground so fast that Rachel nearly dropped me. She chastised me, "Hey! What are you doing?"

But I didn't hear her. I was busy unloading the pockets of my cloak. Several items lay before us as I finished, and they were all things that I had taken on the first trip to Grandma's house. They were all heirlooms that I found important, even though none of the thieves had bothered to carry them off. My grandfather's battered, tin watch. A small, simple painting of my grandparents on their wedding day. One of Grandma's favorite hairpins, the only one that hadn't been taken. Several other small mementos, and Grandma's journal.

I nearly stopped breathing as I reached for the little leather volume and flipped through the pages ecstatically. Grandma had specifically taken out her arrowhead and journal to place them together when she said she wanted to find a safer place for it. My fingers shook as I turned to Rachel. "You made my sword disappear into a piece of fabric! Could Grandma have put the arrowhead in this journal?"

It took Rachel all of two seconds to realize what I meant. She scrambled away from me to stand, pulling me to my feet. "Try to bring it out! I doubt my magic will work!"

With all our screaming, the guys and Princess Mira took notice of us. I put the journal on the ground with its pages open and stood again with my hands above it. I closed my eyes, relying on the lump in my chest, and I instantly felt my magic racing through my veins. My locket began to glow, and then the book on the ground did so as well. A bright light shone in between the pages, and before I knew it, something shot out of the book at high speed, so fast that it went right past my hand. I looked up in time to see the dark blur falling back toward me, and I lunged to catch it with both hands.

When I turned the object toward me, I recognized the strange angular shape with the hollow circle in the middle. I smiled, tears threatening to stream down my cheeks, I was so relieved. I held it up in my hand, and smiles broke forth on all of my friends' faces. Frederick and Mira both seemed proud of me while Rachel and her brothers looked so happy they might faint. Sam's eyes shone, and I knew that he was proud of me, too. I had the arrowhead! We actually stood a chance.

When the wind picked up eerily, I knew that I had spoken too soon. It was like when a spring storm would come through the prairie, the wind picked up in an instant, and the temperature dropped twenty degrees in only seconds, making the cold of Late Winter absolutely frigid. A figurative jacket of magic was laid on my shoulders, and I recognized its signature instantly. Rhydin was coming. My nostrils filled with the stench of sulfur and ash, and the ground began to tremor. I met Sam's eyes in an instant. I knew that this was it. Duunzer was taking Lunaka. Right now.

"We need to get to the castle. It's our only chance!" Frederick shouted over the wind, and that was when the ground truly started to quake with force. I stuffed all of my pilfered things back into my pockets as the shaking became so severe that I stumbled to the ground.

People began running out of buildings left and right, yelling and screaming, their mouths agape and their eyes wide. Every soul was sprinting the other direction toward the center of the canyon even as the tremors threw them relentlessly to the ground. Buildings began to buckle, falling over like people fainting and crumbling to pieces. Not a single brick was left on top of another. The mine began to choke out ink black smoke and spit fire, making horrific noises as it collapsed underneath us.

Ice slid down my spine as a mile away I began to hear the castle bells ring louder than ever before. It was like thunder rolling down into the depths of the canyon, as if the great, heavy bronze bells themselves were about to be smashed in two, they were ringing so ferociously. It reminded me of my dream, and it was happening right now.

The Owenses immediately sprouted their wings, none of the civilians nearby paying any attention in their chaotic running. Rachel grabbed me firmly and jumped into the air as Luke scooped up Frederick and Mira in each arm, and James took Sam. Before I knew it, we were all in the sky!

If it hadn't been for the fact that Duunzer would be arriving any minute, I would have taken more time to marvel at the beauty of Soläna from a bird's eye view. However, this was not the time, regardless of how pretty the snow-white world was.

As Rachel flew rapidly towards the castle, I turned my head to watch the hundreds of people, now little black dots, gunning it for the pulleys like tiny ants trying desperately to reach their hill in a rainstorm. The castle bells continued harshly calling everyone to safety like a shepherd to his sheep. To my dismay, some of the people began climbing over others, holding on to the pulley only to be hoisted up while hanging from their fingers. Still others were being pulled off as everyone fought for their own self interests. The old rusty wheels on the pulleys were moaning so loud I could hear them even from the sky as they were hauling far more than their usual weight limit. Then, I heard the terrible screech and clang as both of them broke and plummeted to the canyon floor, trapping most of the people at the bottom of Soläna.

Unable to watch any longer, I gazed back towards the Darkness. It was advancing rapidly, its smoke overtaking the edge of the canyon by now. Even in the daylight, it was the blackest of blacks. As the ocean of shadow got closer, I noticed Rachel's flight pattern was becoming more uneven, as were her brothers'. We were out of the canyon and within a mile of the castle, flying over top of the people of Soläna who made it up the pulleys before they crashed when I shouted up at her. "Rachel! What's wrong? You can do it, we're nearly there!"

Rachel gasped and made a choking sound. "Rhydin... Rhydin is here! We can't fly when his magic is around to poison us!"

She made one more solid stride upward, the very last of her strength, but then her wings began to dissolve, the smaller shards furthest away going first. That was all we needed though, as we sailed right over the castle wall and down into the courtyard. As we fluttered down to the ground, I heard the boom of the iron gate clanging shut, sealing the castle. Luke and James made it over the wall too as they dropped their wings so nobody would see them. Their passengers hit the ground hard.

Frederick and Mira immediately rushed away from us to the other side of the courtyard where their family was standing outside the great, wooden doors. All five members of the Royal family held their hands upward, and from them shot waves of wind that blew to the tallest tower, initiating a magical star of light that separated and rounded downwards to create a magic barrier around the entirety of the castle. King Adam was even there, with Queen Gloria and Princess Cornflower, all of their eyes closed in concentration, which surprised me. I guessed he still needed to keep up his image.

No sooner than the barrier hit the ground like smooth, shining glass, then the smoky, ash smelling Darkness swept over it in a wave. It was so enormous that it made me feel like an insect under a child's cup. All the light was instantly gone, except for what little shone out from the open door to the castle, as well as what barely emanated from the barrier. The hundred or so people who had made it from Soläna were sprinting past us, hightailing it inside to hide from the danger.

This was it. This was what Frederick and the Owenses had been training me all year for. This was what I'd become an Allyen for. Duunzer was here. Rhydin was here.

It was then that I heard it. An indescribable sound. It was like nails on a chalkboard, a hundred of them. It was such a scream that it crumbled one of the older castle towers to dust and I had to cover my ears, lest I'd go deaf. Sam rushed toward me, but it was then that I saw what had scared me the most in that dream I'd had a season ago.

Two bright red stars, gleaming in the Darkness.

Eyes.

# CHAPTER TWENTY-TWO

Screams of the people huddling inside the castle reached my ears. Out of the corner of my eye, I saw Queen Gloria usher the young Princess Cornflower inside now that the barrier was set. There was no mistaking the fear that overtook her sweet face. The shining, fierce eyes came closer and closer until they were the size of the guards up on the parapet. My breath quickened.

Rachel ripped the arrowhead out of my hand and snatched one of my regular arrows out of my quiver. I watched her speechlessly as she broke the old arrowhead off of the shaft and shoved the Allyen one on in its place. Panic raced through me as large crashes boomed above us. I looked up to see Duunzer banging its sharp claws against the barrier, hit after hit. What would happen when it broke? I had been training for this all year, and now I felt nowhere near ready.

"Lina! Give me your locket!" Rachel bellowed in my ear, causing me to jump.

I reached around my neck and undid the clasp of the chain

Sam had given me, threading my locket off of it in only a second. Rachel took it and fixed it into the small, circular hollow in the arrowhead. It fit perfectly, and it was then that it hit me – I only had the one arrow.

Rachel handed me it, and when I grabbed hold, she looked me deep in the eyes. "You've only got one shot. Make sure you are in the *perfect* spot!"

I nodded at her, still unable to find any words in my fear. Rachel's eyes were gentle, and she pulled me in for a quick, tight, one-armed hug. Behind her, out of the shadows, I saw cloaked people advancing on us. When they lowered their hoods, I recognized nearly half of them as Rhydin's Followers. Eli, the Auklian nobleman who'd tricked me at the Spring Festival. Kino, the woman at the Winter Ball. Even Terran, whom Sam nearly killed that same night.

Frederick and Mira came running toward us as King Adam joined his cohorts, the Lunakan people no longer in the audience. I noticed that Mira had tucked her emerald skirt up into her sash, revealing trousers underneath. Even she was planning on fighting.

The prince's voice was strong and authoritative. "Sam, stay with Lina. Rachel, you and your brothers need to be in the air to distract the dragon as long as possible. Mira and I will be on the ground to take care of the Followers. Keep the dragon busy as long as possible to give Lina a good target! Lina-…"

"I know. One arrow. Got it." I gritted my teeth, the fierce cold of the Darkness beginning to work its way into my body.

Frederick was unable to respond because, at that moment, a huge flash of purple dominated our attention. All of us turned our heads to see the flash of magic coming from slightly above the bright red eyes. To our horror, one clawed hand pushed through the barrier without breaking it. The shining shield above us morphed, matching the contours of the dragon's arm, allowing the creature inside but not the Darkness. It was soon followed by the other, the scaly skin barely tangible, only consisting of swirling smoke.

"Good luck, Lina!" The three Owenses sped off from us, their wings coming to life as they drew their swords, the shining shards reflecting some of the light spilling forth from the castle. I wondered how long they would have in the air after only a couple minutes of break. From the looks on their faces, I knew they were ready to go into full Ranguvariian war mode.

Duunzer entered its big, ugly head into the barrier and let out another ferocious roar, shaking every stone of the castle. Frederick turned on his heel and threw a blast of wind toward Rhydin's Followers, who were continuing their advance on us. Before Mira joined him, she threw one more comment over her shoulder. "Try the bell tower, Lina! It's the tallest!"

With that, I felt pretty much abandoned. Evan should have been here to help me! I turned to Sam, my last companion, about to tell him something dramatic. Before I could even look at him, he had my arm in his grasp, sprinting the other way.

"Save it for later!" He yelled as he dragged me, the first of Duunzer's ebony legs busting through the great stone wall of Lunaka Castle. Gigantic bricks flew everywhere, smashing into the ancient trees in the courtyard. Up above, I saw the flying Owenses doing their best to goad the dragon away from me.

As we ran, I untied my sash and scrunched it into my hand, using magic to pull out my sword as the sash wrapped around the handle. Eli tried to get between us and the bell tower, his big, bulky glasses flashing in the firelight. In seconds, he was lifted and thrown with Rounan magic back toward where Mira could deal with him.

As we were reaching the door to enter the tower, another man in black tried to tackle me out of the blue. I sensed him at the last second and dodged it. The figure quickly rebounded, flexing in an abnormal way. This one wasn't a human. It was an Einanhi. I was beginning to think that Rhydin had so many Followers simply because they were made up of nonhumans he'd created.

Sam drew his sword, and a loud clash resounded as he met the Einanhi's blade. I was about to jump in and help, but Sam yelled at me as he blocked another blow. "Go up the tower! The Owenses won't last long. I'll catch up!"

I swallowed hard before spinning and flinging the bell tower door open. To my dismay, hundreds of stairs awaited me on the other side, but I knew time was against me. I took two or three steps at a time, out of breath before I was even halfway up. Trying to draw on my magic, I kept going as quickly as I could.

When a tiny window passed me by, I couldn't help but stop and look out of it. Mira and Frederick were holding their own against the Followers, and it drove me nuts to not see Sam. Duunzer was fully in the courtyard now, and even though the Owenses were doing their best to draw it away from the bell tower, there was no mistaking where the dragon was headed. I didn't have my feather. Rhydin knew exactly where I was.

With renewed fright, my magic took control, and I hopped up the stairs as if I were weightless. In only a few more minutes, I found myself at the top, emerging amongst at least fifty different sized bronze bells. They were covered with frost the temperature had dropped so drastically, and a couple of them were cracked into two or more pieces. I weaved my way through the giant bowls to eventually find myself on the edge of the tower, high above the courtyard. Duunzer was within a few hundred feet of me as it swiped one of its enormous claws through the air at Luke. The three Owenses were buzzing around its head now, like annoying little flies.

I tried to still my breathing and sheathed my sword into the sash, pulling out my bow and the Allyen arrow. This was it. I could not miss. I. Could. Not. Miss.

I nocked the arrow on the string with my frozen fingers and heaved it back with the last of my strength, the bow refusing to bend in the cold. As I stared at Duunzer, I realized with terror that I didn't know what to aim for! Its head? Its eye? Its heart? The whole thing was a big mass of intangible, swirling smoke!

My fingers were turning numb quickly in the frigid cold and my arms began to burn from holding the bow. As I analyzed the body of the Einanhi dragon before me, my eyes caught sight of one of the Owenses falling out of the sky. I couldn't see who it was, but there was no mistaking the dissolving of their wings. They had been around Rhydin's magic too long. I was running out of time!

Out of desperation, I did what I thought was best. I aimed for one of the shining red eyes, as I used to do with my target practice. Light began to pull out of nowhere around the point of my arrow, the locket beginning to glow strongly from inside. Pulling the arrow back to my anchor, I breathed in, and then as my breath released, so did my fingers.

I hit the eye. Perfect shot. Frederick would have been proud. But the arrow passed right through it, as if it wasn't even there.

"No!" I shouted, waving my bow around like a crazy person, nearly pitching it against a giant bell. I missed, and there was no telling where in the entire courtyard the arrow had landed. My only shot was gone. And with it, the locket, my magic amplifier.

"Good attempt, Linaria."

I froze at the sound of that voice. It was low, sneering, and slightly nasal. It was the voice of my nightmares. I looked up from the tower to see Rhydin perched upon Duunzer's massive head, his billowing black cloak floating to the side. He looked exactly the same as he had last summer, even down to his clothing. His thin, pale lips were curled. Anger built up inside of me so that it rivaled my fear. I barely recognized my own voice as I screeched his name. "Rhydin!"

He chuckled darkly, the evil joy evident in his amethyst eyes. "I perceive you are in quite the predicament. I vow not to harm you if you come quietly. We will retrieve the locket, and you may assist me as I establish my reign."

"Do you *really* think I'll agree to that? After you murdered my family?" I shouted at him, my hatred brimming over. I charged a magical blast of light into my hand and thrust it toward him.

He caught it easily in his left hand. One of my most powerful spells had been caught like a child catches a ball. Rhydin looked at it, as if he were studying it. It was so easy for him. I'd never seen someone block magic that simply before. I realized with chilling dread that I wasn't remotely strong enough without my locket.

"I see you require more convincing." Rhydin muttered, his smirk disappearing from his face as he crushed my magic in one hand, like it was nothing but a wad of paper. Then, he swept the hand outward like a signal.

Duunzer responded to the order and began to put one gigantic foot in front of the other, gaining on the tower. A few hundred feet turned into one hundred, and then into fifty as I desperately looked around me for something. *Anything* that could help me at this point. Magic was obviously not a choice at the moment.

My eyes landed on the bells, and I knew it was worth a shot. It was the only thing that could buy me time. I sprinted back into the labyrinth of bronze until I found the rope, which was as thick as my leg. I clambered up it the best I could with my numb hands and used my entire body to pull it down, initiating the bells.

My ears began to ring with their banging noise, the sounds bouncing around my head until my ears began to go deaf. Duunzer roared with pain, its claws flying upward toward its head as it stumbled, the bells messing with its ears and head as I had hoped. Then with a swipe of its smoky paw, the entire roof of the tower came crashing down on top of me.

I dove off of the rope and threw my hands up above me, stopping most of the debris with magic. A few rocks still pelted me. Choking on the dust, I threw the floating chunks of tower off of me only to come face to face with Duunzer's snout.

Sulfur filled my nose and I couldn't help but hold my breath at this proximity as I backed away as slowly as possible. The dragon's nostrils were big enough for an entire wagon wheel to fit inside, and two long whiskers curled down from either side of them. Its scaly skin continued to roll with smoke and ash, and fixed in its two giant, searing, scarlet eyes was only me.

Rhydin glared at me quizzically as he ran a pale hand through his midnight hair. "Have you reconsidered?"

I gulped. Hard. My breaths became short. I shook my head quickly, continuing to back up until I felt the hard, stone wall behind me.

"Pity." Rhydin spat. His expression fell slightly. He kneeled on the dragon's head once again, and death was in his eyes.

With a roar, Duunzer threw its head up and let out a giant, stream of fire into the night sky. It clashed against the barrier that still stood above, causing the flames to stream out, reflecting in a million directions down the curved magical dome.

I drew my sword once again, trying to get into some sort of defensive stance against this monstrous creature. Before I knew it, Duunzer's claws lashed out again. I swung my sword yet hit nothing. Duunzer's mighty foot slammed against my body, crushing me against the tower wall.

A wave of pain shot through my leg through the numbing cold, and I couldn't stop the scream escaping from my lips. Looking down, I saw that one of Duunzer's razor sharp, midnight claws had pierced through the center of my upper thigh. Through bone. My chest heaved. I bit my lip to keep myself from crying, but there was no mistaking the crimson that began to leak from around the claw.

"Nora was able to shoot the dragon on her first attempt." Rhydin sneered at me. "Maybe you are not the Allyen I thought you were. After all, my Einanhi can only be destroyed if you strike the right target. Now, my dear, I have a locket to procure and an empire to raise out of these ashes."

Down underneath the bell tower, the Einanhi humanoid was giving Sam quite the run about. Sam thought he would be able to dispatch it quickly and join Lina in the tower, but Rhydin had prepared this magical being for more than simple, regular warfare.

The lithe form was difficult to see in the dark and moved like no human Sam had ever battled. It could bend its spine and limbs in sickening ways to dodge his attacks. It wasn't until the bells began to ring that Sam gained the advantage. When the Einanhi glanced up at the deafening noise, Sam aimed a deadly shot that sent the Einanhi flying backwards until it hit the tower wall, dissipating into nothing but sand.

Sam gave a sigh of relief and was about to enter the tower door when he heard fluttering noises from behind him. He turned to see Rachel Owens coming down to the ground, the wings of her flying spell twisted horribly and hardly visible anymore due to the exposure to Rhydin's magic. She held something her hand, but it wasn't until she landed and limped closer that Sam was able to recognize it as the arrow. His eyes widened. Did Lina miss? Was she okay?

Rachel's eyes also went wide at the sight of him. "I thought you were going to stay with Lina?"

"I was! But an Einanhi got in our way so I had to get rid of it!" Sam shouted, wondering why on earth Rachel would ever dare think he had ditched Lina on purpose. "Why do you have that arrow?"

"Lina shot it, but she missed. She wasn't aiming at the right part of the dragon. Luckily, it soared right past me so I grabbed it." The red-haired woman said breathlessly, "I didn't know the dragon wasn't tangible. But when I was flying around, I saw the orb of magic inside its chest that's keeping the whole thing together. You need to get up that tower and give her this so she can try again!"

Sam nodded and was taking the arrow from Rachel when a piercing scream sounded, chilling Sam's very blood. It was the scream of the woman he loved. Before Rachel could say a word, Sam grabbed the arrow and spun on his heel.

He didn't even bother trying the door to the tower. The stairs would take far too long. Instead, using the most magic he had ever used in his lifetime, Sam propelled himself up the side of the tower, jumping like a deer from the different landings or from the thin footholds in the tiny windows. He leaped as if he were weightless, scaling in only minutes the distance that had taken Lina twice as long on the stairs.

When Sam was only one landing away from the top, a second yell broke the air and echoed around the courtyard. Sam raced the last leap, but what he found at the top of the tower gave him the rarest sense of absolute horror. Lina had been shoved against whatever was left of the tower wall, and one of Duunzer's claws had gone straight through the middle of her leg. It had just been withdrawn, the source of the second scream, and Sam watched helplessly as Lina's face grew deathly pale.

I tried to breathe, but when Duunzer pulled out its claw to go with its master to find my locket, the pain grew even more excruciating. I didn't dare look at the hole that had been gouged in my leg, and my head began to grow cloudy. I felt myself falling, unable to stop it. The wall gave way behind me, nothing to keep me from continuing on until I hit Lunaka's soil. My sword dropped first, and I watched it flicker and flash to the grassy courtyard below with my hazy eyes.

Suddenly, two long arms wrapped around my waist and lugged me back along the stone floor before I could fall. My head lolled around and stared blankly up at my rescuer. It was a very blurry Sam. I felt him unbuckle my belt and pull it tight on my leg above the wound. I could barely feel the squeeze through the pain, but it at least helped my vision to clear. I could see Sam's face and the anxiety written upon it. I tried to talk and said, "Sam, we don't have time for this. Rhydin is going after my locket!"

He ignored me and pressed his hand firmly to my wound, sending waves of pain through me again. I gritted my teeth to keep quiet, but it was in vain. Out of nowhere, the pain died out, replaced only with numbness. Sam pulled me to my feet. "Better?"

"Yeah, much." I said confusedly, and looked down at my red soaked trouser leg still buckled with the belt. "What did you do?"

"Rounan healing spell." Sam said simply, but his eyes were still worried. "It's not perfect though, so don't push it! It'll need more healing later."

I spun around, ready to go make my time count, but Sam caught my arm and thrust the very thing I was going to search for into my hands. I stared dumbly at the arrow, wondering if I was hallucinating. "Where did you get this? I shot it at Duunzer's eye, and it sailed right through it!"

"Rachel found it when it went through Duunzer. She told me you aimed at the wrong spot." Sam gripped my arms to make sure I was listening. "She said she saw where you're supposed to shoot it. I guess there's an orb of magic, or something, inside its chest. That's where you need to shoot the arrow."

I nodded, anxious to get going. "Let's go then!"

The two of us trailed out upon the castle wall, running as fast as possible with my bum leg while also dodging missing sections of stone that Duunzer had either knocked over or scorched to a crisp. Down below, I could see Rachel and her brothers on the ground, trying their best to give the dragon a hard time without the advantage of their wings. Frederick and Mira were nowhere to be seen, nor were Rhydin's Followers. I hoped they were okay.

As we rounded the corner, we leaped over yet another missing section of wall. My leg gave a throb, and I knew I didn't have much battle time before it would give away again. We came to a stop when we reached the part of the parapet where Duunzer made its entrance. Even with magic, there was no way we were getting across this gaping mouth in the wall.

Not able to get any closer, I began to scan Duunzer's body almost a hundred feet away from us, especially its chest for this supposed orb. It didn't take me long to find it now that I knew what to look for, and it was no wonder that I hadn't found it the first time. With Duunzer's body constantly shifting smoke and ash, it was hard to study it. Its body neatly covered up the red orb inside just as the clouds could cover up the sun.

When the dragon began to slowly turn back towards us, I realized that Rhydin had discovered I had the locket again. There was no hiding the look of anger that contorted his young, timeless face.

I shook out my fingers, trying to get feeling back into their cold hunks of flesh. As I did so, I couldn't help a little jab as I raised the arrow in front of him. "Looking for this?"

Rhydin shouted at us, his eyes like fire. "Give me that locket, Linaria! You will only miss again."

I ignored him and raised my bow, waiting to draw the arrow back until Duunzer was closer. I *really* couldn't miss this time. The Owenses trailed after Duunzer on the ground, unable to get its attention off of me now, but that was okay. I needed Duunzer as close as possible. But how could I let it get close enough without me being crushed or burned again?

My head started rolling, flipping through every possible scenario I could think of. This was going to take some creativity in order to get close enough to shoot and yet not be killed.

"What are you thinking?" Sam said to me without taking his eyes off of the approaching dragon.

I took a deep breath, my eyes lining up the trajectories between my bow and Duunzer's orb, about seventy-five feet away now. As I decided on what I wanted to do, I shook my head. Sam wasn't going to like this.

Before I said anything, I backed up to the very edge of the wall, giving me six feet of ground to work with. I grabbed Sam's hand and finally looked him in the eye. He was gauging me carefully, but I only saw the little boy in his eyes that I'd had a crush on for years. I tried to smile, even though my heart was beginning to beat faster and faster. My voice was quiet. "I love you. You know that, right?"

Sam immediately became skeptical, his fingers tightening on my hand as he realized I was about to do something stupid. "Lina, what are you thinking?"

"Promise you'll catch me."

All I saw before I ran was Sam's look of confusion, then disbelief, and then terror, all washing through him in succession. I didn't stop. Duunzer was finally close enough. I sprinted that six feet and made it count the best I could before aiming one hand downward to launch myself off of that crumbling parapet.

Time slowed. Fifty feet. I soared over the castle courtyard, my hand reaching to pull the arrow back to my mouth.

Forty feet. Duunzer let out one last roar, Rhydin on top of

its head watching me with his calculating, amethyst eyes.

Thirty feet. Light began to draw toward the arrow once again, the glow strong enough that the smoke of Duunzer's body tried to roll away from it.

Once I was within twenty feet of Duunzer's body, beginning to fall from my leap, my eyes easily latched onto the little red orb within its chest.

I breathed in and let my Allyen arrow fly.

Sam's heart fell into the pit of his stomach as Lina's hand fell through his like water, and he watched her fly off of the castle wall. His hands balled into fists, unsure of what to do as he followed her with his eyes helplessly.

Duunzer opened its big jagged mouth and let out another deafening roar. As Sam noticed its throat begin to glow with fire, he reached out with his magic and snapped the dragon's mouth shut. There was no way he was going to let that thing fry his girl.

Lina timed it perfectly. When she released her arrow, Sam relished in the anger and shock that tumultuously warred over Rhydin's face. The arrow hit home in that red orb, causing the Einanhi dragon to screech louder than ever before. The orb exploded into a ball of light, Allyen light, and sent streaks through Duunzer's smoky body.

Beam after beam shot from the tiny sun in its chest until Duunzer was shattered into a million pieces, the smoke and ash no longer visible as the red eyes faded into nothing. Duunzer disappeared. Sam couldn't hear Rhydin from where he stood now, but after a few seconds, the sorcerer escaped into a cloud of purple smoke. He was foiled today, and Sam reveled in it.

As the dragon ceased to exist, Sam remembered Lina's words with a jolt and reached out with his hands. His Rounan magic stretched into transparent extensions. Just as he had been able to pick up Terran the night of the Winter Ball, Sam scooped up Lina, falling out of the sky, into his invisible magic hand.

She turned and smiled at him, a huge, triumphant grin taking up her entire face. She trusted him, and he had come through. Sam's heart swelled with pride and love. After a difficult, single year of training, his Lina had won against Duunzer!

While Duunzer imploded with light magic, I couldn't see much, being so close to it, yet joy rippled through me when I saw my ball of light shoot upward. Duunzer was gone, and now I watched the light fly up and shatter the barrier that the Lunakan Royals had created. Shining shards like glass fell from the sky, disappearing into stars of rainbow color before ever hitting the ground.

The light became truly blinding as it encountered the Darkness outside, and the noise was deafening with rustling and blowing sounds. I peeked through my white eyelids to see the Darkness being blotted out of existence with more beams, just as Duunzer had.

All at once, blue sky broke in from above, having always been there, only hidden. The castle became blanketed in the beautiful shine of our natural sun, reflecting off of the snow and sending us its warmth. The Darkness had turned everything to such a chill that my fingers began burning with the sudden heat. There was no wiping the smile off of my face at the gorgeous sight of my homeland in the light once more.

I looked at Sam, and he was grinning at me as he slid precariously down the ruined parapet. He looked like he might float himself right off the ground, he was beaming so wildly. When he got closer to me, he began to lower me from where I still floated a decent twenty feet off of the ground.

Sam reached out with his arms, ready to catch me with my bad leg that I had definitely pushed too hard. His hands were firm on my waist, and, when his magic ceased to cushion my descent, he spun me around happily and kissed me hard. Love tinged with a bit of anger was in his eyes as he got all up in my face. "Don't you *ever* do that to me again!"

I couldn't stifle my giggle. "Hey, it worked, didn't it?"

"I would say so!"

Sam gave me a slightly defeated look as I turned to the new voice. Walking down the lane were Frederick and Mira, flanked by the three Owenses, who had masked every sign that they had been a part of this battle. Rachel, Luke, and James looked simply exhausted, each with heavy shadows under their eyes from being around Rhydin's magic too long. Frederick had several sword cuts decorating his skin, now visible through torn sleeves, while Mira's hair was in disarray. A nice bruise embellished her face while her skirt was in shreds.

"Congratulations, Lina." Frederick beamed at me. "I couldn't be more proud of you."

Mira and the Owenses echoed his sentiments, and Rachel walked forward to plop a familiar object into my hand. "You seem to keep losing this, don't you?" She laughed.

I looked down to see the warm metal of my locket, its face seeming newly cleaned after such powerful use. I pulled my chain from my pocket and looped it through, clasping my locket around my neck once more, as it was meant to be. I still felt happy, but I found that the smile on my face was beginning to droop.

"What's wrong?" Rachel asked, her red brow furrowed.

"We didn't get Rhydin, did we?" My shoulders fell, my own weariness beginning to make my limbs feel like lead.

Luke grimaced, his eyes turning a brilliant shade of green. "No. You're right, Rhydin got away." – He walked over to me and took my scraped hand – "But the important thing is that you defeated Duunzer. For now, Nerahdis is out of danger. Rhydin will come back with a new plan, that much is certain. You are a full-fledged Allyen now, and the people know that you are on their side. I would say that is a huge victory."

The corners of my mouth tried to tug back into a smile, but my heart wasn't quite as into it as before. Frederick put his arm around Mira's shoulder and led her back toward the castle. King Adam was nowhere to be seen, but Queen Gloria stood at the threshold and embraced her children warmly.

The three Owenses looped their lanky arms around each other, all around the same height. Rachel straightened James' hair so his ears were covered, and then the three of them started marching out toward where the castle entrance had been enlarged by one dragon's width.

I turned to follow them, but I felt Sam's hand hook onto mine, stopping me in my tracks. I looked at him expectantly, wondering what he wanted as the townspeople began to inch out of the castle into the daylight.

"Lina, I..." Sam stuttered, seeming jumbled. He took a breath, sighing hard as he reached to take my hand with both of his. Whatever this was, it was definitely hard for him. "I nearly lost you today."

I sighed, "I know. I really am sorry. It just seemed to be the best plan that I could come up with."

Sam started waving his hand quickly, seeming embarrassed. "No, it's not that. I understand why you did that. It was a good idea, even if it was dangerous." He smiled.

I quirked my eyebrow, becoming confused. "So, what's your point then?"

His eyes widened and his Adam's apple bobbed as he swallowed hard. He looked down, his thumb began to rub circles over the back of my hand. "My point... My point is..." Sam suddenly stopped his nervous ticks and looked me straight in the eye. "My point is that I could have lost you. With Rhydin still out there, our lives could be turned upside again at any moment, and I want my life to be on the same up side or down side as yours, all the time."

I eyeballed him carefully. I didn't allow myself to hope quite yet that he was going where I thought he was going.

That didn't remain long as Sam abruptly dropped his long leg so that his knee was soaking in the snow. He kept his eyes trained on mine as my other hand flew to my mouth. "Lina, I want to marry you. I've loved you for as long as I can remember, and I don't want to spend another minute away from you. Rhydin could come back anytime, but I don't care. I want to spend every moment I can with you. Will you marry me?"

I don't remember my exact response anymore, but I can tell you with certainty that I dropped down and choked him in a bear hug faster than if someone had knocked my knees out from under me. He was my childhood friend, and I loved him with a love that trumped all others.

Sam made a funny comment about how he was the first Rounan to marry a Gornish woman, but I didn't care. Nothing could have made me happier than knowing that I would have him by my side for the rest of the chapters of my life, both the good ones and the inevitable bad ones when Rhydin returned with a new scheme.

Duunzer was defeated, and Nerahdis was safe for the time being. I could be content with that for now. I knew in my bones that I would be ready when Rhydin returned. I had proven myself against Duunzer and had proved that I was just as qualified as Nora had been. Just as I would love Sam until my last breath, I would protect Nerahdis as well.

After all, I was The Allyen.

# CHAPTER TWENTY-THREE

Early Spring 7th, Year 34 of King Adam's Reign

Today was the day I married my best friend. It wasn't like the dream I've had in my head since I was a little girl of getting married in the barn just like my parents did. It was far better than that.

Maybe a month after Duunzer was destroyed, we found ourselves heading toward northern Lunaka once more, nearer to Lun. We would have married earlier, but I wanted to walk down the aisle, not limp with my leg injury. These were the uncharted prairies where the Rounans lived, and we were happy to get away from Soläna, which held so many painful memories for the both of us.

Instead, our barn was an open field full of newly green prairie grass with only a handful of witnesses. Rachel sewed my dress for me, and it shall remain the most beautiful dress I've ever worn. It was a sky blue color with a white head covering, deep blue accents decorating the cuffs, sleeves and skirt. Also, since I married the Kidek, I wore a traditional Rounan scarf around my shoulders; the blue, purple, and golden stars I've seen so often atop Sam's bandana. Sam gave me his mother's ring, a thin band of stones that were too tiny to see, but it was impossible to miss their sparkle.

Rachel, her brothers, Frederick, Mira, Xavier, Cornflower, and Cassandra were all there. Yes, I said Xavier!

When I destroyed the Darkness with my magic, many of the people that it consumed reappeared in the very spots where they had been taken. It ravaged the continent terribly, many buildings were ruined, but the most devastating blow that it struck was the death of many of the elderly and infants. They simply never awoke from their slumber in the Darkness, possibly because of their weaker bodies. Nerahdis has been wracked with grief ever since Duunzer was defeated, and I feel anger toward Rhydin for this.

However, I was overjoyed when Xavier came from Mineraltir, using the mass confusion to simply disappear. He and Mira have already wed, and the happiness on their faces throughout my own wedding was a joy to see. They are staying here in Lun in disguises, as are Frederick, Cassandra, and Cornflower. Apparently, Queen Gloria told all of her children to leave the castle for their own safety, refusing to leave herself because she still loves King Adam deep down. It makes me frustrated that we're unable to do anything about King Adam, but nobody will believe that their great king is evil.

Frederick and Cassandra have married as well, although I'm not sure any of Lunaka knows. King Adam is still rather peeved at Frederick's choice of wife. I am getting to know Princess Cornflower rather well, and she is spunky and full of the energy expected for a twelve-year-old. We have heard basic reports that Evan and his Ranguvariians as well as King Daniel and Queen Lily are all alive, but nothing too detailed yet.

Cassandra, Mira, and Rachel were my maids in the wedding while Frederick, Xavier, and Luke were Sam's men. I never would have dreamed in a million years that we would have Royals in our wedding.

The Owenses act more themselves after spending much needed time at home in the mountains recuperating from their recent proximity to Rhydin's magic. They are planning to return home again soon after the wedding in order to report to their grandfather, the Clariion, or leader of the Ranguvariians. For a wedding present, they gave us a wind chime made completely out of their shard feathers, which will protect our whole new house from Rhydin sensing us as well as for decoration. Rachel is ever the practical one.

Now that life is quieter, I've taken the time to actually go through this journal that I found at Grandma's. Apparently, it has more magic that I originally thought because, no matter how much I have begun to write, I never run out of paper. Grandma's journal entries are still here in the book, and she writes about how every single Allyen has written in this same book, yet Grandma's is the only other writing I can find.

When I asked Rachel, she told me that the book probably only keeps the current and previous Allyens' writing, so the current can continue to learn from the previous. I love it because it feels like Grandma is still here to teach me how to be the best Allyen I can be. The only thing I seem to not be able to get an answer to is whom the Allyen was between Grandma and I. If there's one per generation as the magic is physically handed down, then who was the Allyen before me and after Grandma? It certainly wasn't Mama or Papa.

I hope to figure this out soon, but, because of the never-ending supply of paper, I feel better about writing my meager life into it. From the day a Ranguvariian saved me from being kidnapped by Rhydin as a child up until today, a month after Duunzer was destroyed. Someday, I will continue the tradition and give this journal to the next Allyen after me.

I wonder all the time what Rhydin will do next. I try not to let it consume me, but it is difficult not to with the recent events. As you can well imagine, Nerahdis is rather chaotic right now. People are waking up from the Darkness to find their grandparents or young children dead, their buildings destroyed, and their animals lost. A world of people terrified by magic are wondering where this dragon came from and are pointing fingers. Lunaka says it was Mineraltir. Mineraltir says it was Auklia. Auklia says it was Lunaka. And so forth.

I don't know what will happen, but it isn't looking good. I hope every day that Nerahdis is not headed for war, but Sam tells me that it is only a matter of time.

We are still settling in our new home. I haven't had a

chance to meet the Rounans who live up here, and so I am hoping that the few hateful stares I've received can be changed. Sam wasn't kidding when he said he was the first Rounan to marry a Gornish woman. Surely, they can't hate me forever, right?

Rhydin continues to inhabit my nightmares. I know he is out there, planning his next move and finetuning it to perfection amongst his army of Followers and Einanhis. I keep practicing my magic and my sword skills every day in this rural prairie. Duunzer was one thing, but Rhydin has been honing his magic for the last three hundred years. I can only hope that Evan and I will be powerful enough to defeat him. There is no doubt that Rhydin will return to take Nerahdis and form his empire. I have to be ready.

Because it is only a matter of time.

## END OF BOOK ONE

# ACKNOWLEDGMENTS

F irst and foremost, I would be remiss without thanking you! That's right, you with this book in your hands. Whether you picked it up because you know me or because you thought the cover looked awesome, I cannot thank you enough for reading my book. I hope that you enjoyed it thoroughly, and that you'll be back for Book 2!

Now, for the people who made this happen. I began writing this book in late 2006 at only twelve years of age. Obviously, this book and my writing have evolved tremendously over the last eleven years, but that time has also been filled with people supporting me who deserve recognition.

First off, I am so thankful to my wonderful husband, Olin, for always telling me to shoot for the stars. He has supported me through everything, and for that, I will be forever grateful.

Secondly, I would like to thank my parents, Mark and Cynthia, for always boosting my self-confidence and pushing me toward publication. I hope to make you both proud.

Also, thanks to the world's best brothers, Matthew and Jason, for always joking around that their big/little sister was someday going to be a famous author. You guys are the best!

Thank you to everyone who has ever read this book before it came to its final state! You guys put up with a lot trying to translate the bizarre ideas of a twelve-year-old into something amazing and a story worth telling. Rachel Evans, who has been there every step of the way since 2006 and for letting me use her and her brothers' names. Daphne Evans, who tore every sentence apart like every good grammar Nazi should.

And, of course, Hannah Robinson and my wonderful mother, Cynthia Riley, for helping me finetune details. Also, Dakota Caldwell for answering all of my millions of questions about publication. This book would not be here without you all!

I'd like to thank all of my faithful followers. You guys make me feel like a million bucks just by following all my random stuff and being excited for me with each stage of the publication process. Thanks!

Lastly, I cannot go without thanking Magpie Designs, ltd. for the amazingly epic cover, as well as L. N. Weldon for the beautiful map of Nerahdis, that they designed for *The Allyen*. Only special people can translate rough pencil sketches into something spectacular.

Now, readers, if you put up with all my acknowledgements, I thank you again. You all are awesome, and I can't wait to continue Lina's journey with you in Book 2, coming soon in 2018!

<br>

Visit my website to learn more!
www.michaelarileykarr.wordpress.com

Made in the USA
Monee, IL
28 February 2023

28655869R00194